Wilderness

ISBN-13: 978-1494211707
ISBN-10: 149421170X

Web: Campbellhart.co.uk
Cover design: Tim Byrne

Part 1

1

February 15th 2010, 2:00am

The engine was still running but the coach was going nowhere. The services' last passenger was resigned to sitting out a long, cold night. Under the faint light from the cubicle at the back of the bottom deck the woman could see her skin was already turning blue. *'I hope they come soon,'* she thought, *'surely the girl will be fine?'* Curled up in a ball with the metal toilet bowl pressed against her skin she stopped shivering and focused her attention on the engine as it purred away reassuringly in the background, this lonely tourist's constant companion these last few hours. Suddenly the noise stopped and the coach shuddered violently into silence. She was alone now, lost in the wilderness.

June 25th 1985

It was quiet and the silence carried its own warning. It was impossible to say how long it had been – alone in the darkness she had lost track of the time. She knew what she was expected to do and was always keen to please, given the alternative. There was no-one to miss her at home, where she was mostly ignored, and when her father came there was little to do but obey. It hurt if she resisted and so she had learned to accept it and now did what she was told. All that she had for comfort was a bed of cushions from a discarded couch and an old, sodden mattress which carried the now familiar smell of decay and parental dereliction. After several hours the hatch opened and he appeared like a fallen angel, with the stars sparkling behind him. She could feel his breath as the cold night air breezed through the room, expelling old air and bringing an end to her long wait. Mary could see his smile and soon she knew that she would taste his fury.

February 14th 2010

It had already been a long day for Mary Clark. The journey from Scotland to Hull had taken 14 hours. Mary met Kovan at the ferry – she seemed safe and well on arrival which had been a relief given the circumstances. Kovan had been shy at first, the way that 5 year olds can be, and at first she didn't seem to want to talk and had hid behind her guardian. But slowly she came round. They talked for a long time. Mary gave the child her phone to play with which seemed to win her over. Within an hour Kovan was laughing and looking ahead to the long promised family reunion. The train would get them back at Glasgow Central for five, leaving plenty of time to put her mind at rest. The road back was uneventful. Her little girl had arrived, and that was the most important thing.

***

Onur Kocack was looking forward to seeing his daughter. They had been apart for a long time and there were things she needed to know about how their new life would be. Onur had come to the UK from Turkey on a sponsored Visa. He had been working as an engineer in Istanbul on the new Metro system when the trouble started. He had told his wife that it had all been down to debt, but there was more to it than that.

Onur had landed on his feet and had found a job with the Madoch Group, a fledgling Scottish firm with a growing international reach and which was badly in need of his expertise. The firm had paid to have him flown over to Britain and he was now making more money than he had ever dreamt of back home. Onur had been taken under the wing of Eric Sanderson who seemed to be a bit of an outsider but his help and guidance had been invaluable in those first few weeks. Onur's background meant that he had been the ideal candidate for the role. He dealt with the drilling and blasting needed for this current project to overcome foundation problems for the wind farm which was being thrown-up on moorland outside the city. The granite bedrock below the surface meant there was a lot to do but it was rewarding work for which he was well suited. Although Sanderson was much older it was good to work with someone that he really felt he knew, and that was going to make all the difference.

***

Mary and Kovan made the connecting bus in Glasgow by 6:30 that night. The train had been delayed and the weather was changing with a forecast for heavy snow, although there was still little sign of it. It wasn't long, though, before the blizzard whispered into life and slowly but surely enveloped the west coast. The bus was busy. They were heading to the end of the line at Shotts, midway between Glasgow and Edinburgh, which traditionally bore the brunt of the weather in every season because it lay on higher ground. As they settled down in the top deck the driver's voice crackled over the tannoy to announce his name was Stevie and that the weather meant their bus being diverted. Stevie explained that the motorway was now a no-go area – it hadn't been properly gritted and the company couldn't vouch for their safety. *'Fair enough,'* Mary thought. Commuters in their wisdom, Stevie continued, had all rushed to beat the traffic but had only managed to create a jam. The express bus was cancelled so we'd be getting treated to a rerouted service that ran parallel to the motorway taking in Rutherglen, Hamilton, Motherwell, Wishaw and Newmains before they'd reach home. At roughly four times the normal travel time this was not good news but at least they could still travel and the snow could not be helped – all the same, though, it was going to take a long time.

Mary smiled at Kovan, kissing her gently on the head as she slept, exhausted. Five miles out from the city centre the traffic had slowed to a crawl. At Buchanan Bus Station the coach had been full but the numbers had gradually fallen away as the coach snaked-on through the night. Given the amount of time they were spending onboard Mary was glad this was a luxury touring coach and not a basic local bus which would have been uncomfortable and a worse way to end what had already been a taxing day. The

3

information sign on the inside of the bus above the drivers head said this was a Van Hool double-decker. She passed the time trying to remember what it looked like from the outside. It had white livery with 'Dales Travel' on the side, tinted black windows while the rear part of the bottom deck was covered over for reasons of luggage and comfort, giving the bus the strange look of being an oversized single-decker. Outside Mary noticed a man struggling along the pavement bent into the freezing wind while his white haired terrier battled along against the elements barely visible in the snow.

***

John J Arbogast was in the mood for celebrating and had a big night planned with Sandy Stirrit – an old friend with a shared history. When they were both married they met socially as a foursome, making the most of the night life but these days, with less in the way of domestic responsibility, they tended to stick to Glasgow's fine array of hostelries. Tonight it was Rab's in the Merchant City, part of town which had been transformed from a forgotten sea of broken down warehouses to emerge as one of the more fashionable parts of town. Looking around as he made his way to the pub Arbogast thought it might be going too far to call the area sophisticated but when compared to the free for all drunken brawls he had dealt with as a police officer on Sauchiehall Street this was a much better bet if he was looking for a quiet life. Tonight he was. Rab's was fine for a February evening. A roaring fire, fine food, and a good mix of people meant there was never any hassle and his line of work was never a problem with the people he met.

Friends from childhood, Sandy Stirrit had gone into journalism while Arbogast had focused his talents on police work. While their careers hadn't crossed early on, in more recent years their friendship had become mutually beneficial on both a professional and personal level. Not that they remained friends simply for the added value but it helped. It was Valentines night tonight and John realised they might be the only non-couple in the place. He hadn't even thought about Valentines. Tonight Arbogast was celebrating something far more important than love – it was

4

his last night of freedom. He had been promoted to the Major Crime and Anti Terrorism Unit at Strathclyde Police. MCTU operated across the Strathclyde force area, which was by far the biggest in the country. He would join the ranks of around a dozen people who had been picked out to travel to hotspots across the area. For him though it was a prime chance to escape Glasgow's murder merry-go-round and get his teeth into something more interesting. After 14 years on the force he needed something different. Lost in his thought he noticed Sandy standing beside him at the bar and pushed across the first pint of the night.

***

By the time they had gone through Newmains they were the only ones left on the bus and the weather had deteriorated badly. Kovan was happy enough playing games on her newly acquired phone, but Mary was starting to get worried. They had passed a large number of abandoned cars and the snow was lying deep by the side of the road. Mary had taken the time to ask the driver if he thought they would still get through to Harthill and he seemed confident they would make it, although he couldn't say how long it would take. This wasn't good. If they didn't get home on time there would be a lot of questions to answer and a lot of unhappy people. They were all there for Kovan. The bus juddered after losing traction on the road and moved to the side, sliding as the brakes struggled to keep the vehicle from spinning out of control. Kovan screamed. Mary thought the coach might topple over like a scene from a bad disaster movie. She tried to look ahead, to figure out what was going on but as she faced forward the world spun round making her feel nauseous, terrified.

After what seemed like an age the bus finally found the verge of the road and got lodged in drifting snow. The only sounds she heard were the gentle purring of the engine and her own breathing. Then from the bottom deck Mary heard the doors opening with the gentle swoosh announcing the arrival of winter into their air conditioned sanctuary. She watched as the driver went out in the road looking for damage before disappearing from sight. About ten minutes passed and with each passing second the coach became colder. Mary felt the coach lurch slightly to the left as someone came on board on the bottom deck. From below she heard a determined stamping as snow was shed from footwear. When the driver appeared Mary felt uneasy although she couldn't say why and this was something Kovan seemed to sense too, her tiny hand gripping tightly around Mary's. The driver, stooped to accommodate the low roof, rested an arm each on the top of the empty chairs on either side of the aisle in front of them.

"There's been a change of plan."

**

John and Sandy had really gone to town. Pints had led to cocktails which led to shorts which in turn had led to bad behaviour. They had been demonstrating a now forgotten theory involving vertically stacked pint glasses to two young students when an almighty crash heralded an early exit from Rab's, forcing them out into the billowing snowstorm which had wrapped itself around the city.

"Where did all this come from Sandy? I could do without it that's for sure – let's not hang about for too long – where are we heading?"

"Devil May Care?"

"Sandy," John protested, he knew where the conversation was going.

"Go on JJ – just for one."

"I can't – you know I can't."

"Are you saying you won't?"

"I'm saying I shouldn't," John smiled and Sandy led the way.

Devil May Care was the latest in a short line of 'exotic' bars which had opened up in the last ten years but it was by no means in the top tier. Fashioned into the ground floor of an otherwise derelict tenement block it had at one time been a thriving club but was now home to the less exclusive end of what was supposedly a luxury market. Every time Arbogast passed it he was reminded of a short-lived topless hairdressing salon which had opened amidst howls of protest. They said they weren't sure if it was a backdoor brothel. It was and it had been his smiling face which had closed it down, his picture on the front page of all the

6

papers, making him the butt of a thousand jokes. The picture in the papers was far from flattering and the copy painted the snippers as slappers with faces to match. To say that Devil May Care was bottom of the barrel would be unkind but you could still see it if you looked hard enough. Badly hand-drawn outlines of unlikely dancing girls announced the club's mission statement from the off. When they arrived outside it was still only 11:30 and the place had just opened. If the club's doorman was sober he would see the first guests of the night were far from it. John had met Sandy straight from his weekend shift at 4:30pm and they had drank straight through, so it felt later than it was. When the doorman asked if they had been drinking they said 'just a couple' and by the time they made their grand entrance it was hard to say who was most disappointed. The circus began in earnest with one girl taking lazily to the pole in a move which was supposed to pique their interest. Three girls mobbed Sandy at the bar, with flattery disguising a dogfight for tips and the start of business on a cold winter's night. Arbogast got talking with a dark haired eastern looking woman with eyes he could not see past.

"Will you dance for me?"

"Come with me."

She was sallow skinned and wore light blue lingerie which made a showcase of an arse which rocked from side to side as she led him by hand to the red room at the back. A figure at the door told him 'look but don't touch.' As she sat him down she undressed him with her eyes and herself with her hands. He knew he shouldn't have come. He lent to touch her right breast which was now just inches from his face but had his hand brushed away. He was quite drunk and definitely in the mood for more than was on offer. Drunk and turned on he reached behind her back and grabbed her, bringing her body towards him. He kissed her violently. She screamed, turning from goddess to banshee in one easy breath. The next thing he knew she had fallen back. Arbogast was hoisted from his seat by two men he hadn't noticed before. He felt a sharp pain in his armpits as their ham fists dug deep. He couldn't quite work out what was going on although he knew this hadn't been part of the plan, as he was dragged through the hall and was unceremoniously thrown through the fire doors.

"You were told no hands – so don't come back you stupid prick," was the last thing he heard as the city whirled by in a haze, his head hitting off the side of an industrial bin which was perfectly positioned to break his fall. As he lay face-down and unconscious in the snow a small trickle of blood oozed from his forehead which dripped to the ground, mingling with the rest of the garbage from the day before.

2

George Rome had been farming for 25 years and had never seen anything quite as bad as this. He'd spent early evening rounding up the sheep from the higher pastures with his son Gerry, shepherding the animals back to the warmth of the barn and out of the reach of the thickening storm. That way at least he would be able to feed them and they would be safer too. If the weather front continued for any length of time George knew that it would soon become impossible to reach the animals and he couldn't afford to lose stock at this point in the season. Herding sheep in the snow was no easy task and it had taken four hours to find them all, with white on white being a hard ask. Finally they had accounted for the entire flock and had driven them all safely back down the two mile journey to the farmhouse. By this time the snow was heavy and drifting deeply and it looked likely to get worse overnight. Satisfied they had done everything they could the family settled down for the night and waited.

It was 2:00am when George opened his eyes. Something had got his attention. Hauling himself from his bed George could feel the freezing cold bite at his arms and feet. He quickly pulled on his robe and crept out of the bedroom, taking care not to wake Jean. The kitchen thermometer showed -14c which was colder than he had expected and worse than he feared. George went through the house to check no-one was there. It struck him as a ridiculous routine, creeping through the house with a poker from the hearth, but it put his mind at rest. It could just have been the cat or probably more likely a noise from the barn, which tonight was full of sheep not used to being there and certainly not used to the temperature. He pulled trousers and a jumper from the laundry basket and made his way over to the barn to check.

The snow was deep. There must have been more than a foot in the courtyard, which was sheltered from the wind so he could only imagine what it would be like in open country. George Rome checked the barn. Nothing. There were no tracks so he ruled out foxes, *'It's unlikely any animals will be out hunting tonight,'* he thought, *'and if they did try, how far would they get?'* Cursing his intuition George knew he had wasted his time and also lost half an hour's sleep which he would regret come morning. After knocking the snow from his boot he made his way back up the stairs to bed. He rubbed his face which was numb from the blizzard outside. And it was then that he noticed. Outside in the gloom he saw a row of lights and what appeared to be a bus.

George woke his son and the two went to work. Gerry fired up the tractor and together they attached their snow plough. The Rome farm was near to the Kirk o' Shotts, an ancient church in central Lanarkshire which sat on a hill, dominating the skyline for miles around. This was the high ground between the east and west coasts and snow was a fairly regular feature in wintertime. Normally they used the plough on the poorly maintained single track back roads to clear avenues for their cattle and to open up access around the farm. Theirs was a supply and demand business and they needed to keep their assets in good condition or they could quite easily face financial ruin. Tonight looked like being an entirely different prospect.

"I knew I'd heard something," George said, "Depending on which way the wind blows you can just hear the engine of the bus rumbling away in the background. The lights are on so there must be someone on board."

"You don't know that dad," but George just shook his head.

"We need to reach the bus."

The coach was on the main road around a mile away from the farm and the snow was deep. The coach sat in a dip in the land and the snow was drifting deeply on one side, which was now partially covering the windows on the lower level at the driver's side.

"It's going to take us a while to get there," Gerry said, "The plough isn't really designed for snow this deep and I can't see that we'll make it all the way. Maybe we should phone the police?"

"There's no time for that," George said. He was becoming impatient with his son's reluctance to help, "It would take the emergency services hours to get here in this weather. We've seen this before and we could end up being cut off for a time, so we need to try and get there now. OK?"

It was hard going and the snow got deeper as they worked their way downhill. There wouldn't normally be a bus on this stretch so George guessed it must have been diverted onto the old A8, which ran parallel to the newer motorway. *'It must been closed down,'* he thought. George knew from experience that planners never planned for weather like this. At this temperature the normal way of making roads safe didn't work. Grit and salt were only effective up to temperature of around -10c and it was way below that already. George looked at his watch which read 2:45am and he wondered if the main road might reopen. There would be little point in clearing the motorway during the blizzard as the snow was coming down at such a rate that any progress would be undone in a matter of minutes.

They had managed to dig through about a quarter of a mile in the first hour when the lights went out in the bus and the engine stopped. They saw it shudder to a stop and the chassis swung on its suspension from side to side as the pistons stopped firing and the engine died.

"That's bad news son. If there's anyone on there, it's going to get cold pretty quick," George said, trying to convince himself the coach could still be reached more than anything else. The closer they got the harder the task became. The sheer weight of the snow was causing problems for the plough blade and they had to take it in turns to physically move snow by hand to relieve the pressure on the plough and allow it to keep moving. After a while it became clear that they were facing a thankless task. In the end the tractor gave up, the dark diesel fumes spluttering into the night against the tractor's arc lights, a stark contrast to the whiteout which surrounded them. The pressure was too much and the machine overheated and died. They still had a reasonably clear route back to the farm but still had 300 metres to go before they would be able to reach the bus.

George phoned his wife Jean who was now wide awake back at the farm, "Hi...yes but its bloody hard work...listen could you get over to the barn and attach the trailer to the quad bike and get it down here?... it should be fine...listen we're having to dig by hand...the tractor's died...no it's not ideal...but it's the only option we have and we're close now, so close...OK yes...of course...yes OK...speak soon. Hurry, Jean."

Both father and son were both exhausted and freezing by this point. Their jackets weren't made for these conditions and their hands were numb and their faces ruddy and blank as the biting icy wind robbed them of expression, the cold bringing tears to their eyes. Two hours later they were close, inching ahead using shovels and grit, determined to reach the bus – finally they got there.

"Thank Christ," Gerry said, "I hope there's someone in there after all this."

Following the instructions on the side of the bus he turned the emergency access lever clockwise beside the door. Nothing happened. He took off his gloves and forced his hands through the rubber seal between the double doors. Slowly they juddered open until there was enough room for them to squeeze through.

"Pass the torch, will you?" George said.

The bright beam shone a halo into the interior. Outside there was no light and the grey skies left the coach looking black inside. It took George time to find a focal point as the torchlight swept through the bottom deck. It seemed there was no one on board after all. The driver's seat was empty. The key was still in the ignition.

"There's no one here but why would they have left the engine running?"

"It's strange right enough – best check the top deck too," He watched his father make his way up the steps. When he reached the top floor the low height of the roof forced George to stoop.

"There's nothing here," George said as he paced the isle, "Wait – what's this?" he said bending over to pick up a pair of jeans on the floor and then a jacket and jumper. "Women's clothes?" he added sniffing the garments in a gesture Gerry found odd but didn't mention.

"I wouldn't have thought you'd be leaving much behind on a night like tonight," Gerry said, but that was all there was and both men then returned to the bottom deck and sat down.

"Well that was a complete waste of fucking time," Gerry said but wished he hadn't when he caught the glance from his father.

"We had to try – what if someone had been here?"

Then from the back of the bus came a soft thud. Both men were startled and Gerry screamed despite himself.

"What was that?" he said, whispering, concerned that he might have given himself away.

"Snow falling from the roof perhaps? Although it sounded like it was inside – somewhere at the back?"

"I'll check," Gerry said, trying to appear a bit braver as he edged forward, torch in hand.

The bottom deck was split into three compartments. The first two quarters were reserved for seats which were arranged around three sets of tables as was standard in the luxury model. At the back a boxed off area at the side revealed a spiralling staircase which led to the top deck, while at the end of the aisle on the bottom there was a door for the onboard toilet. The rest of the bus was given over to luggage space at the back and was only accessible from outside. The door of the toilet, which was covered in black material and matched the interior walls, was closed. But it was obvious this was where the sound had come from.

As he opened the door he peered round with fearful eyes. When he saw her, he wondered if it was already too late.

3

When the coach was an hour overdue John Dale started to worry, but given the blizzard he knew it would take time for Stevie to make it back to base. When he still hadn't returned after two hours, he became anxious and had an uneasy feeling something had happened. The radio was dead, with white noise the only response. As a last resort he had checked the travel websites and although there were multiple road closures there were no major incidents reported and he could not figure out why Stevie had not arrived back. John Dale had taken a lot of stick when he had taken Stevie on because of his background but he had reasoned that you couldn't label someone for the rest of their life just because of one mistake however serious. Stevie had already paid his dues. He had been a great driver these last four years and always stuck to the timetable, until now anyway. That he hadn't heard from him in since he left from the bus station in Glasgow was worrying but the motorway had been closed and it would have taken time to wind through the city and the surrounding countryside for what should have been a 25 minute trip. Dales Travel catered for tourism but the company had branched out to provide a limited commuter service between Lanarkshire and Glasgow. Business had been slow of late and when John Dale saw the forecast he sensed he might have been gifted with a golden opportunity to generate some good PR and extra cash. There would be a lot of people stranded by the weather and additional coaches would be in high demand. By stepping in and providing a lifeline for commuters John Dale knew he was facing a win-win situation. *'But where the hell was the coach,'* he thought. He tried the radio one more time but again all he heard was static. All the other drivers were home and dry and he was alone now at the Shotts depot having sent everyone else home.

John only lived a few streets away so he could afford to stay on, but the weather was hellish and he knew the business would be shut down for at least the 24 hours while the authorities tried to beat back mother nature and restore normality. Having paced the shop floor for half an hour, checking his watch every minute, he bit the bullet, phoned 999 and reported the coach as missing.

***

N Division was the branch of Strathclyde Police which covered North Lanarkshire. The area had once counted among the industrial powerhouses of British manufacturing but that had been a long time ago. Today the region was still nursing a long term hangover after the collapse of heavy industry in the 1980s. Unemployment was higher than average and the promise of an IT boom had disappeared virtually overnight, with the lure of cheap labour in Eastern Europe proving too big a temptation for business, despite the Government millions which had been pumped into their coffers to come to Scotland in the first place. And after the boom, came bust. The first signs of decline came when civic leaders ran out of cash and were unable to maintain the region to the level it had become accustomed. Parks became overgrown, services closed, potholes scarred the streets like tarmac acne. The signs of decline were apparent. Everyone talked of progress but somehow life never seemed to change. Each new facelift was more like a coat of makeup, destined to be washed off by the end of the night. Pockets of affluence could be found, as they can in any area, but so far there had been no phoenix like renaissance for this forgotten stretch of ravaged hinterland. It was here that Frank Simmons worked his beat. He had only been a Constable for two years and still had a lot to learn. He had always wanted to serve his time in Glasgow but he had been sent here instead. Pouring out his fourth coffee he sighed, puffing air into his cheeks – he knew he was in for a long night. The snow was thick and lying which meant problems for the overnight desk. They had been dealing with abandoned cars and lorries for the last four hours. There had been 34 minor accidents reported on the roads and now that the motorway was closed his less fortunate colleagues had been sent out to travel along the carriageway to mark off all the vehicles that had been searched and found to have no-one in them. It was hard work but there would be hell to pay if someone was found dead behind the wheel, simply because there was no-one to find them. Eight years ago a man had been found sitting at Buchanan Bus Station waiting for a bus home from Glasgow. He had waited and waited, but in the end he didn't leave. Eventually someone from the control centre had gone down to tell him there the station was closed but the advice came too late. The traffic controller had tapped on the sitting man's shoulder but instead of turning round he slid off the bench and tumbled onto the concourse like a bag of old clothes. The coroner's report suggested he had died of the cold and had been sitting dead for as long as five hours. No-one had noticed. People had come and gone and he had also been spotted on camera. No-one did anything. That was his final moment – staring into space at Stance 46 waiting for a coach that never came. In his inside pocket they had found a small wrapped necklace for his granddaughter. The papers had loved that and questions followed asking why this could have been allowed to happen and what was wrong with the world that people could stand by and do nothing. It filled half a page but was forgotten by the next day. Thinking back Frank knew that was part of the reason he had signed up, because he wanted to try and do something for the victims, for the people no one cared for. Tonight, though, he knew he would rather be in bed. Getting home tomorrow might be more of a problem than it should be. Frank's office was in Motherwell which was the regional HQ. The phone rang. Control again.

"Frank?"

"Yes," Frank said, "I'm still here – what have you got for me this time? Six old ladies stranded on their way to the bingo perhaps or maybe Miss Scotland has picked the wrong day for a bikini shoot?"

"Very good," said a blank voice at the other end. Frank didn't know who it was, it must be someone new. He had meant to ask but they had had so many conversations tonight that it seemed the time for introductions had passed.

"We've had a report of a missing bus. It was travelling from Glasgow through to Harthill but had to take a diversion through the City's Southside after we closed the motorway. The owner has been on to say he expected the coach back between 9:00

and 10:00 but it hasn't shown up yet. He can't raise the driver but says he's one of their best. He's hoping there hasn't been an accident – you could hear he was worried. He said he had been waiting by the phone in Harthill. Traffic doesn't seem to be moving much past Newhouse now. The snow's three or four feet deep in places. I've never known it to be so bad. I just thought you should know about this one. It's a luxury coach with all mod cons so even if they do get stuck they should at least be warm. I'll keep you posted if anything else comes in but it looks like this one might be a problem."

Another phone was ringing from a desk at the far side of the room, "Thanks Control," Frank said, "I think it's going to be a tough night but as you say it's probably nothing." *'Strange the driver hasn't been in touch by radio.'* Frank pressed the flashing red light to take the next call in what was likely to be an eventful evening.

***

On the coach George and Gerry were still staring down in disbelief.

"What the fuck is this?" Gerry said, pointing.

When they had opened the door at the back of the bottom deck they had uncovered a figure lying curled around the stainless steel toilet bowl wearing only her underwear.

"That explains the clothes on the top deck," George said.

The woman was handcuffed with her hands pulled behind her back. Her bare stomach was pressed against the metal fittings. Her skin was blue grey but she was not shivering.

"Is she still alive?" said Gerry.

George was crouched over her, checking for a pulse.

"She's still breathing but her heart rate seems slow. She won't have had any heat on this bus since the engine died and that was hours ago – I think she might have hypothermia. We're going to need to get her to hospital as soon as possible but let's get her back to the house and try and get some heat through her. Phone your mum and tell her to get a move on – we need to act fast."

***

17

Arbogast didn't know how long he had been out cold for but it couldn't have been long. When he awoke he wasn't sure where he was but he did know he was freezing. His sense of smell was overwhelmed by the strong stench of urine and rotting food. As he opened his eyes it was obvious he was not at home. He threw up, retching until it seemed as if there could be nothing left inside him. Saliva dripped from his chin as he propped himself up on one arm, his hand going numb as it sank beneath the snow. Looking at the thin film of snowflakes building on his jacket he started to come to. *'My head is thumping,'* he thought, *'and there's the taste of blood. I must have been in a fight? No the blood is dripping... My head is bleeding – where am I?'*

As he regained some sense of composure he knew he was still quite drunk although he was sobering up quickly. The alcohol was already starting to leave his system, marking the start of what he suspected would be a rather unpleasant hangover. Grasping onto the side of the industrial bin he hauled himself up to a standing position. The snow had seeped through his clothes but he knew he had also pissed himself. *'That explains the smell.'* Slowly the evening's events came back him. He had been was lying between two industrial waste bins in the lane directly behind Devil May Care. *'What have I done?'* Arbogast didn't see himself as a problem drinker. He liked a drink; it was true, but not generally to excess and rarely through the week. Groaning at the state he was in he finally remembered that he started his new job tomorrow – later today in fact – with the chances of creating a good first impression getting slimmer by the second. Looking around Arbogast knew he was out of sight, safe from prying eyes in the alley. Glasgow was a Victorian city with the centre based around a grid system. Between the blocks ran a network of lanes mainly meant for access and deliveries but which by night served a range of functions ranging from outdoor toilets through to prostitution. The council were trying to redevelop these areas so they would be used by people in the same vein as Barcelona's Gothic quarter but given it was always either freezing or raining Arbogast didn't see much hope of a cafe culture taking hold anytime soon. Looking down at his sodden trousers he felt deeply ashamed. *'Some fucking elite I'll make.'* He checked his watch: 2:23am. *'Fuck.'* He knew he'd be lucky to get a taxi in his current condition so he made a start on the long walk home. Arbogast avoided the main streets and kept to the alleys, keeping a low profile and avoiding the eyes of the occasional passerby. As he walked down by the banks of the Clyde in heavy snow he shivered and thought of Japanese films. Snow usually represented death, a habit which had slowly infiltrated western movies. Tonight he felt like death itself. If he were in a Japanese film he would be dead within five minutes. As he trudged on contemplating his own self inflicted misery he noticed a light glowing in the distance through the gloom. His saviour tonight was to be Kerry. Kerry's snack bar was a city institution. An all night van selling many cultural fried delights, most of which were conducive to an early heart attack. But tonight as he held the roll thick with sauce, dripping fat and running egg he welcomed the impromptu meal as being fit for a King. He washed it down with a scalding hot cup of third rate tea, rising up on the balls of his feet and savouring the moment. Then he remembered groping the girl in the club, "What an arse you have been tonight John, what a complete and utter arse." Kerry looked up from serving the next customer, "Did you say something," but Arbogast was already back on the road.

***

Jean Rome had been getting tired of the constant calls from her husband. First off he had woken her. He said a bus was stranded but that the snow plough wasn't up to the job. It had always been the same with George, ever since they'd got married. Why buy new when you can make do with second hand gear. She knew she could be harsh and that they were living through tough times but business had been good for them so far. The snow plough had been 12 years old when they had bought it. Well she said bought. She had gone away to visit her sister for a weekend and found on her return that her one year old Mercedes had been traded in for a tractor and plough. And now here we are two years later and it's knackered, when the car would have lasted a decade at least. She laughed at this despite herself. Well now he wanted her to get the quad bike hooked up to the trailer. She had never done it before and it was hard going in the cold. Her hands were bleeding from a gash from the tow bar. Then the phone went. But it wasn't George it was Gerry.

"Mum, we've found a woman on board and she's not looking too good. Bring down blankets when you come but get them fast. Dad says he's worried she might die if we don't get help soon."

"My God," Jean said, "will this night never end?"

It took Jean ten minutes to reach the bus. Her boys had cleared a path to the bus but it was still snowing and the way through was starting to cover over already. The snow was piled up more than six feet at the sides and she couldn't really see for the swirling snowstorm that had swept across the land. She used the dim torch light in the distance as her beacon and by the time she reached the bus she could see her family were not in a mood to hang around.

Acting as one all three of them uncoupled the trailer and tried to spin it round. But there wasn't enough room to turn so they had to physically lift the machines, first the bike and then the trailer. When they were set they cleared the trailer and laid a blanket for a mattress. George and Gerry laid the woman down and then covered her in the duvet Jean had brought down.

"Could you stay with her in the back Jean? Keep her warm and I'll drive. Gerry, you too," he said as he fired up the bike and roared back to the warmth of the farmhouse.

They laid the woman on the couch at home and got the fire going immediately. Their guest looked half dead. She was mumbling incoherently "Not this time," she seemed to say.

"You'll need to phone the ambulance and police right now George. This isn't right. Why would she be down there handcuffed like this?" Jean looked quizzical as she mulled this over, "We can't care for her here. She needs help," George nodded and went to phone from the kitchen.

***

When the phone rang again Frank Simmons cursed under his breath. 'Phone call number 456 here I come.'

"Motherwell Chinese laundry," he said, expecting another minor incident.

It was control, "We've got a problem. The bus I told you about earlier?"

"What about it?"

"It's turned up but there was woman handcuffed on board. She was practically naked. A local farmer phoned it in. He's dug her out but says he's scared she might die. He says the area is completely cut off and he doesn't know what to do. We're going to have to get someone out there. You better get on it."

Frank's left hand massaged his temple back and forth as he stared at the receiver. His heart sank as he knew this was not going to be easy.

"No problem," he said, and hung up. It was 6:00am.

4

February 15th, 6:00am

The storm had engulfed N Division. The snow had fallen thick and fast for nine hours and there were drifts of up to ten feet in some isolated areas. Unfortunately the bus was right in the middle of it, with an eight mile section of the M8 from Newhouse to Harthill now completely inaccessible, getting there was proving difficult. It was -14c outside which provided its own problems. The gritters and snowploughs were still out working around the clock but were struggling to make a difference. The snow kept falling and they kept trying to clear it. People complained that they didn't understand why Britain always ground to a halt when a severe weather cast its shadow over the country but the truth was the UK just didn't get prolonged periods of any kind of weather. While their Scandinavian neighbours could fit snow tyres and prepare for longer periods of this kind of natural treachery, Britain was likely to bear the brunt of a bad spell for a couple of weeks at best. That didn't matter right now, though, and Frank Simmons could see the headlines already. He had counted 230 cars either abandoned or broken down overnight and with every call came more administration. He looked at his in-tray and wished he could just roll over and go to sleep. It was going to take at least a couple of days to get the roads back to normal and a lot of effort to clear the cars that had been left unattended. There were more than 15-thousand people living in the affected areas and with no supplies likely to get through for some time they were facing a logistical nightmare to keep people alive for as long as the weather continued. Frank drummed his fingers against the desk trying to work out his priorities. *'And now we have this bus.'*

Sergeant Ellen McRae was having a hard time keeping track of everything. Technically she was meant to be handing over to the day shift in half an hour but problems with staff getting to the office and the sheer volume of work still to be done meant she would be here for a long time yet. On balance it seemed as if the coach was their biggest short term problem. The call had come in that a woman had been found in the coach. The Scottish Ambulance Service emergency helicopter was making its way there now. The conditions were not ideal and visibility was poor. The pilot would have to take a judgement call on whether icing was going to be a problem for the blades. At the moment it was looking good to land at the farm which would let them pick up the woman. Sergeant McRae had spoken to the farmer George Rome and asked him to try and clear a good space for the helicopter to land. He had said the snow was deep but not so bad within the farm itself, which was fashioned around a courtyard. She hoped the woman could be reached.

***

Sandy Stirrit had a blinding hangover. He wasn't sure what had happened to JJ last night but the last thing he remembered was lap dancing. *'Why did we go there? It's a shithole, we spend a fortune and I always end up feeling like this.'* Sandy was father to a baby girl. When he got home he remembered this and put his clothes straight into the wash basket to mask the scent of five different women which lingered on the fabric. His wife Karen would not understand why he went there and to be fair neither did he, not entirely. Sandy had an early start. He was still drinking at 1:00am. Fast forward five hours and he knew he shouldn't be slotting the car keys into his Vauxhall Astra and heading off to another early shift. In a vain attempt to rid his body of alcohol he drank three pints of water before going to bed and a triple espresso from the pot as soon as he got up. He knew he shouldn't drive but taxi expense accounts were practically non-existent these days and he had to rely on his own transport to get from A to B. When he got to the office no-one raised an eyebrow. Everyone working at this time of day said they hated the shift but they never considered trying anything else. Sandy had been doing a round of check calls to the police duty officers when he had picked up a tip from Motherwell. He had met Frank Simmons once before at a press event. He had been a young cop trying to impress an experienced hack but had seemed decent enough and Sandy had liked his company. It was also never a bad thing to get more cops on side when good leads could follow.

"Alright Frank," Sandy said, "I imagine you have been caught up in the snow hell overnight?"

"Oh aye, It's been murder. More than 200 cars abandoned and we're also missing a bus somewhere."

"A missing bus," Sandy interrupted sensing he could be onto something.

"Yes we have a coach unaccounted for near to the M8."

"I thought the motorway was closed?"

"It is but the driver will have taken the route near to the motorway along the old A8."

"Is anyone missing?"

"Well the driver obviously but no word on anyone else at the moment."

"Interesting....do you have anyone out there just now?"

"Yes, but its hard work. As I said we have hundreds of incidents out here but it's one of our priorities. If you try phoning back in about an hour I might have more details before the shift change."

"I will do Frank," Sandy said, "Thanks for the heads up."

***

It would be fair to say that George Rome was not enjoying himself. He had been out grafting in the snow for six hours already and was now having to create a makeshift helipad. Gerry helped as Jean looked after the patient. There was enough room in the yard for the air ambulance to land but clearing a good amount of space was going to be difficult in the time they had. The ambulance said that they should be there within half an hour. He improvised. George and Gerry turned over a flatbed trailer they had sitting in the yard and pushed it over using the larger of their two tractors. They then pushed the trailer along on its side, acting as a massive shovel. Judging by the scraping of metal on concrete the process didn't

24

sound particularly healthy and George knew he would regret the decision tomorrow when he assessed the damage. However, it was a small price to pay if they could help to save a life. Father and son managed to clear the space of around a squash court. They stood outside with their torches pointed towards the maelstrom and waited for their relief.

***

Detective Chief Inspector, Rosalind Ying, had taken control of the morning meeting at N Division. She had sent uniformed constables out to the farm who had searched the bus and reported back. What they had found changed everything and a forensic team was now on its way out.

"Good morning all," she said scanning the room. There should have been more people here and they would need much more than this as the day went on. Half had been here for ten hours already while those who had made it through the snow so far accounted for roughly two thirds of the normal total.

"First up I'd like to say it's been a great effort from the overnight team. It's been a long, hard shift but we think we've managed to keep everyone safe and there were no major accidents to speak of. However..." DCI Ying left the word hanging. "...however we have a developing situation near to the Kirk o' Shotts which looks likely to have major implications for us."
Colleagues glanced at each other, unsure of what might be heading their way.

"As you may know a coach was found abandoned. At first it didn't look like there was anyone on it – a farmer and his son managed to get to the coach and found a woman handcuffed in the toilet. Why she was there we don't know, but what we do know is that she was left there in her underwear and now looks to be suffering from hypothermia. The woman, Mary Clark, is being treated in Glasgow's Royal Infirmary and at this time it's unclear how long it will be before we can speak to her. In the meantime we've sent two uniforms out with the Air Ambulance to conduct a preliminary investigation. We identified the woman from a passport in her handbag. We also found two tickets for the journey

– one for the woman, and one for a child. The child has not been found and neither has the driver."

"That's all we need," snarled an anonymous voice from the back of the room, "a fucking pervert. With any luck he'll be dead already and buried in the snow. He won't have got far."

"That's enough," DCI Ying said, "Let's not prejudge this before we even get started. We'll be setting up in the major crime incident room here at Motherwell, active immediately."

The addition of extra space at the headquarters had been controversial to say the least. The decision had been made to ensure there was always a spare room capable of handling a major case but operational staff had complained that space was already at a premium. They had lost the argument and on days like these no-one really complained.

"I appreciate that a lot of you have been here overnight but additional help will be needed."

Everyone in the room nodded. In practice no-one claimed for overtime. It was cases like these that made the job worthwhile. What's more a similar case two years ago had failed and they had ended up dragging the body of a 12 year old boy from the bottom of a quarry. He had been beaten to a pulp and dumped in a weighted sack and forgotten. The press had had a field day with it. One of the tabloids had dubbed it the 'Cat Sack murder'. The label had no doubt sold a lot of papers but the family had been furious. DCI Ying wondered if this time would be different.

***

Sandy had been caught up in a round of calls to the emergency services all morning as he tried to establish the scale of disruption the storm had caused. Bored now, he had retreated from the newsroom and was sitting outside having a cigarette and coffee, freezing in the morning chill when he remembered the bus. His brain was running slowly this morning and he reminded himself he was getting too old to be out on the town on a Sunday night.

Five minutes later he rang Motherwell again and was surprised when Frank answered.

"You still there Frank, thought you'd have been off for a wee kip by now?"

26

"It's been a bit hectic."

"Anything to do with the bus?"

"After a fashion."

"Oh come on don't dry up on me now."

"I can't say Sandy."

"Did they find someone?"

"........"

"Frank"

"All I can say is that they have found someone on board."

"Male or female?"

"Female."

"Age?"

"Thirties."

"Injured?"

"No comment Sandy. Look there will be an official statement going out on this in the next hour. I'll get bollocked if I say anything more to you just now but keep in touch."

Frank hung up and left Sandy holding the phone about twelve inches from his face, looking down the receiver as if some hidden gem was going to jump out and give him more information. He was intrigued and wondered what the police were hiding.

***

Rosalind Ying had that sinking feeling. The results from the Police National Computer had not been good. The driver, Stevie Davidson, was listed on the Sex Offenders Register. More than that he had tried to abduct a girl ten years ago when he was only fifteen but had been caught by a passerby and arrested. He had done two years but was released early on good behaviour. It seemed the authorities felt he was no longer a risk.

"Fuck," Rosalind knew this was going to be a massive case and that she had to make the right decisions now if they had any chance of finding the pair alive. The first thing to do was to appoint a team but she knew N Division did not have the resources to police this adequately. She picked up the phone and contacted Chief Constable, Norrie Smith. It was agreed that he would assume overall control of the investigation while she acted as Senior Investigating Officer. Norrie Smith told her he would select the team with the best experience in this field, bringing together IT, intelligence, family liaison and someone from the Major Crimes and Terrorism Unit (MCTU). They agreed to liaise with the media team who would call a press conference within the next two hours to issue an appeal for information. They both agreed that there had to have been more people on that bus who could help. When the conversation ended Rosalind sat back and took one long deep breath, slide her hands back through her hair. *'I have to get this right.'*

***

Arbogast felt like death. Why was it that every major moment of his life always coincided with a hangover? A friend from England had once suggested the Scots had a self destruct mechanism which seemed to have a habit of kicking in at just the wrong time. He had protested against that at the time arguing it was nothing more than a petty prejudice but perhaps it wasn't too far off the mark. Arbogast thought the weather played a major part in the national psyche – the further North you went the worse the boozing became. He was surprised once, when visiting Thurso, to have found a sign on the main street pointing the way to the Samaritans. The suicide rate there was high but he wasn't that bad yet was he?

Normally he would have driven to work but now that he was based out of Pitt Street he no longer had the luxury of a parking space. If he needed transport he'd use one of the pool cars. Leaving early he felt fresh in the winter wind. It was not snowing in Glasgow anymore and he knew it wouldn't be long before heavy footfall and concerted effort would transform the city streets back to their everyday condition. His first appointment of the day was with the Chief Constable and the DCI. He imagined the first week would be induction heavy and work-light which suited him perfectly. He was only half way there when his phone rang.

"Arbogast?" It was a tinny voice at the end of the line, number withheld.

"Speaking,"

"Chief Constable, Norrie Smith, here. I need you in the office. Presentable – and within the hour."

"I'm just on my way in. I thought our meeting was at 10?"

"There's been a change of plan Arbogast. I've seen your record and I need your expertise for a developing case. We seem to have a child abduction case out in Lanarkshire. I see from your files you dealt with the so-called Cat Sack case two years ago."

Arbogast winced. It had been a difficult case to work and not one he liked to remember. They had tracked down the suspect but the boy had died. He should have done more.

"We all remember the case and there's nothing more you could have done. You have recent, relevant experience which we can use. I'll fill you in on the details when you get here. DCI Ying from Motherwell will be taking the lead. The team are meeting at Pitt Street. I want you to sit in on the press conference. The timing's not great but we can't pick the cases – you're on the team."

"Well I'm not sure how I'll look. I...eh...fell in the snow last night and I'm not looking too pretty."

"Too bad Arbogast"

After a heavy intake of breath Arbogast managed a "right" in reply

"Oh and Arbogast,"

"Yes sir?"

"Welcome to Major Crime."

5

Arbogast looked out over the assembled press pack and wished he was in a better frame of mind. The conference room was an oddly proportioned space framed by a stage at the front with stairs leading up from either side. It had been digested into the bowels of the Pitt Street headquarters and was best known to the public as the backdrop to many a night of misery on television news bulletins. It reminded Arbogast of church mainly due to the countless sermons he'd heard here, that and its size. The room stretched back about 40 feet but was easily the same in height. Halfway up pale cedar panelling gave way to expansive windows which in turn flooded the room with light. He entered the room from a narrow corridor to the right of the podium. For these occasions the stage was always redundant, replaced by a more intimate Strathclyde Police stall which was made up of two long tables sat side by side in front of a triptych of branded boarding, which made it feel like a post match football interview. For the first time today it was Arbogast who was sitting up front as part of the top team. Three of them sat at tables laden with radio and TV mics along with the dictaphones of the press corps. Chief Constable, Norrie Smith, sat centre stage with Rosalind Ying at his right hand. Arbogast sat uncomfortably on the left trying to make himself invisible. This was a big story. The press release had gone out first thing.

Missing persons Shotts

Detectives in Motherwell are appealing for witnesses after two people went missing overnight.

They had been travelling on a bus which became stranded in heavy snow when they appear to have left the vehicle.

One other person was found on board. This third person is presently being treated for exposure in hospital.

A press conference will be held today (Monday morning) at 10am.

Interview opportunities will be available.

For further information please contact Media Services on 0141 332 4789

The information was vaguely sensational and had attracted a full house. There were four TV crews, several radio stations and all the major local papers, as well as staff from selected UK agencies. Of all the snow stories doing the rounds this was the only one that was actual news. Rosalind Ying had insisted Arbogast obscure the cuts and bruises from his nocturnal adventure with makeup. He had protested but when she showed him his face in the mirror and asked whether that was what he wanted to show the national press for his first assignment in Major Crime he had given in. He still didn't look particularly healthy but he was as ready as he could be. Arbogast didn't expect to say much if anything at this stage in the investigation given he knew exactly nothing about it. His heart was racing and he was gripped by a fear he might be found out on day one. 'Stay focused,' he chanted to himself as Norrie Smith got the conference underway.

"Ladies and gentlemen thank you very much for taking the time to be here today. It's encouraging that we seem to have a full house and I can assure you that your help is needed. Last night a coach became stuck in a ten foot snow drift near to the Kirk o' Shotts on the old A8. On board we found a woman in her thirties suffering from the effects of hypothermia. She is currently being treated for this at Glasgow Royal Infirmary. From evidence found at the scene it seems there was also a child travelling with her who was not on the bus. The driver is also missing and we can assume the two must be travelling together. Given the temperature overnight dropped as low as -14 Celsius we are extremely concerned about their welfare and are appealing for witnesses."

Sandy Stirrit raised his hand and was the first to ask a question. "Are there any concerns about this child going missing with the driver?"

Norrie's reply was brusque "We have been unable to speak to the woman found on board and we do not know her relationship to the child at this time. I can make no further comment on this matter as it is part of an ongoing investigation."

"And when do you expect to speak to the woman," Sandy said, "Does she have a name?"

"Naturally she has a name," he stopped and smiled around the room, "but her details will not be released until such time as we have spoken to her next of kin."

"What about the driver – do we know much about him?"

"We have been in touch with the coach company and they are co-operating fully in our inquiries. I must stress we are at a very early stage in this investigation and our primary objective is to find the two missing people. There is a lot of snow in that area and we still haven't been able to fully open up access to the site yet given the conditions. The area is largely cut off and this is causing us problems. If anyone listening to this in the area saw or heard anything they might think is useful please contact us immediately. We need to know if anyone travelling on the bus beforehand remembers seeing the woman and child. We need your help," he said, looking directly at Sandy's camera. 'He's good,' Arbogast thought. "This investigation is being handled in Motherwell by DCI Rosalind Ying who is heading up our team there. To my left is DI John Arbogast who will be offering the expertise of the Major Crime squad who have dealt with similar cases in the past. We will be updating the media as and when we have more information and thank you again for your time."

Norrie stood up, nodded to the room and left with a press officer by his arm furiously scribbling notes and taking instruction. Rosalind Ying was left to deal with the mass of interviews, repeating the same information again and again. It was obvious there was something being left unsaid but this was going to be big news and the fact the satellite broadcasters were there already alongside network correspondents meant it was going national.

45 minutes later Rosalind Ying and Arbogast left the press briefing and rejoined Norrie Smith at his desk. Despite the fact that this was supposed to be a paperless office there were reams of reports and files. A dark wood table which had known many owners over the years formed the focal point.

"Right, sorry for leaving you with all that but I had some information flagged up to me through my blackberry which needed immediate attention," Chief Constable Smith said by way of apology, "As we know the driver, Stevie Davidson is on the sex offenders register but considered low risk. I've called in his social work reports so we should know more about his background shortly. The woman we found on the bus has been identified as Mary Clark. We've checked her files and she's married to a John Clark. They live in Shotts area. More importantly though is that she doesn't have children, so who was she with?"

Arbogast and Ying looked at each other and then back at the chief.

"I sense there may be something more?"

"Yes Rosalind," the Chief Constable said, "For the most part Mary Clark seems a model citizen. Interestingly, though, her maiden name was Sanderson," The revelation drew blank faces all round, "Her police file show that she had made a complaint about her father Eric about 20 years ago. She had claimed he had been sexually abusing both her and a boy on the Sanderson estate. She made claims about some sort of hidden room where her father abused children, herself included. The claims were never substantiated but it made a lot of news back in the 80s. The boy involved in all this was Stevie Davidson."

"You have got to be kidding," Arbogast said smiling incredulously, "You mean to say that a child has been taken from the daughter of someone accused of molesting him as a child? I've never come across a revenge attack so far down the line. It all seems a bit too fantastic. I mean how would he know?"

"Agreed, but on the face of it the facts we have certainly seem to connect. It looks like we might have a revenge snatch on

33

our hands. Admittedly it does all seem a bit bizarre. What are your gut feelings Arbogast? Do you think Mary Clark could be in on this?"

"And leave herself to freeze to death on the bus? Doesn't seem likely does it but it wouldn't be the strangest ploy I've come across. I don't know, is the short answer, but we need to be able to speak to her as soon as possible, we won't be able to keep this under wraps for long."

Rosalind Ying nodded in agreement. "I'll update the people we have on hospital watch at the moment. Arbogast, I suggest you speak to the father. I'll deal with the driver side of things and I'll get a family liaison officer ready to tackle the husband. We're going to have to pull our resources."

Mary Clark was being cared for in the intensive care ward at Glasgow Royal Infirmary. She had been diagnosed with moderate to severe hypothermia. When she had been found she was freezing with a body temperature of 29c, which was 7 below the norm. Doctor Ellen Fitzpatrick considered her lucky. Having been found practically naked in that weather she was fortunate not to have died. The only thing that had saved her was the length of time the engine had kept running. That and the fact the farmers had heated her externally with blankets and duvets. This was smart thinking and in the two hours it took the medivac to get there her temperature had already risen by two degrees. Mary had been semi conscious although she hadn't been making much sense. She was mumbling about Turkeys and honour as she slipped in and out of consciousness. The doctors opted to proceed with an internal warming technique. The doctor placed a mask over Mary's head allowing the gas to enter Mary via life support. If it all went to plan her temperature would rise by 2.5c an hour until she reached 40c. Only then would they know the extent of the damage. The patient was still shivering. As Doctor Fitzpatrick watched from the bedside she could see that Mary's pale blue face was starting to regain some colour but it would be several days before she was completely back to something approaching normal. "You're going to have quite a story to tell when you wake up," she whispered. In the corner of this private room PC Frank Simmons watched and waited.

Arbogast was surprised when he arrived at Eric Sanderson's farmhouse, or rather surprised at what remained of it. The address he had been given was for 'Sanderson Farm' on the outskirts of Bishopton in Renfrewshire, about sixteen miles south west of Glasgow. Arbogast had been paired with Detective Sergeant, Mhairi Reid. The farm itself was typical enough. A two storey sandstone affair which had been pebble dashed at some point. To the side was a small one floor extension which looked like it might be used as a kitchen. What was striking however was that the building seemed to be collapsing in on itself. There was a large crack from the middle of the house which began at the lintel for the front door and continued up through the height of the building. It looked like the hand of god had pressed down on the house and forced it down with the middle maybe half a foot lower than either gable end. The snow lent the scene a strange fairytale quality. Someone had been busy as the driveway and front court had been cleared. A man appeared from the right hand side of the house carrying a snow shovel in one hand and a cigarette in the other.

"Mr Arbogast is it?"

"Eric Sanderson?"

"The very same – I had a phone call to say you'd be coming. I see you've been looking at the house. It's been in my family for 150 years."

"What happened?"

"The past caught up with her. This area's covered in old mine workings. Everything after about 1872 was officially recorded. There were so many shafts littering the landscape that they needed to know where everything was. Unfortunately everything before 1872 is something of a mystery. Many of the pits simply fell into disuse and were covered over and forgotten although the pits and shafts remained. It must have been about a year ago that it emerged rather dramatically that this house had been built on top of old works. It had been snowing and when the big thaw came the ground gave way beneath us – there's limestone bedrock which gets eaten away by water – and as you can see the

35

whole structure simply sank. The council came out and surveyed the area. They found the mine workings alright – they're right beneath the living room. We were fortunate not to crash into the abyss but I fear the whole house might disappear this year once the next thaw comes, so I'm in no hurry to see the spring."

"But you're still living here?" asked Arbogast

"Well not really, I've a caravan round the back that I've been staying in. I do venture into the house now and again but it's really not safe. It's still home though – where else would I go? But enough of my misfortune, I gather you're here about Mary?"

"Yes and no. We're still waiting for your daughter to come round although I'm told that should only be a matter of time. It's the circumstances that we found her in that have brought us to you Mr Sanderson."

"Call me Eric, please."

"You know the circumstances Mary was found and we still have a child unaccounted for. It's the driver that's really brought us here."

"The driver? I can't imagine I'll be able to help you with him."

"The driver was Stevie Davidson."

Eric Sanderson focused intently on Arbogast and his knuckles turned white as his grip on the snow shovel tightened. Suddenly he seemed to become self aware and his body relaxed.

"Well officers, if it's Stevie Davidson you want to talk about you'd better step inside."

The first thing Mary Clark saw when she opened her eyes was her husband John. He was sitting at the side of her bed with his elbows resting on his knees, looking at the ground.

"John," she tried to say, though it sounded more of a rasp through her thickened throat.

"Mary – you've come back to me. I was so worried. I'm sorry."

Mary focused on trying to form her words and whispered "I'm sorry too."

PC Frank Simmons had been stirred from his stupor and was writing everything down. The first thing he did was to get in touch with control. There was more to this than met the eye. As he watched the reunited couple he couldn't help but be moved. Husband and wife cried and held each other tight but there also seemed to be a note of apology about the way they acted, as if they had parted on bad terms. While he mulled this over and waited for DCI Ying to arrive his train of thought was broken as the Doctor burst through the doors and asked everyone to leave.

6

The Sanderson farm was circled by a ring of birch trees covering about an acre of land which, in summer, must have given the family a sense of privacy. In the depths of winter the trees lent the property an eerie feel, with the white barked trunks camouflaged against the snow – it reminded Arbogast of a druid worship site he'd visited as a child which had been built around a rocking stone – not unlike the crooked house he could see now.

Arbogast realised he had come to a standstill, lost in his own past and struggling with his hangover when he saw that Mhairi Reid and Sanderson had left him behind. Jogging to catch up he found them at the back of the house. The detectives were surprised to find a large static caravan pitched about 30 feet north of the house itself. Behind it was a long slated building which Sanderson told them was a shower block which had once served a long gone camp site.

"Quite a set up you have here Mr Sanderson," Mhairi said, "although I'm surprised you choose to live like this, so close to the house."

"It's not ideal but it does. The building at the back has showers and electrics which supply me with all the power I need. There's also an outdoor tap but it's useless in this weather as you can see," he said pointing ahead of him. Beside the outhouse was a freestanding lead pipe which was capped with a copper tap. The water hit the ground, frozen in mid flow. "The weather's been so bad that I've been buying bottled water these last few days," he seemed amused by the story but cut himself off when he realised he was rambling. "And now if you please, welcome to my humble abode," Sanderson gestured for his guests to go inside.

Last through the door Arbogast stopped and scanned the narrow corridor which ran the length of the 40 foot tin can. The inside was even worse than he imagined. The walls were tatty and pockmarked with holes that looked like they had been punched through. The doors were of the plastic concertina variety and looked like they had played their last tune a long time ago. To his right Arbogast could see a door at the far end of the corridor which presumably led to the master bedroom. The next door sat at 90 degrees and was presumably another bedroom while directly in front he assumed the damp smell seeping from under the rotting, mouldy door must be the bathroom.

"Did you get lost Mister Arbogast?" Sanderson waved him through to the living room cum kitchen. The three of them sat down at an aluminium rimmed formica table top set into the far end of the caravan. There were fitted seats forming an L shape round the table, with the long end of the room framed with two panoramic windows which currently looked out onto the undulating snow fields of rural Renfrewshire.

"I picked it up for next to nothing from a travelling fair that used to camp here during the winter," he said, "It's more than 30 years old and as you can see is not fit for much these days, but it'll do me. But anyway I digress, what can I help you with? You mentioned Stevie Davidson?"

Arbogast generally preferred a bit of preamble but he could see his guest was in no mood to dance around the issue at hand, "Stevie Davidson is missing along with a child that had been travelling with your daughter. We know your connection and we believe you might be able to shed some light into the history between Mr Davidson and your family?"

Eric Sanderson sighed and shifted his weight back into the seat. "I thought I'd heard the last of Stevie Sanderson. This goes back to the 1980s and I'm sure you're well aware of the circumstances."

"I've read the reports but it's your version of events I need to hear today," Arbogast said, "I appreciate it's a topic you'd probably rather not delve into but I'm afraid on this occasion I'll have to insist."

"OK, well I'll give you a potted history of how we came to meet," Sanderson said, "As I've already told you my family's lived here for generations. At one time we had around 400 acres which we put over to sheep. We made a living from it for many, many years but then came the attack from Russia." Arbogast was in no mood for the ramblings of a lonely man and had already raised his hand ready to protest when Sanderson explained what he meant, "The Russians and their nuclear fallout was what put us out of business. The Chernobyl disaster in '86 polluted the animals – it meant we couldn't sell the sheep. There was a blanket ban on the sale of meat – those damned toxic clouds drifted over the land and rained us right out of business. Do you know there were farms still under restrictions as recently as last year? It was a real hammer blow to us. We tried to diversify with crops and then leisure but nothing seemed to work and eventually we sold the majority of the land. Some to the Forestry Commission – you can see the woodland about half a mile away. With the rest I put up a small wind farm. Maybe you saw it? There are only three turbines but if I had known how much money you could make I'd have kept more land. It's worth it just for the subsidies. The UK Government has promised to create fifteen per cent of our power from renewable by 2020 but they need to pay people to do it. It's crazy really but on top of any money you make from energy they also have 20 years guaranteed income just for having turbines. It's making me a fortune." He was lost deep in thought when a cough from Mhairi Reid brought him back.

"Apologies, that's got little to do with young Stephen. My family always liked to keep good relations with our nearest neighbours in Bishopton. For years we allowed community groups and local schools to use part of the land for annual camping trips. We have local water supplies here and it's a safe place for children to roam away from the danger of heavy traffic. In those days people weren't so bothered about letting their kids run free. In 1985 around twenty boys from the local High School came to camp as part of a three day trip. I remember it well as they called it 'frosties'. It was sort of a rite of passage where they would camp under the stars and not under canvas. They'd light fires and keep them burning through the night and be taught basic survival techniques, staying awake wrapped in sleeping bags. I remember

40

the teacher telling me they loved it. 'They all think they're Indiana Jones' he'd said. At that time we still had the sheep and I was only too happy to give the boys a talk on what we did, gave them a chance to work with the animals and experience farm life firsthand. Most of them would think they were too good for that kind of thing – they were beginning to be interested in girls and music, so work still seemed a long way off. Then it happened that one of the boys – Stevie Davidson – went missing, which, as you can imagine, caused a great panic. I assumed he must have gone off exploring but he didn't reappear. We searched everywhere – in the outhouses, in the animal pens – but he'd vanished."

"The police were here, though," Arbogast said, "there must have been quite a search?"

"Of course the place was crawling. There was a lot of talk that maybe he'd fallen down a mine. I had always heard there were hidden shafts in the area but at that time I had certainly never seen any so and I told them that although they didn't listen. But then after about 13 hours, just as quickly as he had vanished, Stevie Davidson reappeared. They found him walking along the M8 motorway, disorientated. He couldn't remember where he'd been...or so he said. I was just thankful that they'd found him as I felt partly responsible."

"Why would you feel responsible? Did you have anything to hide?" Arbogast was curious to see if he would get a reaction.

"I hardly think I'd allow school children to camp on my land then abduct one of them Detective. No that incident was the start of the end of my relationship with Mary – that was when all the trouble started." Eric Sanderson stopped and massaged his temple. He screwed up his face as if he were trying to block out the memory.

"Could you explain please?" Mhairi said, looking to Arbogast to make sure she wasn't acting out of turn. Arbogast nodded.

"The next thing I knew the police were knocking on my door saying they had a 'few questions to ask'. To this day I have no idea why she did what she did but she accused me of molesting the boy and her. My own daughter said that."

"It's a serious allegation but what grounds would she have for saying that?"

"None that I'd know of – her mother Joan, god rest her soul, had died from cancer the year before. Mary had taken it badly as they'd been very close. It was difficult for me caring for a girl of 12 after that – it's a hard age not to have a woman around. Things just sort of deteriorated and then after the 'incident', completely out of the blue, Mary accused me of rape. She told the police that I had taken Stevie Davidson to what she called 'a secret place' and 'happily abused' the pair of them. She said she had seen me with him the day he was found. And if that wasn't bad enough she said I had molested her too – done terrible things to her. I don't have the words to express what that did to me."

Arbogast was intrigued by the detail and thought it a nice touch that Sanderson had managed to look glassy eyed as he recounted his story. Perhaps he was getting too cynical but he couldn't help but feel he was wasting his time. He took a deep breath, "And where did she say this 'secret place' was?"

"That's just it, she never could say. It broke my heart to have her accuse me like that. The police took it seriously and searched the property but found nothing. The paper's got hold of it and my name has been tarnished ever since, even although there was never any evidence. To this day Mary claims she was telling the truth. She moved out of here as soon as she was able and I haven't spoken to her in about ten years. She's lost to me. I'm told she works helping hookers in the city – you know women that have been attacked – so I've heard anyway. As for Stephen Davidson well I haven't seen him since the day he disappeared and his family never made a formal complaint – only Mary did that."

"Could Mary and Stephen have kept in touch?" Mhairi said.

"It's possible I suppose, but why would they? To the best of my knowledge they had never even met. It wasn't long after that that the farm hit bad times."

Arbogast persevered "Let's try and stick to the matter at hand. I take it you don't think that Stevie and Mary would know each other today?"

"Why should they?" Sanderson said, his voice getting louder, "It's a hell of a coincidence that they'd be travelling on the same bus but what do you expect me to say? If they had ever met before, they were kids, nothing but kids. Would you remember

42

someone you had met once when you were a child, 20 years later? It seems unlikely to me."

"Yes..." Arbogast considered his next question carefully. He wanted Sanderson to be calm so he smiled with his eyes in a carefully rehearsed show of understanding, even if it was just theatre. "Do you get on well with your grandchildren?"

"Grandchildren? I don't have any unless you know something I don't?" Sanderson said, laughing.

"We need to know who was travelling with your daughter."

"Well she doesn't have any children that I know of. As for any friends she may have had or their kids, well I suspect you'd be better asking her husband. He'll know about her life now. I'm ashamed to say that I can't tell you anything about my daughter."

Arbogast sensed he would get nowhere with this today and he knew he had other people to speak to, "We've asked enough for today Mr Sanderson and I need to get back out to Lanarkshire which will take time in this weather. I have no doubt that we will need to speak to you again. Where can we reach you?"

"I'm working as an engineer at the new wind farm development on Eaglesham Moor. They're putting 200 turbines up there. It's one of the biggest projects in Europe you know. When I used the money from the sale of my land to put up my turbines I felt something of a pioneer. There weren't many around at that time and I used the money to retrain. I saw a boom industry in the making and it's turned out that way I'm glad to say. I'll give you my mobile number. We're doing some blasting at the moment as some of the turbines are being built on granite bedrock, which is causing more problems than expected. If I can't answer straight away I'll get back to you as soon as possible. Have you had any word on my daughter's condition?"

"Haven't you been to see her?"

"I don't think that would be appreciated."

"You could still phone."

"DI Arbogast, while I appreciate your concern for my family affairs, my daughter and I parted on extremely bad terms. We fought for over four years after the 'incident' but she was unrepentant. She still believes I've done her wrong and she can't bear to be anywhere near me, and I've come to accept that. I don't like it but that's the way it is. Having said that, though, she is still

43

my daughter and if you could keep me updated on her condition I'd appreciate it."

"I will do. Thanks for your time. We'll see ourselves back to the car."

Arbogast and Reid left Eric Sanderson mulling over the past, sat in his ancient caravan.

"Eric Sanderson," Mhairi Reid said, "the fun never starts." She laughed at the absurdity of her own comment although Arbogast found it hard to see the joke.

"What do you mean?"

"Well, look at him, a man in his mid-50s living in a wrecked old carnival caravan, sat back watching as his family home sinks into the ground right before his eyes. It's bizarre and yet he says he's rolling in money. Why would you stay here? If you ask me his story doesn't quite ring true."

"It's a strange one right enough," Arbogast said, "I mean why would a daughter accuse her father of sexual abuse – and not just her but a complete stranger – if there was no truth to it?"

"He did seem genuinely upset that he has no contact with his daughter but I still don't get why she'd put him through all that for no reason. Do you think the death of her mother maybe sent her over the edge?"

Arbogast considered the question for a moment before answering, "You do hear of children blaming one parent for the death of another, but with cancer I'm not sure that would hold. It's not like it's anyone's fault. But look at this place. It's in the middle of nowhere. You could get away with a lot out here if you were minded to – just the two of them."

"Oh come on Arbogast, do you really believe that? They checked at the time and found nothing."

"Yes you're right but that doesn't mean there's nothing here. The technology in 1985 was prehistoric by today's standards. Sanderson said in there he'd discounted the possibility of there being a mine in the area but look at the house, it's being sucked into the earth by a crumbling mine shaft so the stories were true. What else could be hidden here, waiting to be discovered? I think one thing is perfectly clear though."

"What's that?"

"We really need to speak to Mary Clark."

7

At the end of the first night Arbogast was going to stay and work but was told he needed to be fresh for the next day when they expected to be allowed to speak to Mary Clark in hospital. He left the office and made his way back home listening to Nick Drake's 'Bryter Later'. The sweet melancholy of the music fitted his mood perfectly as he wound his way through the frozen Lanarkshire landscape. He focused on the songs, isolating instruments to try and deconstruct how it was pieced together, trying to put the investigation to the back of his mind. He was a big believer in this way of working, leaving an issue to one side for a while and then coming back to it with a fresh mind. Psychologists called it incubation – you would have the genesis of an idea but forget it and then hopefully find inspiration from your subconscious. He wouldn't say no to an idea.

Arbogast was glad to be home, even if only for a few hours. He turned his attention to what constituted his drinks cabinet – a lone bottle of Glenmorangie left on the fireplace – and poured himself a generous measure into Caithness crystal. It was a thick, heavy glass and the last of six from a prior engagement, although there was no-one left to toast. He promised himself one complete, undisturbed hour of relaxation and made for his Project Genie III turntable, which was his pride and joy. His previous record player had shuffled off this mortal coil after a late night visit from Sandy who had been blind drunk when he arrived and who had immediately fallen asleep on the couch. Arbogast had woken the next morning to find Sandy standing in a trance emptying his bladder over his TV and stereo system. He was prone to sleepwalking but had been ejected from the flat, like a drunk at last orders. Everything had been destroyed, although the plus point

45

meant that everything had to be replaced and upgraded. He dug out his old Otis Reading LPs and sank back into his well weathered leather armchair as the strains of 'You left all the water running' oozed out from the speakers and deep into his soul. Slowly but surely he slumped into a good place, feeling the knots wash away. It had been quite a first day but at least it was over.

On cue the phone rang. He was in two minds about answering but he knew it might be important.

"Mr John J Arbogast?" the voice said at the other end.

"Speaking"

"Mr Arbogast its Janine from the Woodlands Rest Home – I think you should get here as soon as possible – your mother has taken a turn for the worse."

The trip to the care home was only a three mile drive but tonight it felt longer. As he drove through the city the bright lights and late night activity shot past in a blur. John J Arbogast had been born on the 8th of October 1973. His mother had left it late and was considered a very old mother at the time, giving birth at the grand old age of 41. He had no father that he knew of and no brothers or sisters to keep him company and so his formative years were spent primarily with his mum. 'Me and my mum,' he had always said when he was little. It had never seemed that he was missing out on anything as they did so much together and to be fair he had been quite spoilt. Or as spoilt as you could be when your mother spent half her time as a teacher and the other half making up for being away so much. But when she turned 70, things started to go wrong. At first he thought she'd turned to drink and it had been a great joke between them, her sitting with whisky in hand and him berating her for being such a lush. But a year later what he had thought were drinking binges turned out to be galloping Alzheimer's. That had been the term they'd used – galloping. The word conjured the prospect of a race to the finish and it hadn't been wide of the mark. Her mind at least was long gone and she'd been here in Woodlands for three-and-a-half years, in body if not in spirit.

When he arrived he pressed the buzzer and was admitted by an anxious looking nurse, "Janine?" he said

"Yes I'm so glad you made it. She's taken a turn for the worse."

"She seemed OK when I last saw her," Arbogast said, trying to remember when exactly that was. In the early days he had tried to visit every day. It had seemed so cruel to have her here with no-one to speak to and she was still fairly chatty at that point. But recently it had turned into once a month. Once he didn't come for twelve weeks and this was something he would never try to justify. He just never spoke of it to anyone. Apart from him no-one even knew she was here. They would sit for hours just the two of them. Arbogast knew he was talking to himself, but he told her what he had been doing, while she sat staring off into space with her hands clasped together on her lap, looking as if she were watching an invisible fly hovering around in front of her somewhere. Sometimes there would be flashes of recognition. She would suddenly burst into a smile and say, 'There's my wee boy,' or touch his cheek and tell him that she loved him. So shocking were these experiences that they more often than not reduced him to tears. He would hope against hope that it might mean she was getting better; that she might come back to him. But of course she never did and as the months went by she was gradually lost to him.

He usually saw her in what the nurses said was her 'favourite' seat by the window, surrounded by about twenty more of the lost generation. Today she was in bed, attached to a drip with life support machines doing what they did by her side. The red emergency cord seemed somewhat redundant given there was no one capable of pulling it.

"Mr Arbogast?" the voice broke his train of thought, "Mr Arbogast, are you OK?" asked Janine the night nurse on the ward. "You're mother is rejecting her medication and it's affecting her breathing. It's possible she may not last the night but we will try and stabilise her."

"What for?" Arbogast said, "She's a vegetable and she'll never been anything else. My mother died years ago, it's just that no-one's told her. Please don't give her any more medication – this is no way for her to be kept, paying your bills while barely being alive."

He thought Janine might be shocked but all she did was dip her head slightly before looking up at him through slightly narrowed eyes. "Mr Arbogast we have a duty of care here and we will do everything in our power to keep your mother alive. It's illegal just to 'let her go'. You of all people should understand that. I called you as it's possible we might fail. She might die tonight and if she does...well at least you can be with her. It's morbid I know but I've seen people who didn't come and regretted it, so you've done the right thing by coming tonight... in my opinion."

Arbogast knew she was right. "Well if you don't mind I'll sit here and wait."

Janine nodded. Doctors came and went doing their tests and measuring their successes and failures. Arbogast was ready. He thought it would be a blessing for his mother if this was the end of the road. Not that he believed in life after death but it had been a solace his mother had always clung to and he would never forget her so she would have that fleeting immortality if nothing else. As he sat with her he tried to remember her as she was, and one image kept returning to him. They had gone on holiday to the island of Arran, off the west coast, where they rented a small flat. This was their annual treat. People might laugh at the notion now but it had been such an adventure to him as a young boy. He had felt like an explorer, the laird of the island. But it was their routine that he remembered most fondly. There was a spot by the coast where a fresh water stream met with the sea where they would drive the car to wash it. They took washing up liquid from the kitchen and dowsed the car with buckets of fresh mountain water. It seemed such an exotic thing to do at the time and they always enjoyed it. He would 'race' his mum in the car, leaving 15 minutes earlier than she to reach their destination and of course she always let him win. She had climbed onto the bike, which was far too small for her, and cycled round and round in circles, both of them laughing. She wore a yellow pastel quilted jacket and beige slacks. Round and round she went until eventually she got too dizzy and fell off. They had fallen about laughing; it had been the perfect day and possibly his lasting image of his mother in her prime. He smiled as he thought of it and then slowly was taken by sleep and the exhaustion of the last few days.

He had been dreaming about running over cobbles when he was awoken by a gentle rocking. It was Janine. She had been trying to wake him, but for how long? In his stupor he said, "I

48

don't think it's time yet," as his mind lingered on his childhood days.

"I think you might be right," she said, "Take a look," as Arbogast looked up his mother was sitting upright in her bed, being fed some sort of gruel by the nurse. "You see I think Ella Arbogast will be with us for a while yet." John J was both relieved and disappointed. It was great to see his mum alive but this was her condition now. He asked if he might be able to feed her and the duty nurse agreed. "Not too much now and don't force it please, she might choke." He felt immensely sad as he carried out this task but at the same time he knew he had made a breakthrough of sorts. He still had memories to cherish and he could still be part of his mother's life. After about an hour he left the care home and got back in his car.

Arbogast sat for another 20 minutes, shuddering at the prospect that what had happened to his mother could happen to him too. If it did there would be no-one to come and see him. He turned on his phone which rang immediately. It was DCI Rosalind Ying.

"Where have you been?" The sound was so loud that Arbogast had to move the phone away from his ear, "Get yourself to the hospital – Mary Clark's woken up."

The call disconnected and Arbogast put the car in gear and left his mother behind him.

8

February 16th 2010

Ever since Stevie Davidson had failed to return to the depot many of his colleagues had already convicted him of every conceivable crime. More than a few eyebrows had been raised when John Dale had decided to take him on – a man who had been sent to jail for trying to abduct a child from the side of the street. The boss had argued that he had been young and that everyone deserved a second chance. He was like that, a bit of a social champion – he liked to see himself as someone who was better than the rest. 'But now look what's happened,' they said, 'No Stevie, no coach, and no child.'

'Was it a boy or a girl?' thought Jean Jessop, her mind was working overtime. Jean had worked with Dales for 22 years and had more experience of working in the business than the current owner. She had been taken on when there was just one bus and John's dad Phil ran the show. Jean knew what had happened. She might not have any proof but she knew. They'd been trying to catch Stevie out for years but he'd been clever. He'd kept his cards close to his chest. But now, well now they had him and he'll be going back to jail where he belongs. This time he'd gone too far.

The company was closed because of the weather. No-one could get into work and the roads were too blocked to cope with coach traffic so Jean had ended up with an unexpected couple of days off and too much time on her hands. *'Why haven't the papers named Stevie yet?'* she thought, *'I mean he's got previous and that kid will be in danger – possibly already be dead.'* Jean had already made her mind up that the world deserved to know exactly what they were dealing with.

Linda Davidson wasn't sure what had happened. The police had been round to tell her that her son was missing and that a child may be with him. A woman had been left to die on his bus? Linda didn't think it sounded right. Stevie had had his problems but that was all in the past. Even so the evidence wasn't looking good. She had tried to phone his mobile but it went straight to answer phone. The police woman had been nice. She had said they couldn't find him either but she was quite insistent they needed to find him soon – although there was no need to assume the worst. Then she'd gone and Linda was left, alone, in her lounge. 30 years ago the room would have passed for modern. The old brown mottled covers on the couch were tinged with damp and the furnishings were really now just functional rather than smart. This was the house of a 69 year old woman, living alone and with no need for the high life. Linda could feel that a deep depression was starting to take hold and she sat and wept at the unfortunate string of events which seemed to have dogged her son through the years. Linda stood by her fire place looking at aged and weathered pictures of her family that now seemed lost to her, when the silence exploded into a wall of sound. She was aware of a crash which sounded like glass. Cursing her haphazard cat she made her way into the hallway where she found a brick lying on the carpet. She stared at it not really knowing what to do. Turning to face the door another brick came smashing through the living room window, shards of glass tearing through her life and bringing Linda back to life, as fear gripped her to the spot.

News of a disturbance at Maplin Drive in Motherwell came not from the police but through the internet. Sandy Stirrit had been looking to find new lines on the deserted coach case when he turned his attention to his Twitter account. He had been sceptical about using social media as recently as six months ago but he could see the medium had obvious merits. He often gleaned leads from tweets and online discussions while he had been given more than one story through direct messages to his own account. People were now videoing incidents and posting them online immediately. Even though a lot of content tended towards the libellous you could still find interesting and immediate reaction to all manner of stories within seconds. Today he was surprised. Someone calling themselves @HotGossip had made a number of interesting entries under the trend topic #snowpaedo which, if there were anything to them, threatened to blow the case wide open. He had struggled to get any information from Arbogast but this might force his hand. A story is a story after all. @HotGossip had made a number of tweets over the last three hours including:

#snowpaedo bus driver is known sex offender Stevie Davidson from Dales Travel

Justice 4 #snowpaedo Stevie Davidson police do nothing then we will demonstr8

#snowpaedo Stevie Davidson @ Motherwell Maplin Drive 2:30 4 justice DM me for details.

Sandy was intrigued. He phoned Dales Travel and asked to speak to Stevie Davidson anonymously. He had spoken to the owner earlier who had nothing to say but it would be interesting to see the reaction. John Dale answered again and said Stevie Davidson was not working today and the depot was closed. He could pass on a message. *'Well Stevie seems to exist.'* Sandy phoned Arbogast to sound him out.

"Alright JJ how's the case going?"

"I can't speak now Sandy."

"You'll want to know this. Does the name Stevie Davidson mean anything to you?" The brief silence meant that it did.

"Thanks JJ, you might want to check up snow paedo on Twitter. Looks like there's a storm heading your way," and hung up.

With a cameraman in tow he headed over to Motherwell. Something was happening there and he might just get there first.

Arbogast was still driving but he wasn't happy. DS Reid had checked the social media sites on her personal mobile and when he heard the information being posted online he blew up.

"What are these people thinking – what are they thinking? Just sit back and wait for the backlash Mhairi – this isn't going to be pleasant."

This was a tricky case and the last thing they needed was vigilante attacks. If they didn't make progress soon they would need to put some kind of ID out for Stevie. At least that had been the plan. Messages about Stevie's identity in relation to the case were now being freely distributed online with some messages having been re-tweeted more than a thousand times. Someone had even made the leap and connected Stevie to his previous conviction. Nothing yet on his childhood but it was now only a matter of time before that came. *'Fuck.'* He knew they'd have to bring forward a press conference and update the media if they were to keep on top of the coverage. The messages were libellous but Arbogast knew Stevie's reputation was already tarred and he wouldn't have a chance of winning a court case. But there was no warrant out for Stevie so technically no-one was breaking the law. Sandy was already onto the case and this was certain to be all over the press before the day was out, regardless of anyone's guilt or innocence. They would need to name him but it wasn't his call. He phoned into Motherwell and told DCI Ying. She was furious.

"While I can get royally pissed at the press at least they check their information, this is just gossip and there doesn't seem to be anything we can do. We'll get hammered for keeping the public in the dark on this one but we haven't even spoken to Mary Clark yet. Get to the hospital and see what you can get from our mystery woman. I'll call a presser to tie in with the late night TV bulletins and we can hope for some damage limitation."

"Good luck Rosalind," Arbogast said, but the line was already dead.

By the time Sandy Stirrit arrived at Maplin Drive what looked like a full scale riot had broken out at a seemingly innocuous semi-detached council house. It was a quiet residential street which had erupted into a fury. There was a crowd of around 150 people, mostly children, mobbed around the house. All the front windows were broken and rocks and abuse was being hurled in its general direction. Sandy wondered if Stevie Davidson might be here, hiding. As he skirted around the mob police sirens cut through the noise of the rabble who knew their time was up. As the crowd ran the camera rolled. Someone had set fire to a pile of rubbish and left it burning on the doorstep. He could hear screams from inside. He'd seen this kind of thing before. It was peculiar to this area but when someone got wind of a sex offender living locally the mob turned ugly. Some of the local papers liked to print names and addresses but it inevitably ended up like this. Mothers would take their children down and families would unite to rid their community of its unwanted guest. It was horrible and ugly but he wondered what he would do in the same situation. He knew for a fact he wouldn't take his kids to hound a pervert. These people were out of control but all the same he could understand their reasons.

The TV news that night made for compelling viewing. The opening shots of a mob running from the shattered facade of an urban home made for great footage. Sandy had managed to get a quick sound bite from Linda Davidson who sobbed as she was led away by ambulance staff and under police escort, "My Stephen's done nothing wrong. It's all in the past. Why can't you leave him alone?" This was followed by confirmation from DCI Rosalind Ying that they were seeking to find both a Mr Stephen Davidson, who had been driving the coach, and an as yet unnamed child. No she could not comment on previous offences but they were treating this case as a force wide priority. They had yet to speak to the woman found but hoped that would happen shortly. The next day the papers were full of lurid details with past case notes 'mysteriously' appearing. It was trial by media. Although no charges had been raised against Stevie Davidson whatever happened next he was going to be blighted with scandal of the worst kind for the rest of his life.

Jean Jessop had got up early the next day to see what people were saying. She hadn't thought her campaign would have received so much attention but when the TV guy had turned up it had all gone stellar. But maybe she had got it wrong. Not about Stevie. He was guilty no doubt about it. But she'd expected him to be at his home but it had only been his mum. She had stopped when she saw her, tears streaking down her face, brought to her knees in her living room. But at least people knew now. At least they knew that it was Stevie that they were looking for.

9

February 17th 2010

Mary Clark looked frightened. Although she was past the worst she still felt dazed and her audience was having trouble making out what exactly she was trying to say through slurred words and vague gestures. She was like a drunk at the end of a long night of celebration and this wasn't going to make for an easy Q and A session. Arbogast and DS Reid had pulled up chairs and were sitting staring at the patient while her husband, John Clark, sat at the other side of the room.

"What were you sorry about?" Arbogast said.

"Sorry?"

"When you woke up you told your husband you were sorry – what about?"

"It's personal," Mary wouldn't look Arbogast in the face and was focusing all her attention on the hospital ID tag strapped around her wrist.

"Mrs Clark, we will have plenty of time to talk in-depth about what exactly happened but right now we have a child missing with a known sex offender. We know you were travelling with the child. A number of people on the bus have come forward to say you were travelling with a young girl. The driver of the bus was Stevie Davidson who I know you know. I've spoken to your father."

Mary's eyes opened with a look of pure disgust, "My father...what have you been speaking to that bastard for? Be in no doubt Detective that he does not speak for me."

In the background the husband, John Clark, tried to intervene, "I really don't think this is—"

"Oh it is very necessary Mr Clark," Arbogast said, "and I would ask you to keep quiet or I will have you removed."

John Clark looked at his wife and then the DI. He realised this was a battle he would not win and sat back down.

"Who was the girl Mrs Clark and why is she with Stevie Davidson?"

Mary sat silently while she worked out what she was going to say. She looked close to tears.

"You have no daughter," Arbogast said, "so who is she?"

"I can't say," Mary's voice was a whisper, "I just can't say."

Arbogast was getting angry, "You can't say – really? A little girl is out there Mrs Clark. Where you were found was under ten feet of snow. Now it's quite possible the girl and the driver may already be dead. Someone took the time to undress you and left you for dead and I have to make the giant leap that someone had good reason for doing so. Does it please you that the girl might be dead or being abused? She could be in the hands of paedophiles," Arbogast knew this was a risk but hoped the threat of abuse might spark some kind of reaction, "she could be getting molested right now, this very second. We need to find her Mary and you need to help."

It was at this point that Doctor Fitzpatrick intervened, "Please DI Arbogast this really won't do. I need to speak to you for a moment – outside please."

Arbogast glared at the Doctor with unconcealed contempt, "That would be most inconvenient Doctor," he spat out the two syllables of Doc-tor with a venom which surprised DS Reid and the Clarks.

"Nevertheless if you would join me for a chat I think that might be best." Outside Doctor Fitzpatrick was unimpressed. Her stance was belligerent with arms folded right foot forward and shoulders squared in a gesture of defiance, "Just what do you think you're doing in there? That woman is lucky to be alive. We still don't know what happened to her but she was, as you say, left for dead in a bus and has still obviously not recovered. You need to go easy on her – she's still in shock. Keep on at her like that and she might breakdown altogether. Do you understand?"

Arbogast realised he had been holding his breath and exhaled through his nose and nodded.

"And if you had bothered to ask," the Doctor added, by way of compromise, "the bruising she has is historic. I'd say they were a few days old. Certainly she didn't pick them up on the bus," Her voice softened, "I appreciate the situation here but please just use some common sense."

Arbogast thanked her and they returned to the patient was crying, buried in her husband's arms.

Arbogast stood at the bottom of her bed and apologised, "I'm sorry to have gone off like that Mrs Clark. I appreciate what you've been through, but please be under no illusions about the seriousness of this situation."

"It can't have been Stevie Davidson. Surely I would have recognised him. If you've spoken to my father then you will have been given an idea of what happened in the past. It ripped our family apart but I stand by what I said. That bastard has got away with a lot over the years and I'll have nothing more to do with him. But as for Stevie Davidson, I haven't seen him since I was a kid. I can't imagine he'd recognise me either."

"It's a hell of a coincidence don't you think?" Arbogast said, with the slightest of smiles.

"I'm sure I don't know what you mean officer, but I can assure you I do not know that man."

"Well that as may be but we still aren't any further forward trying to find the girl. Who is she?"

"I can't say."

"You will have to say Mary. If you don't you might be charged with perverting the course of justice and possibly as an accessory to murder."

Mary flinched at the M word, "I can't tell you everything officer – believe me I would if I could. I don't know how much you know about me but I work with prostitutes in Glasgow. The Phoenix Centre helps women in crisis, gives them alternatives. You have to understand that a lot of them are forced into what they are doing and addiction can be a one way street for a lot of them. I feel something of a bond with the way they live and try to help when I can."

58

"Mrs Clark, please stick to the point – we don't have much time."

"Bear with me. About a month ago I was approached in the street by a woman, Hanom Kocack. She's Turkish and had been smuggled into the country by her husband Onur who works here as an engineer. She told me her family had got into trouble with debt in Istanbul – very serious debt. She said Onur had borrowed from loan sharks. It's a familiar story but the debt soon added up and it was obvious they'd never be able to pay off what they owed. They had a daughter too – Kovan – and they made the decision to get out while they still could. Onur found work here in Scotland. He was sponsored by the Home Office to work with the Madoch Group. He left first, about six months ago. He tried to get his wife Hanom into the country but couldn't get a visa so he opted for a different route. She travelled west through to Bulgaria where she linked up with people traffickers. To cut a long story short she arrived in the UK with about twenty other women in a container on a cargo ship. She told me it hadn't been a good journey but she made it all the same."

"So the two are now both living here in Scotland – I'm assuming then I know who the girl is?"

"Yes but its more complicated than that. Hanom is in Scotland. In Glasgow in fact but her life has not worked out the way she planned. The women who were brought in are being forced to work in sex clubs. They are given no money and have no papers. They know if they go to the authorities they will be deported so they are virtual slaves. People don't realise what goes on. Onur is living somewhere in Glasgow but hasn't seen his wife yet. This is what brought Hanom to me. Hanom found my number through Google in an internet cafe. She told me she needed to find her daughter. She said they would have travelled together but the traffickers insisted it wasn't they way they did things, that it wasn't safe. Kovan was brought to Britain in a van. She was forced to sit for 16 hours in a space hollowed out under the dashboard. The poor girl was stiff with cramp, terrified she might be electrocuted by the wires which held her in place. But she got here and I met her off the ferry in Hull two days ago. We travelled back to Glasgow by train and were travelling to meet her mother in Shotts when we got stuck in the snow."

"How was it that you were meeting her mother – I thought she was a virtual prisoner?"

"There was nowhere for them to go but they do get breaks. They could walk about in the city but where would they go? She knew the people that brought her to Glasgow still had her daughter."

"So you would have me believe that the people holding Hanom hostage would just hand over her daughter to a complete stranger?"

"I can't talk about that but I made sure I got her."

"Mrs Clark you realise your story sounds rather unlikely."

"It's the only story I have. I'm not lying. You have my word."

"So what happened on the bus? Why were you left behind?"

"I don't know. It wasn't part of the plan. I knew I might meet a third party. Hanom was going to try and run away. She said she'd try and leave."

"You've met her then."

"She found the address for the Phoenix Centre and came in one day on one of her breaks. She seemed nice and I agreed to help. I had to – the way those women are treated would sicken you detective – I had to try. Hanom said if she couldn't meet with me on the night I collected her daughter then someone else would. She said I'd know."

Arbogast was far from convinced but sensed this is what he was going to have to work with. "So I'm assuming Hanom didn't show up?"

"The bus stopped in the middle of nowhere and a car drew up behind us, it must have been a jeep of some sort to get through the snow. The driver said the coach couldn't go any further. He seemed nice and gave Kovan his jacket. He was very concerned for her. And then someone else got on the bus and, well, I just can't remember anything else. Kovan was quite relaxed about the whole thing. I think she was excited at the prospect of seeing her family again and all that snow, it was a novelty to her. I think she felt her journey was over."

Mary looked exhausted. She'd been talking a lot and had no energy. Her face was still very pale and drawn and it looked as if she needed rest. Arbogast could tell there was some truth to her tale but he wasn't sure how much.

"I'll leave you be for now Mrs Clark but I'll be back. You will have to remain here until you can be released. DS Reid is the family liaison officer for this case and she'll keep you up to date with what's going on. You will also be seeing me again. Before I go however I need you to tell me where Hanom works. It is essential I speak to her as soon as possible. She may have pictures of the child which will help us too. All I have to work on at the moment is that the girl is missing with a known sex offender with a history which ties closely into yours. This case isn't looking too tidy just now and if, as you say, there is another person involved then it looks even worse than I had expected. Where does Hanom work?"

"I promised not to betray that."

"Do you know what's happening here?" Arbogast said, his voice rising, "You are an accessory to abduction, trafficking and failing to report multiple crimes. You need to start cooperating."

Mary stared back for an age before replying, "I need you to help me. The last thing I want is for that girl to fall into the hands of dirty, filthy, perverted men. I've been there and I wouldn't wish that ordeal on anyone. If this is Stevie Davidson we're talking about then it would surprise me that he was mixed up in something like this, given what I know about his past. But I worry about Hanom Mr Arbogast. If you turn up at the club as part of an investigation she may well disappear. These men don't mess about."

"I will be discreet. There are ways round this. It may be that we already have some kind of contact there. A lot of the clubs are very cooperative. They're lucrative for the people who run them and they like to keep us onside."

"Very well," Mary said, she was shaking now and afraid of the potential consequences of what she was about to say. "Hanom has been working out of the Devil May Care club. It's possible she may have been moved as the women are rotated to make sure the regulars have fresh meat to ogle. If I were to try and find her I'd start there but tread carefully."

Of all the places this investigation was heading the last one Arbogast had expected was the venue of his recent humiliation.

Mary was right, they didn't mess about there and less than 48 hours ago he had been one of lecherous punters ogling fresh meat. *'How am I going to be able to go back without being recognised? First things first – I'll have to get back to Motherwell to update Rosalind Ying about where we're at.'* Arbogast was pleased that he had made a breakthrough. He remembered all too well having failed the last child he had been tasked with finding. The last kid had died and that couldn't be allowed to happen again. But then again perhaps it was already too late.

10

DCI Rosalind Ying stared at the paperwork and knew that on the third day of the investigation things were only going to get worse. The researchers on the HOLMES team were collating every piece of evidence which had been gathered so far. Witness statements; evidence from door-to-door enquiries; and crime scene analysis; but it was still early as far as getting results were concerned. She was hoping the leg work would throw a fragment of progress her way as the press coverage had gone ballistic after Stevie Davidson's identity had been confirmed. His past record hadn't been mentioned but that hadn't stopped the vultures from tearing strips from his bloodied reputation. This was both a blessing and a curse. Although the case was now leading news bulletins across the country they were also under more scrutiny than ever. Rosalind had pulled Stevie's social work record and his police files. He wasn't the worst, she had explained to Arbogast, and he didn't seem to pose a threat. She was interested in the information that sprung up on his disappearance in 1985 and she and Arbogast had discussed this at some length, "It does seem quite a coincidence. Do you think Eric Sanderson could be involved?" but Arbogast, or John as he asked to be called, wasn't sure, "There's something wrong with his story but I'm not convinced he's directly tied into this. If the allegations from the 80s are true then Sanderson certainly played a part in shaping Stevie's life. What I can't figure out is how this all fits together? It doesn't make sense but maybe there's more to him than meets the eye?" They'd got Stevie's mobile number from his work and tried to trace the handset but it hadn't been used since the morning before he went missing, which his mother had confirmed had been a call to her. The number was still being monitored but it seemed likely at this point that it wouldn't be used again. The weather was still holding them up. While it had stopped snowing, travel conditions hadn't improved. Overnight temperatures had been a constant -12c, rising to only -5c in the day. The snow masked any evidence there might be at the bus and it had been snowing all night. By the time they reached the coach there were no tracks to suggest anyone had either left or entered the bus from any direction. The bus itself had been another problem. They had to wrap and lift it and bring it back to Motherwell for forensics which was a major operation in itself. The roads were still bad and the vehicle so big that the flatbed sent to carry the bus had slid off the road and into a ditch and ended up needing rescued itself. In short it was all taking longer than it should. Frustrated, Rosalind Ying gathered her papers and made her way to the morning meeting.

The debrief room was full which reflected the size of the case and the priority which it was getting. In reality the scope of the case was now national with forces across Scotland on the lookout for Stevie Davidson and the girl. There was a quiet chatter among the various teams as they waited to hear if any progress was being made. One side of the emergency incident room was floor to ceiling glass masked with internal blinds which were open. This allowed Arbogast, sat at the head of the room, to see Rosalind Ying powering along, papers in one hand, deep in conversation on her mobile in the other. The door opened slightly then stopped with Rosalind's foot keeping it from closing. He hadn't appreciated it before, perhaps he had been struggling with the case, but she was an attractive woman. With a Chinese mother and Scottish father DCI Ying had a classic dress style and a confident nature. She wore figure hugging designer suits which flattered her shape. As she pushed through the throng she caught him staring and smiled. He tried not to blush. *'This is not the right time to be leering over your boss.'* Rosalind had a laptop to plug in for a powerpoint presentation. As she bent over to plug the computer in he couldn't help but be impressed by the sight of her and found himself wondering what she was like when her out-of-office was turned on. He wondered what it would be like to have her like that, bent

64

over and permissive before cutting himself off, embarrassed by his own inappropriate daydream. He hoped no-one had noticed although he could feel his face had reddened.

Rosalind stood up, "Right let's get started," she paused while the room quietened down. "First off I'd like to say thanks for everyone's efforts so far but as you will be aware we are still far from the finish line."

She was interrupted by Craig Marshall from CID. "Let's face it, the paedo has probably already killed the kid – when we find the bastard he'd be best off having an accident. It's not like it's his first time, the prick."

There were murmurs of assent around the room but the reply was blunt.

"If I hear any one of you repeating shite like that, you will be off the team. We do not know what Stevie Davidson's motives were although on the surface there is a link to Mary Clark. We still don't have a picture of the child but I'm hoping we'll get one today from the CCTV footage we're reviewing from Buchanan Bus Station. The girl, Kovan, was smuggled into the country so there may well be links to child traffickers either here in Scotland or overseas. It is unhelpful to come to this investigation with the mentality of tabloid outrage. Keep a clear mind guys and we might just break this case – is that understood?"

The silence was all the answer she needed. "At the moment we are questioning all known sex offenders but so far have turned up nothing. Everyone we have spoken to about Stevie Davidson has said that they trusted him a hundred per cent, although we suspect one of his colleagues has been leaking information to the press. The online entry naming Stevie came from a Twitter user called Hot Gossip who rather stupidly had kept contact details on her profile despite an attempt to appear anonymous. We will be speaking to one Jean Jessop in due course. Meanwhile the search goes on. So far we've had more than a hundred uniforms out there but progress has been slow and the fact there's so much snow has been a nightmare. DC Small I think you might have more information from the scene?"

"We haven't turned up anything from the bus at all. So many people have used the coach that it's difficult to tie anything down. Interestingly we have one lead from the Kirk o' Shotts

65

church which we missed first time round. A door had been forced at the back of the building. We hadn't seen it first time as snow had obscured the wall," this was met by groans and disbelief, "So we know someone has been in the church recently. The door to the bell tower had also been forced but we found nothing to suggest that anything else had been damaged."

Rosalind turned her attention to DS Reid as family liaison officer, "What do you have for us?"

DS Mhairi Reid had questioned the husband John Clark as soon as the investigation had been called in. She travelled to his home with one of the duty PCs whose name she couldn't remember. The couple had a modest home in Shotts, just a few miles from where the bus was found. The estate was one of those non-descript brown brick affairs that were thrown up on vacant plots across the UK. While the area once had a distinct industrial feel post war reconstruction had seen an explosion of council estates and more and more of these areas were becoming commuter zones, with pokey homes being thrown up with little space between them and not much in the way of sound insulation. DS Reid had a gut feeling that John Clark would not be home, suspecting he would have already left for the hospital but she wanted to see what she could learn before she spoke to him in person. The house itself was semi-detached with an out of place Tudoresque wood and plaster effect covering the top floor. She saw nothing so out of the ordinary. Inside was an explosion of IKEA and brown leather and it had a distinctly masculine feel, like a bachelor pad which had morphed into a married home but still hadn't decided on a style. It wasn't so different from her home in Shawlands. Going round the back garden she saw there was a boarded up window in the kitchen. A box stood out from the snow which contained large shards of glass so it would appear that the damage was relatively new. As she peered into the kitchen a voice sounded from across the hedge.

"Can I help you officer?"

It was the neighbour, a 50-something woman, with a cigarette in one hand and a smoking mug of tea in the other. The mug read 'horny bitch'.

"Do you know when this happened?" DS Reid said, "It looks recent."

"Two days ago that was. Those two are always fighting. The walls in here are so thin you can hear everything." *'And I bet you fucking love it,'* thought DS Reid. Horny bitch continued, "They were screaming at each other that night. It was something about a kid. I don't know if she can't have any or he won't let her but they were wild that night. There was a lot of noise and it sounded like they were throwing things. I was out having a smoke when an ash tray came crashing out of the window. I was quite frightened to tell you the truth. And then I heard her screaming so I knocked on the door and it all went quiet. He answered and said it was all fine but I told them if I heard anymore I'd have the law round. And that was that."

Mhairi left horny bitch tapping fag ash into thin air. About a half an hour later she was back at the hospital where she found John Clark sitting by his wife's side.

"Mr Clark if you have a minute I'd like a word," he looked round absent-mindedly and patted Mary's hand and kissed her forehead as he left. Mhairi explained her role as family liaison officer and that she would be his first point of contact for any developments.

"I'll be honest with you Mr Clark we are still at an early stage with this investigation but I can assure you that this case is our number one priority," John nodded but looked as if he was bemused to be having the conversation at all. "First off I have to ask you a couple of very direct questions and I'd appreciate an honest answer."

"Of course."

"Did you know the child your wife was travelling with?"

"No."

"We don't believe that Mr Clark. What were two of you fighting about the night before?"

That got his attention.

"Sorry. What?"

"I have reason to believe there had been a violent disturbance in your home the night before this all happened. I visited your house before I came here. There was a broken window."

"It's the bloody neighbour that's been talking to you isn't it, the bitch. Look DS Reid it's no secret that we've been having a bad patch and that night, well, let's just say we went beyond the pale. Mary and I desperately want to have a child but my wife can't. She wants to adopt but I'm not sure. She got so angry that she drew a kitchen knife on me. I'm sure she didn't mean anything. She wouldn't have actually stabbed me but it shocked me and I—"

"Did you beat your wife Mr Clark?"

"—Hang on that's a bit strong. I lashed out at her. She had a black eye and left for a friend's house in Glasgow. I haven't seen her since. I've been waiting and waiting and now this," he gestured behind him, "I know I was wrong but this is unbelievable. I can't believe she would steal a child though if that's what you're getting at."

"I didn't even suggest that Mr Clark. Let's just keep calm."

DS Reid's report came as quite a revelation to the group. Rosalind Ying knew of course, but to many in the team it sounded like a promising lead. DS Reid explained, "On the face of it seems as if Mary Clark might have the motive to abduct a child. She knew Stevie from when he was a boy but denies they've kept in touch. I'm no psychologist but this wouldn't be the first time that someone complaining of child abuse turned out to be an abuser themselves."

"A female child abuser," Arbogast said, "would be very unusual."

"Agreed," Rosalind said, "but not impossible, and we must keep an open mind. We will need to keep Mary in hospital for as long as possible. If she recovers fast enough we may be forced to arrest her to give us more time to pick through this one. Her story is full of holes and her husband seems to be a problem too. The bastard's lucky he wasn't reported for assault."

Everyone nodded. A huge amount of time was spent by the force dealing with domestic abuse and warring couples. It was never pretty but had become part of their day-to-day lives.

"Our other lead is the information we got from Mary Clark. How reliable this is we don't know but it seems the mother might be working as a lap dancer in the Glasgow area – forcibly if the story is to be believed. I need to know who owns this business. It goes without saying that means a trip to the Companies Register. Also we need to double check the women's identity – this Hanom Kocack – we'll be trying to find the husband. Onur Kocack is apparently working on a wind farm through a Home Office sponsored scheme so he should be easy enough to find. And in the meantime DI Arbogast has an interesting assignment relating to the mother. Arbogast over to you..."

The possibility of human trafficking in the case posed several very real problems for Arbogast. Firstly everyone he was trying to track down did not exist, not legally anyway. There were no pay slips, national insurance contributions or health records – nothing that would point to where they could be found. Over the years there had been many warnings of the dangers of people being smuggled into the country but so far no-one had been caught, which made him think it might not be such a big problem after all. Arbogast phoned his old CID pal Richard Evans.

"Hey Rich, how's it going?" Arbogast said. He could hear a sigh at the other end of the line.

"What is it this time?" Both men had worked together as rookies in Glasgow CID in what felt like a lifetime ago. In 2001 Rich had moved into the then newly formed Scottish Drug Enforcement Agency. At that time it was all about sending a public message that drugs were being taken off the streets, although in reality they were only chipping away at the corners. Time had seen the agency expand and it now had responsibility for certain serious crimes and border protection in partnership with the UK agency, SOCA. In short Rich's stock had risen and he was among the more influential frontline police in Scotland.

"Rich you'll be aware of the coach case I'm on?"

"The Snow Paedo you mean? You've been doing yourself proud there so far."

"Don't be a dick," Arbogast said, "there's still a kid missing. I have information on this case which ties into the Devil May Care club."

"The titty bar?"

"So eloquently put but yes. I think the child's mother may – and this is only a 'may' – may have been smuggled into Scotland from Turkey. Do you have anything on the club? Who runs it? I'd owe you one."

"Ah behold the sight of the lesser crawling Arbogast – a sight so rarely seen in these parts. Well as it happens we have been keeping tabs on Devil May Care. It's part of the Madoch Group – do you know it?"

"I've had dealings with Mister Madoch in the past."

"These days he's Mister Teflon. His business appears to be a legitimate company, but in reality he's tied into so much shit that it's only a matter of time before we get something on him. John Madoch started out carving up his rivals with kitchen knives but he got wise fast and he's built up a pretty impressive empire. Madoch has a sizeable holding in the Moorland Wind farm out at Eaglesham. He's also been putting up speculative office developments in the financial zone, not to mention a couple of city centre hotels – you might know them – the Cooperage and the Gold Star?" Arbogast didn't know them, "but the thing is all the cash comes from drug running and prostitution. Madoch is as bent as they come but he has good people and we just can't trace his money. His only nod in the direction of dodgy these days, on paper anyway, is his chain of lap dancing bars. He has six – one in every Scottish city. We think he brings in girls from Eastern Europe and rotates them round the clubs a couple of weeks at a time. So far we haven't been able to catch him out."

"Have none of the girls been able to help?"

Rich snorted down the phone like a bridled horse. "We've tried John but they're scared stiff. They all say the same thing, that they're well paid and thankful for their jobs. If they say there's no problem it leaves us with a headache and we've no evidence to suggest they're here illegally. Politically it's a bit sensitive as no-one wants to admit the trafficking issue is alive and well. We just keep saying we're doing well policing the borders and everyone's happy."

"Except the girls," Arbogast said, "Look Rich thanks for your time. I'm going to try and make contact with this woman, if she even exists, I just wanted to pick your brains and check I wasn't stepping on a live investigation?"

"Not so that you'd notice but if you get anything on Madoch I'd appreciate being kept in the loop."

Arbogast spent the rest of the afternoon going through case work and arranging a timeline of events as they had them so far. Then when he had paid a visit to the communications team to check for an update on press interest he left for Glasgow. It was going to be another late night.

Hanom Kocack was worried. Things had not gone as planned and she had heard nothing about her daughter. She had trusted the woman from the refuge, Mary Clark, so what had gone wrong? She hadn't made the rendezvous and now she didn't know what to do. Hanom had stolen a mobile phone from one of the men in the club the next night and tried to phone Mary. More often than not, the men were so drunk you could slap them on the face and they'd still pay up. But the line was dead. No answer. So what was happening? She knew her husband was here somewhere. In this foreign city, he was here somewhere, so why hadn't he got in touch? Something must be wrong. They had planned for this and nothing could go wrong – that's what they'd said. Tonight she had to keep on doing this disgusting job. Thrusting herself on those drunken slobs, with their erections rubbing against her thighs, trying to touch her, wanting her. The first night she had been sick, she didn't know how much longer she could keep going. The girls she stayed with kept changing and they never spoke. There were fourteen of them living in a large damp room in a tall building. They each had a mattress and sleeping bag but that was all. They allowed them out at night for half an hour but they were told not to disappear, not to speak to anyone or their families would pay the price. Poor Kovan. Where was she now – dead maybe or left to rot somewhere. Oh god no, please not that, please let my baby be OK.

Arbogast parked a couple of blocks away from Devil May Care. There was a good chance the car would get broken into but it was a chance he was willing to take. Across the road from the nightclub was a gap site. The building had been a well known department store in its day but had burned down about 35 years ago and had never been redeveloped. This part of town remained quite unfashionable despite the fact it was only two minutes walk from the city's main shopping precincts. He waited at a safe enough distance so that he would not be seen by the bouncers on the door. The girls arrived in a mini bus at 10:00pm. They all wore long coats so he assumed they were already 'dressed' for the night. 'It's another way of keeping them on the leash,' Rich had said once. He thought the girls were coming in from Eastern Europe. Arbogast saw one girl who he thought fitted the bill. She looked familiar. The club opened at 10:30 and was open until 3:00. It was midweek and he wondered how busy the club would get. People drifted in and out until he spotted his chance. A large stag party of around 25 boozed up blokes turned up ready for their titillation. It had obviously been an all day session but the management had let them all in all the same after a quick grilling. *'There is nothing as stupid than a drunken man with a cash card,'* Arbogast thought as he filed in behind them, an anonymous friend.

"It's the business this eh," he said pretending to be one of the lads, "Best part of the night mate best part of the night. It's just a shame you can't take them home but you never know eh?" It made Arbogast ashamed of himself. He had been here himself barely able to stand just the other day and he'd been just the same, thinking he owned the girls, that he could paw them. Inside he bought himself a drink and sat down. He was wearing a suit jacket, a striped white shirt, and jeans. He couldn't see his target yet and would have to bide his time. He paid a girl for a dance and was back at his table in a few minutes. This endeared him to the crowd with the stag saying to him, "You don't mess about you dirty bastard – It's my stag you know. It's supposed to be me first." Apparently he thought he was with him. And then he saw her and rather than waste any more time he made his approach. Arbogast had to admit this was a good looking woman. Tonight she was wearing all white lingerie – she looked like something out of a 1980s porn film, which appealed to his baser instincts. She looked at him with fuck off eyes and said "Shall I dance for you?" She took him by the hand and they left the bar and into the corridor which led to the parlour. He couldn't remember having seen that before. She stopped and turned to face him.

"You were in here the other night. I remember now – you tried to touch me, to feel me. You're supposed to be barred. In fact I think it's time you left – wait here."

This was his moment, "Hanom?" he said. He knew from her reaction that she was the one he was looking for, "I can't speak for long but I'm with the police. A girl has disappeared and I've been told you might be the mother?"

Hanom moved back a step "Who are you. Is this some kind of joke?"

"No joke – I've spoken to Mary."

"We cannot speak here there are cameras," she said looking around to see if they had been noticed, "Speak to me while I dance, but quietly." She took him to a cubicle that was enclosed on the left and right with a red velvet partition. There was no door and at the back of room sat a security guard. If it was the same security man from the other night he didn't seem to recognise Arbogast. When he sat with his back against the wall Hanom straddled him with her legs on either side of him, knees down on the seat. As she writhed over him he had to struggle to focus his attention.

"I have a police mobile in my jacket pocket. I will leave the jacket here so take the phone. That way we'll be able to talk and I'll be able to find you – we can trace your movements but only if the handset is on." Hanom was still dancing and Arbogast coughed to try and hide his embarrassment.

Hanom was following every word now, "Where is my daughter? What has happened to Mary Clark?" she was bent over Arbogast now and had taken off her bra.

Arbogast tried to look turned on, for appearances sake, although under the circumstances this was no great feat. "She's OK," he said, "but in hospital. She says she doesn't know what happened but I think she knows more. Will you help me?"

She stood up and smiled at him, bending over to kiss on the cheek, "I have no choice – please get me out." He paid her the money and left as the stags partied on. Everyone was too busy to notice Hanom going back into the corridor and taking the phone from the inside of the black suit jacket which had been dumped on the floor.

73

11

February 18th 2010

He met her at the Adelphi at 2:53. He was smoking a cigarette and she tried to disguise herself with a large brimmed hat with a dark band around it and a long overcoat. She asked for a light but she only wanted to see his tie. A man with a hat and cane was watching. He looked a bit like an aged Charlie Chaplin but they hadn't seen him, yet. They hailed a cab and left. They didn't notice the man with the cane stub out his cigarette and follow on behind. Two others watched him leave too, but that was another story. In the cab they talked about this and that, about a man called Reardon and another called Jake but they were skirting around the issue. 'Right at the next corner,' he said. He hadn't told her where they were going and she wanted to know. 'The Green Cat,' on Saughton Street he said. She thought he wouldn't like it there but he said that was only when he wasn't expected. The green neon sign outside meant they had arrived and as they entered the car left. He took her arm and led her to a table but they didn't see what the mirror saw: a limping man, with a Charlie Chaplin cane. The piano jingled on but no-one really listened. As they ordered they should have seen the cane, the lunging limp and the man who was taking his hat off but they were still making small talk, no time for the outside world. The piano played on. She hadn't eaten all day so she ordered a glass of milk – hot, while he wanted a steak sandwich, rare, and a glass of beer. She hadn't looked at the menu. And still they didn't see him. He was looking now, looking all around. He had come for a reason but they didn't know what it was yet, although we did. He asked about money but she didn't know. Charlie Chaplin left the bar; his back was aching, too much

74

for one day but it hadn't ended yet, not for them. He'd found them and soon he would bring the others back... the Killers.

It was 3:00am. Arbogast smiled as he watched The Killers, a Film Noir from 1946 starring Burt Lancaster and Ava Gardner. It was Lancaster's first movie. He loved this scene most of all. It was subtle for its time. If you watched the main characters and their small talk you would miss the bigger picture. It all happened in the background. *'It's all in the background,'* he thought, *'what's happening in this case that I can't see – the connection that's missing? Where's my limping man, my missing link?'* Arbogast swirled the ice in his glass and hoped that Hanom Kocack would soon be able to fill in some of the blanks. It had been three hours since he had left the club and he suspected would not be able to phone until it was safe. He had been brought onto the case as 'the expert' from Major Crime. He snorted at the thought of it. If you could call finding a missing child after he'd died an accomplishment then he was definitely the best man for the job. He didn't want to live through that again. He remembered having to tell the mother her son was dead and how she had pounded his chest 'you said you'd find him,' she screamed, 'you promised you'd find him.' He would never forget that. All the family had been there that day and every one of them had looked at him in that one moment in a mixture of disbelief and hatred. He knew it wasn't his fault, knew they were all caught up in the moment but she was right – he had promised to find the boy and he supposed that he had, although what use was a corpse to a loving mother? What was worse was that the 'Cat Sack' killer was never found – all in all a resounding success. Arbogast still hadn't been formally introduced to the Major Crime unit but they obviously had faith in him. The rank and file hated Major Crime which had formerly been Serious Crime but was changed in one of the regular departmental reorganisations, which in reality amounted to nothing more than a smoke and mirrors reshuffle which was supposed to point to progress. He knew from his time in CID that some of the constables didn't like the 'big guns' as they called them. They saw only an elite group that they weren't part of, people doing the glamour work, but that wasn't the case at all. The truth was that they were the best in their field. The unit worked across the

Strathclyde Force area, with officers parachuted into investigations which best suited their experience. Regional CID teams were usually glad of the help and that had certainly been true this time. But was he overreaching with this ruse with Hanom? What if she didn't phone and he never heard from her again? The Killers had ended now and he saw on the late night news that a CCTV picture of the missing child had eventually been found. *'Thank god for that,'* he thought, *'it's taken three days to get that out of the system.'* The picture wasn't great quality and wasn't in continuous video capture, rather the stop-start time lapse shots you sometimes see on TV during cases like these. There was Mary, hand in hand with the girl. Kovan had no luggage, no bags but was clutching something in her hand. The sequence showed footage from three separate cameras and followed their journey from outside the bus station through to the departure board and then onto the coach that would end up stalled and stranded in the worst blizzard in 50 years. The TV announcer said the Police had asked for anyone with information to come forward. They had had a good response the first time round but it was good to keep this in the public's eye. Arbogast hoped it would do some good. He waited until about 4:00, but it was clear the call wasn't going to come. He woke up later that morning, still fully dressed in yesterday's clothes, and immediately left the house.

Arbogast thought the investigation was going well. That is to say everyone was busy all the time even if they had yet to make that major breakthrough. The public appeal had helped fill in some of the blanks and they were fairly certain now that Mary Clark had at least been telling the truth about her movements. Witnesses had seen them leave the train and make their way to the bus station. More than sixty people had got in touch to say they'd been on the bus although only about a dozen could remember seeing the pair on board. They hadn't appeared to be talking much on the bus but Arbogast didn't think that unusual. How much English is a 5 year old from Turkey likely to know? Rosalind Ying had also identified the van the child had been smuggled into the country from CCTV footage taken at Hull. The border control people said it was far from an exact science and that this must have been one that 'slipped through the net'. Just that day, they had explained, they had found a container in a cargo ship with five dead Afghan nationals onboard. They'd suffocated and probably paid thousands for the privilege. Back in Lanarkshire the team still hadn't tracked down 'Hot Gossip' who wasn't at her home address but they agreed they would need to warn her off and set an example. Arbogast hadn't ruled out that she could be involved in the case but that information would follow in time. They had now interviewed everyone at Dales Travel and one common theme had emerged: although people had been wary of having Stevie Davidson on the staff, they had all said 'he'd been alright.' It seemed Stevie had gathered his colleagues together and told them about his past and that it was something that was not going to happen again. Most had respected his honesty but it seemed that Jean Jessop had been bad mouthing him for years, waiting for something to trip him up. Jean had been identified as Hot Gossip and Arbogast knew that they would find her eventually. Meanwhile the door-to-door enquiries continued and more and more paperwork found its way back the HOLMES team who were busy logging and cross referencing data from across the country, searching for correlations on anything that might spur them forward – but so far no joy. This was the grind, the real police work. People think of crime and punishment, but success is determined mainly through hard work and a little bit of luck. Arbogast looked at his phone for the 25th time that morning but still had nothing from Hanom. At the morning briefing he updated the team on the evening's work and they all hoped now it had been the right thing to do. Later, sat in the canteen with an undersized cup of powdered machine coffee, Arbogast looked out at the ice and snow, "and the piano played on," he said to himself, "just tell me what's in the fucking background please – I can't see for looking."

Sandy Stirrit had a feeling he might be onto something. His report last night had helped to generate fresh leads for the Police and more and more people seemed to be coming forward. Newswise it had been a quiet couple of months and it was great to finally get something juicy to sink his teeth into. The weather had been stretching their resources. Usually when it snowed everything stopped and the bulletins felt more like extended weather forecasts. People he met would always say 'you must love it' as they'd have their pick of snow stories, but in truth everyone hated it. Reporters hated finding snow stories and viewers quickly reached the point where they hated hearing about it, but they kept on doing it anyway. In the last 20 years bad winters had become rare, until recently when they had had three ferocious winters in a row. *'Maybe the climate is changing after all,'* he thought, making a mental note to chase up the science after the big thaw had set in. This time had been different though and they had a bona fide drama which just happened to coincide with the weather or 'snow hell' as they called it in the newsroom. He had cut out the offending tabloid and stuck it to the wall. The 'Snow Paedo' headline had become legend. Sandy knew it was probably a mistake that would cost the paper dearly in court but the name had stuck. If they found the guy and he hadn't done anything he could sue but then they probably made the call that a convicted sex offender wouldn't want to bring any unwanted attention on himself, as if he could avoid that now. And so it seemed he didn't matter. Stevie Davidson had turned into a commodity. There were no arrests so technically they could say what they liked. Arbogast had been keeping quiet on this and he didn't want to cause him too much grief, *'But Jesus, give a dog a bone would you JJ?'*

Today's big break had come quite unexpectedly. He'd been speaking to the Police media officer last night at the press call where they'd unveiled the CCTV footage. He had been told about the break in at the Kirk o' Shotts but that they weren't sure if it was connected to the case. The press officer assured him they had combed the area and found nothing, largely on account of the snow having masked every movement. There was nothing to suggest the church had anything to do with the investigation.

Eric Sanderson took a deep drag from his cigarette and shook his head as he watched the lunchtime news. The reporter said the police had botched the investigation. That they had searched a church less than quarter of a mile from where they had found Mary and missed a forced door and weren't sure what, if any, relevance this might have to the wider case. The TV guy said this was despite there being more than a hundred officers in the area and despite the fact this would be an obvious place for two people trying to shelter to go. The reporter was on screen now, standing by the wrecked door which had been cordoned off with police tape. He said, 'Could this have been sanctuary for the bus driver Stevie Davidson and for a young girl who have not been seen since? Sources at Strathclyde Police say there doesn't seem to be evidence to connect this but, if they missed it first time around, what else might they have missed?' Eric had seen enough he switched it off. 'They know nothing, nothing at all.'

Rosalind Ying was furious. "Did you see that news report?" she said as she burst through the door. She stopped at Arbogast's desk, hands on hip, towering over him. Arbogast was distracted by the swell of her cleavage before he remembered he was meant to be working. ·

"News report?"

"You're fucking pal Sandy – saying we'd made an arse of the crime scene, had missed an obvious clue and didn't know what we were doing," she glared at him accusingly.

"Well in fairness Rosalind, we did miss a big bloody sign."

Rosalind breathed deeply and shook her head. She raised an accusing finger, "Was this your doing?"

Arbogast stood up now and put his hand on where he though his heart might be, "On my life I don't talk shop with Sandy, not during a live case anyway. He knows the score."

Rosalind wasn't convinced but her anger subsided, "I've had Pitt Street on the phone. The Chief Constable has made it very clear he's not happy with the way this is going. It's four days in now and we haven't made any real progress. I think this might get passed over to him. I might be replaced."

Arbogast could see the situation but took a different take on it, "It might be just what we need. If Stevie is out there," he corrected himself, "if whoever is responsible for the disappearance of Kovan Kocack and Stevie Davidson is following all this it might work in our favour."

"What do you mean?"

"Well, look at it this way – if you thought the police looking into this didn't know what they were doing wouldn't that boost your confidence just a little?" He brought his thumb and index finger together as he said 'little'. Rosalind could see he was off on a new train of thought.

"Perhaps,"

"Let's hope so Rosalind. If he gets sloppy now it might be just the break we need."

They looked at each other as if trying to guess what the other was thinking, to guess what leads might be uncovered if it played out that way. Arbogast become aware of a low rumble, a pulse of sound. He was still lost in the thought of landing a lucky break when he realised that his phone was ringing on vibrate. They both looked at the handset which was slowly making its way to the edge of the desk when he caught up with it.

"It's her."

There had been a church on the site of the Kirk o' Shotts since 1450. Perched on the top of one in a series of low undulating hilltops in the area, the remnants of much older glacial decline, this had seemed a good spot for worship. The building was plain to see for miles around and the chapel served to bind the people together. Through time Catholicism had become less catholic, giving way to the reformation and the 'heretic' Protestants. Wars had been fought and rebellions lost. The old chapel gave way to a new church in 1560, and sparked the start of a long pointless struggle with people who all knew they were right. Today the Kirk o' Shotts hosted a congregation of less than two hundred, with more and more of the locals looking for answers elsewhere, but for those who remained the church retained a special sense of history. Today a new congregation had found its way to the building. Not concerned with theological discussions or of moral well being, but of the rights and wrongs of a live investigation. The press corps had descended en masse to the Kirk following last night's insights.

Camera crews vied for space. Styled in the Jacobean-Gothic style the church had distinctive ridged gable ends, which gave the effect of steps leading to a central point. In the middle sat a small copper topped bell tower and weather vane. No-one knew today which way the wind blew as the metal cockerel had been frozen solid for a week. There was no real reason to be here other than to report on the lack of progress. 'Perhaps there was nothing new in the investigation,' one seasoned hack said, 'but maybe this will give the police the kick start they need to get things moving.' The Kirk's minister had been tracked down but had nothing to say. From the car PC Frank Simmons wondered why he always got the shit jobs, as another reporter knocked on the patrol car window looking for an update.

Arbogast answered the call with his left hand so that he could still write with his right.

"Hanom?"

"Mister Arbogast," Hanom said. She spoke with an accent but her English was excellent. Rosalind leant into the phone to hear. Arbogast wanted to turn on the speaker phone but he knew he would run the risk of drowning her out. Hanom didn't wait for a reply.

"I cannot talk for long. I tried to phone you last night but it was not possible. We have been moved. We are being kept in some kind of skyscraper if that's the word? It's not so nice. The area looks very poor and maybe no-one really lives here," Arbogast wondered if she might be in a tower block somewhere, "You must find my husband, he will help me. We are locked in a struggle to free our family. I would leave Mr Arbogast but I cannot. They have my child, I am sure of it. I do not know why this is happening. We escaped Turkey for a new life away from our debts but these people would have me live like a whore. I cannot stand it but I must – for the love of Kovan I must endure this."

"How can we find the girl, who did you deal with? Mary Clark told us that you wanted her to meet with you on the night your daughter disappeared. Who was she going to meet?" Arbogast could sense he wouldn't have much more time, he needed answers.

81

"It was supposed to be me but I could not leave the club that night – it was too busy. I tried to believe me, but they would not allow it. I had agreed with Mary that her husband could help, that they hide my daughter somewhere. Mary said she had a safe place. Somewhere that could not be found. I trusted her Mr Arbogast. You must help me."

Arbogast thought for a second. There was something he could sense, something she knew that could help them. He grasped the phone tighter and then it came to him. "Hanom does Kovan have a mobile phone? I think I saw her with a handset at the bus station but I couldn't make it out at first. The footage was grimy but she held something, could it have been a phone?"

"I don't know. She's too young to have a phone. She didn't have one at home but maybe Mary gave it to her to get in touch with me?" There was a rattle on the phone, the sound of a hand being put over the receiver.

"Hanom, HANOM. Are you still there?"

Her voice returned, distracted, "I am sorry I must go, find my husband," and she was gone.

Arbogast stared into space.

"Well that was food for thought," Rosalind said, "John and Mary Clark were tasked with hiding the child in a secure place. They played us well didn't they?"

Arbogast bit his lower lip as he chewed things over, "It would seem so. I'll need to get the Home Office to confirm the husband's address if they haven't already got back."

"No they haven't – not so far. It seems he's moved about a bit. The address they have is out of date."

"I think we're going to have to play a little game of Mr and Mrs. I'll phone the hospital and let them know we're on the way. Get DS Reid to do her family liaison bit, but make sure she's got someone else with her. We might need to bring him in but we'll grab him for a chat first." He smiled and looked up, a wide grin spreading over his face, "At last, something to go on."

He didn't buy that Mary and John would kidnap a child to raise as their own but he thought he was starting to see the bigger picture thanks to his brief conversations with Hanom, and he knew that he would need to try and find her. He sent her a text on the phone which he assumed would be switched off now. It would help them to have a decent picture of her and he asked her to send one if she could – even a copy of a physical photo taken on the mobile would be better than nothing. He thought it might also be time for a raid on the club. His mind was racing with the possibilities the case now offered when his day took a completely unexpected turn. PC Frank Simmons knocked on the door to tell them that Stevie Davidson had been found.

Amid the furore and the public soul searching about how a known sex offender could have been allowed to drive a public bus, why psychologists hadn't picked up on this or that, years ago, emerged the latest version of the truth. As search parties scoured the country looking for Stevie Davidson he hadn't managed to travel more than half a mile. The discovery had been made by a cub TV reporter at the Kirk o' Shotts who had, in a careless moment, slid on an ice patch and knocked over both his camera and cameraman, causing all three to tumble to the ground. As the cameraman tried to get his breath back, sitting spread eagled and wet arsed in the snow he felt his hands find the rim of what he thought was a rock. The combined 30 stone collision had displaced a lot of snow and was to make an even bigger impact on the case. Around two hours later the forensics team had uncovered the body of Stevie Davidson who had been lying face down in the snow. His neck was broken and it was assumed he had fallen from the bell tower, which would explain the break-in and the open door above. Stevie had lain there undiscovered while the snow had continued to fall, masking all that had happened in its wake. In the next 12 hours all the snow around the church and its graveyard was removed with expectations that the girl's body would be the next to be uncovered. But despite the hours of manpower and extensive searching nothing more was found.

Part 2

12

Istanbul, Turkey, June 4th 2003

Stopping at the kiosk to buy water and magazines Hanom made her way to Sultanahmet Park. She had no plans other than to enjoy what was turning out to be a fine summer's day. It would soon be noon, meaning the call to prayer would sound out across the city, but the thought did not stay with her long. Hanom had become preoccupied with plans to celebrate her 18th birthday a week today. That and the small matter of what she planned to do with the rest of her life. Hanom wanted to become a lawyer but medicine was also an option. She had excelled at school and gained top marks in her exams but she wanted to wait and see something of the world before going back to study at University. *'So much to do and so much time ahead of me,'* she thought, *'what can't I do?'* Hanom took her cold water from her bag and as she screwed the top off she counted the number of times she could hear the tiny plastic slivers giving way. Someone had told her once that if you heard thirteen clicks it was a lucky bottle but as usual she couldn't keep count, it all happened too fast. She smiled as she drank, knowing that in about an hour the water would be warm from the day's heat and so she decided to enjoy the moment while it lasted. As Hanom sat and thought of her future she also basked in the city's past. From the peace of the park Hanom looked over at the Blue Mosque, a building she loved. As a child Hanom imagined the Mosque's six towering minarets as rockets aimed at an unseen enemy. 'You have quite an imagination child,' her mother would say, 'but try to stay in the here and now.' Her mother was traditional in every sense of the word and had raised her daughter at home while her husband toiled long hours at the family business.

She was planning to visit her father at the Grand Bizarre later in the day to surprise him.

"I wonder if he realises I am not made for his world?" she said, thinking out loud.

As she pondered her imagined life, a voice from behind cut through her daydreaming

"Talking to yourself – perhaps you'd like some company?"

Hanom thought she recognised the voice but when she turned she was blinded by the sun and had to raise a hand to shield her eyes to try and make out who it was. As her vision adjusted she could see that it was the Kocack brothers, who she knew as family friends through her father's business. Onur and Karim were immediately recognisable as brothers, although separated by a year in age they looked very much alike. Hanom knew that Onur worked as some kind of engineer and was only too happy to bore you to death with his underground tales from the city's new Metro network. Hanom thought Karim a different prospect altogether and was impressed by the fact that he had travelled, which was something she wanted to do more than anything else in the world and the sooner the better. She would listen intently, hanging on every word as Karim recounted in vivid detail his trips to Thailand and America which always sounded so exciting. When she spoke to Karim she felt that she wanted to leave Istanbul that very day and jump on the next flight out, but of course so far she hadn't.

"Ah the mysterious Kocack brothers," she said as her eyes adjusted to the bright midday sun, "what brings you here today?"

Onur began to answer but was cut off by Karim, which was just the way Hanom preferred it. "We are celebrating today my dear Hanom and what a day of celebration it will be – fine dining and the best of the city." he said, his arms spread wide as if he had taken to the stage, causing Hanom to giggle. Onur said that his brother was fuller of himself than usual as he'd just landed a new job.

"A new job brother but you don't tell the whole story," Karim turned and winked at Hanom.

"He is jealous as I make much more money than he does now – 100,000 lira a year to do with as I please."

Hanom was impressed, "And what do you need to do to earn this princely sum?"

"I am to be the personal assistant of one Mr Eser Ozan – you may have heard of him?" Hanom certainly had. Eser Ozan had a reputation as a rising businessman, tipped to join the Turkish elite but his reputation was mired in scandal and it was widely rumoured he operated in partnership with the city's organised crime network.

"Is that a good idea Karim?" Hanom knew her friend had been wild in his younger days. Karim had once put a man in hospital after being insulted at a party. His actions had landed him in serious trouble but Hanom imagined she knew what kind of man he really was and that violence was not in his nature. Karim always treated Hanom like a sister and she was content to see him happy.

"Oh don't believe the gossips Hanom," Karim said, laughing, "Mr Eser is going places and so am I. He invests in the Metro that Onur here has been toiling so hard over. One day soon I'll be paying my brother's wages, isn't that so?" Onur was clearly unconvinced.

"One day at a time brother. One day at a time."

Hanom was lifted by these little confrontations. She always felt the two were in some way competing for her attention although nothing had ever come of it. She wondered if she would mind if one of them made a pass. All three had known each other for about ten years and it seemed odd to Hanom to think of the brothers as people who might feature in her love life. She blushed at the thought of it and was caught out immediately.

"Ah but Hanom you are turning red in the sun, you must remember to protect that beautiful face of yours. But we must leave now. Until next time," Karim said, turning to leave with a wave, leaving Hanom to her thoughts once more. She hadn't noticed but the fountain had come on in the pond and her small world now seemed more alive than ever before. Hanom made a mental note to make sure Karim would be able to make it to her birthday party. Of course she would have to ask Onur too as it would be far too obvious just to ask Karim to come alone. *'I am a lady after all.'* As she picked up her water to feast on another burst of fresh cool water Hanom didn't even notice that the bottle was warm. Hanom did not know it yet but her world had already changed forever.

Bishopton, Scotland, February 20th 2010

Eric Sanderson did not know what to make of the discovery of Stevie Davidson's body. The initial press reports suggested his death had been accidental. It seemed that Stevie had broken into the church and taken refuge in the bell tower before somehow falling to his death. It didn't make sense. Eric was sure the truth would emerge before too long but he was feeling particularly agitated today. He had been getting angry at the slightest of things. Earlier for no good reason he had smashed a chair off the floor after dropping his laptop. He had been surfing the internet looking for more information on the news sites. There was no doubt the stress of the last few days were starting to get to him. *'Stevie bloody Davidson, what good ever came of you?'* Eric locked his caravan door and made his way to the Range Rover. He looked over at the house and wondered if it hadn't changed shape again, dipped deeper into its own foundations. His reference point was the TV aerial which was no longer standing straight up but leaned over to one side, and the more it dipped the more anxious he became. As he drove Eric decided he would try to put the investigation to the back of his mind. He hadn't taken any time off work as he knew this week was going to be an important one at the wind farm. They had reached a delicate part of the process which would require blasting through solid granite, which eventually would form a level base for a 400 foot turbine. He had been surprised at how much he loved the work. Having spent 20 years on the farm he had found he had hidden talents and getting involved with the Madoch Group had been a godsend. The fact that he had money to invest had of course helped his cause. Mr Madoch had been keen to speak to him after he knew the colour of his money. Eric Sanderson had fallen in love with wind power. With expertise in the area from his own small scale effort he had been immediately taken on and was now a senior partner in Moorland Wind, which was majority owned by the Madoch Group. The past no longer mattered, or at least it hadn't until that copper had turned up and that bloody boy had died. Eric Sanderson cursed the turn in his fortunes as he turned off the M77 and onto the newly laid tarmac road which marked the start of the Moorland Wind site.

The wind farm was already amongst the biggest in the UK with 99 turbines erected and with another 150 to follow. Eaglesham Moor was a bleak and blasted place, with few plus points save for its one abundant asset – the wind. The site office, and Eric Sanderson's base for the next eighteen months, was a series of drab grey portacabins which had been formed into an onsite village. There was a fully functioning canteen, which catered for the 215 people working there. Once the project was completed there would only be a handful left to maintain the turbines but before that there was land to be cleared and turbines to be erected. Despite everything that was going on around him it was this task that occupied Sanderson as he pulled up outside his office.

"Hi Gill, anything I need to know?" His secretary gave him an accusatory glance as she surveyed the mounds of snow Eric had brought in from the short journey from car to office and then proceeded to scrape off on the carpet.

"Nothing that's not in your diary, although the weather looks likely to have delayed any blasting we might have planned. Also your partner in crime is running late."

Eric Sanderson shared the hut with Onur Kocack, a Turkish businessman Mister Madoch had brought in from Turkey on a personal recommendation. He had a first class degree from the Teknick Universitesi in Istanbul and had years of experience working on the Istanbul Metro system. Eric thought they were lucky to have him. Onur seemed distant at times and his English sometimes left a lot to be desired but there was no doubting his value to the operation. Looking at his mobile Eric noticed that Onur had sent him a text saying he was due in half an hour and that they had 'serious business to discuss'. Eric Sanderson cleared his mind and tried to focus on the day ahead.

Arbogast had been called to an emergency meeting with DCI Rosalind Ying at the Chief Constable's office about four hours after the discovery of Stevie Davidson's body. Norrie Smith had been silent when they arrived. His was a large office, clad mainly in antique mahogany. Norrie would complain, to anyone that would listen, that it was a highly impractical office but that he had been unable to change it because the furniture had been there since the building had opened. Dragged from the 1960s through to the 21st century, the fixtures and fittings struggled to cope with the demands of modern policing. Computer cables were tied together with tape, with a vast array of wires leading to the room's only socket which was inconveniently located at the door, on the wrong side of the room. Arbogast had been staring past the Chief Constable trying to get an idea of where exactly the panoramic window looked out onto. He could see tree tops so he assumed the office must be at the front of the building looking out onto Blytheswood Square. Norrie Smith poured three small cups of coffee into ornate red edged Wedgewood porcelain tea cups which he assumed had once been meant for special occasions but now looked ready for a charity bin.

"I'll get straight to the point," Norrie Smith said. He stopped and looked at Arbogast and Ying, failing to get straight to the point, but they could see that it was in the post. "I'll be taking over as the Senior Investigating Officer in this case. DCI Ying you have done a great job on this so far and please don't take this as a personal criticism. After a slow start I think we're making good progress. But the discovery of Stevie Davidson has changed things. For all the furore of the press about paedophiles on the run, it doesn't look like our Mister Davidson is the main man in this case. He may have been involved in some way but this is now starting to look like a much bigger deal. Maybe the girl has been abducted by a paedophile ring? For all we know she may not be in the country. This is now an international case and we will have to broaden our scope. With respect, DCI Ying, while you've got clout out in Lanarkshire I can get more done more quickly. We'll be dealing with Europol now while forces across the country are actively looking for this girl. This girl—" he searched his desk for inspiration.

"Her name's Kovan Kocack sir," Arbogast said, mainly to save Ying from having to answer. He knew she would be gutted by the decision but she would also understand the reasons.

"—Yes the Kocack girl. DCI Ying, I want you and DI Arbogast to continue as lead detectives, but you will be reporting directly to me on this now on a day-to-day basis. I'll take the controlling role in the investigation. We're a few days in now and I'm going to be reviewing the case to see where we are and, if appropriate, make suggestions on possible new avenues. Understood?" The question was rhetorical and they all knew it but Arbogast and Ying both nodded their assent, like plastic dogs in the back of old cars. "OK good, well where are we now?"

Ying began with Stevie Davidson "It was a major shock to have found him where he was, but it looks like he fell from the bell tower. We have matched DNA samples from the splintered door. I'm not sure why he went there and I'm not convinced he was alone," Norrie Smith nodded and gestured his approval for Ying to continue in a movement which reminded Arbogast of a Royal wave. Arbogast was starting to get angry as he saw the investigation getting bogged down in ego, split loyalties and too much talking, but forced himself to bite his tongue.

"I'm not sure," Ying said, shifting in her seat and looking at the ceiling, "that Stevie would have left the bus with the child and then immediately gone their separate ways."

"Unless something happened before then?"

"Well yes but what could have happened? Why not just go back to the bus where it was warm. There must have been someone else there, a third man if you will. Perhaps they met at the church? It's an easy landmark to find. I think we can rule out anything having happened to the girl early on. We've had half the force over that area and we've turned up nothing."

Arbogast had had enough, "Look we've been bursting our arses over this case. The weather out there is atrocious. The snow has covered all tracks and there is literally no evidence from the scene. We should have an autopsy report from Stevie Davidson by lunchtime although it does look as if he's fallen and broken his neck. I'd agree there must be someone else involved here and the pointers at the moment are looking to Mary and John Clark."

"Of which I hear there has been a further development?" Norrie Smith said, although the question was more of an accusation than anything else.

"He's gone missing," Ying said, wondering who in her team had been leaking information, "We haven't been able to get a hold of him yet. Arbogast's source says he was supposed to be meeting with Kovan Kocack and Mary on the bus. We're still trying to track down the girl's mother but that should just be a matter of time. I've got the tech guys onto it and we should be able to pin her down through mobile phone tracking."

"But she's scared boss," Arbogast said, "She's scared her daughter will be harmed. I'd say it's significant she thinks the girl is still alive."

Norrie Smith was unimpressed, "But you still haven't been able to speak to her face to face yet and the father also seems to be eluding your powers of detection?"

"John Clark you mean well yes I was coming to that," DCI Ying was starting to get annoyed. This had been the biggest case she had handled from Motherwell and it wasn't going to look good that it had been taken off her – she needed to get a result. "The Home Office has finally provided us with a new address but it hasn't led to anything yet. We've tried the house but there doesn't seem to be anyone home. We have a patrol car outside the flat on Crow Road. It's been rented in Onur Kocack's name but his neighbours say they haven't seen much of him. He'll turn up. In the meantime we're trying to locate him at his work. He's a registered engineer with Moorland Wind which is managing that wind farm at Eaglesham."

Norrie Smith knew the one she meant, the turbines could be seen from his window springing up on the horizon to the south of Glasgow.

"Arbogast will be going out there after this meeting to try and find him."

It was Arbogast's turn to talk, "It's something of a coincidence that the father of the missing child works with Eric Sanderson don't you think? I don't know if they work closely together or not but they are in the same field, if you'll excuse the pun." His joke went unnoticed or if not it was certainly unappreciated. Arbogast made a mental note to keep the puns for the pub. I could use a drink now, he thought, "but where was I?"

"You were telling us about the Sanderson tie in with the family," Norrie Smith said, "although I must say we are putting a

94

lot of stock in the word of strangers. The only one of us to have met with any of the Kocack clan is you, Arbogast, and that was in a strip bar. Meanwhile the person that put us onto the family is currently one of our main suspects, namely Mary Clark – you have to admit it doesn't look good."

It was Norrie Smith who was becoming impatient now and the atmosphere in the room was becoming uncomfortable.

"Mary Clark is the key to this," Arbogast said, "She's refusing to speak to us just now so we'll have to apply more pressure. I'm going to put out a missing persons appeal for the husband and hope we get something back from that. In the meantime I'm going to go and see Sanderson again. There's something in this relationship he has with his daughter, I'm sure of it. She complained in the past that he abused her in a secret location and now we have a missing girl. I also think John Clark's involved, I just need to establish how."

When they left the room Arbogast turned to Ying and reassured her that she was still in the driving seat, but she wasn't interested. Arbogast wasn't happy either. He had quickly come to trust in Ying. She had welcomed him to the team but more importantly she had let him take risks when he felt they were needed. It was her that had sanctioned the mobile phone drop at the club and it was her direction that had allowed the case to get started. He had thought Rosalind Ying might have had problems with the change in personnel but she was more driven now than before.

"Listen Arbogast I don't really know you that well as a person but you seem to have good intuition. We need to work fast and find the girl – preferably alive. I suggest we continue to pool our resources and tie these strands together. Norrie's just doing his job, I know that but it still feels like a kick in the teeth. He'd get carpeted if he let this go on without getting more closely involved. I mean just think about all the bad headlines this has been getting and not just in the local press – I saw the story on the New York Times website – this case is making news in the US, Australia – it's everywhere – but we're here and we need to get this done. You've been here before and failed and I don't want that to happen twice. Arbogast watched as Ying let rip. He could see that the meeting had got her adrenalin going and she was as committed as he was to closing this case.

"Fine," he said, "let's go."

He waited and watched as the police went about their business. They had found the driver's body but that didn't matter. He knew they knew nothing. The weather had been a gift from god. The child was his now, to do with as he wished. The driver had been unfortunate but it had proved a stroke of luck. How fortunate to find a paedophile just when you needed one. He had watched the TV news when the body was found. He couldn't always understand the accents but so many people were shocked. One woman 'Jessop' had said she would miss 'her Stevie' so much. 'Such a nice man to work with,' she had said. I could not agree more. Hanom, he noticed, had been acting strangely. She obviously has not realised what has happened yet, perhaps she never will. But of course things have to move on. He had plans for so many people and so long as the police stayed four steps behind he would still be able to make the connection, to escape from this miserable freezing country and so far it had all being going to plan. Satisfied that he had done everything that had been asked of him, he checked on the girl, who was alone. She was quiet of course, as was to be expected under the circumstances. That might change when she was reunited with her mother. But it was not going to be the bright new life they'd hoped for. As he left the room the little girl looked up, he caught her glance for a fraction of a second as the light from the hall was quickly extinguished from her room. He wondered if she might come to hate him. That would be good, and just – let her learn the meaning of hate. It was all her fault after all.

13

Istanbul, Turkey, June 11th 2003

Hanom's family had lived in the same place for the last four generations. The house was built in 1843 and over time the weather had changed the wooden framed building into a weird, warped shambles within the similarly well worn Canturkaran district of Istanbul, overlooking the Sea of Marmara. When Hanom walked these streets she felt part of something bigger, older, something she felt that others did not have. Originally her family home would have been covered with a lime facade and as such was prone to salt erosion from the sea air. Her father had told her that it had been a proud day when they put up the timber cladding to protect their home and still in this street there were few other houses that looked quite like theirs. The timber had shrunk and twisted through the years, giving the three storey structure the look of having melted in the sun. As a child Hanom had thought of it as a fairy tale gingerbread house. Her mother had told her not to be so morbid, but she hadn't understood what she meant. The top floor had an overhang and perched over the street below as if trying to find a better view of the shimmering horizon. This was a common arrangement in the city which allowed more space upstairs while also giving shade and protection for those passing in the street. And it was here that Hanom spent her 18th birthday. Although the house stretched to quite a height there was surprisingly little space inside, although that had not stopped the influx of friends and family who had squeezed in to the narrow rooms to help her celebrate. Aunts and uncles from the country, friends of her fathers, and people she had known from school, all were here. Hanom blushed at the thought of it, she wasn't used to so much attention but for all the fuss there was only one person she wanted to see and he wasn't here. It was about 8:00 when Onur arrived, with flowers in hand and a smile.

"I'm afraid Karim might be late tonight. He asked me to send you his love. He has work to finish and couldn't get away. I hope you can accept my apology on his behalf."

And then he did something that took Hanom quite by surprise. Onur went down on one knee and took her left hand in his right. He clasped it and she could see his eyes welling up as he lifted his head to meet her eyes.

"Dear Hanom I know you have only eyes for Karim but I feel I must tell you my heart. Since we have been children I've looked on you as someone special. I know I have neither the bravado nor the money of my brother but I'm not a poor man. I have brought you this gift dearest Hanom so that you know that I am here for you. I love you Hanom and if you would have me you would make me the richest man in all of Istanbul."

Hanom was so shocked that she didn't know how to react. Onur had got the attention of the room and prying eyes watched on as he waded ever onwards with his declaration of love. Looking back Hanom remembered being angry at his having ruined her day. She had cursed Onur and chased him from the house. They had all laughed at the foolish boy and the laughter had fuelled the atmosphere for what had been one of the greatest days of her life. Karim never did show up and although she could never explain quite why, Hanom could not stop thinking about Onur.

Glasgow, Scotland, February 20th 2010

John J Arbogast drove as Rosalind Ying contemplated her future and Arbogast knew better than to pry. Instead he switched on the local radio station to catch the hourly news. There was nothing about the case and he thought that perhaps they were losing interest. But he knew in his heart that it was only a matter of time before the headlines would return. Driving through the city you would never have known that half the country was still deep under the cover of snow. The daily temperature had risen slightly and it was now reaching -3c through the day but in the evenings it stayed

98

cold, -12c every night. The weather was the only thing anyone ever talked about and Arbogast wished it would end. The main roads were clear now, thick with grit and rock salt, the carriageways brown with the treatment it was hoped would keep the cars running. Arbogast drove west along the M8 and then veered off onto the M77 after crossing the River Clyde on the Kingston Bridge. His turn-off came about five miles after they reached the higher ground around Newton Mearns, but Arbogast cursed after missing it. He had been expecting a better signposted exit but it was a farm road that led directly from the hard shoulder and wasn't easy to see due to the amount of snow piled up at the side of the roads. It took about 15 minutes to double back and find the place where they should have turned off. The diversion had done nothing to improve either his or Rosalind's mood.

"Do you think you'll be able to find the wind farm OK John?" she said to Arbogast's obvious chagrin. Eventually as they crawled along the untreated back roads of Eaglesham Moor they came to a small bright orange sign which indicated that they had reached their destination. The Lexus that Arbogast had commandeered from Pitt Street HQ wasn't designed for off-roading and the vehicle struggled along the make shift track which had been put in place to link the main road to the site headquarters.

"I thought these roads were meant to be good for dragging bloody wind turbines along," Arbogast said to himself. This at least got a smile from Rosalind who was looking out of the passenger window trying her best not to laugh.

The reception area had taken them by surprise. Instead of the shabby works hut they had been expecting they entered into what was advertised as the 'Showroom'. The interior was decked out in dark wood laminate flooring with the walls covered with artistic shots of machinery in motion. In one corner sat a scale model of one of the turbines with what looked like a potted history of the site above. The girl on reception was young – she looked about 21, with bobbed black hair and heavily made up. She reminded Arbogast of someone who might work at a perfume counter. Her manner, however, showed her to be more of a Rottweiler than a Poodle as Arbogast and Ying tried to get her attention.

"Yes Mister Herbison I understand that you have made an appointment but the team are all out in the field today – we're at a very delicate stage in the operation and I'm afraid you will just have to wait on this occasion." It looked as if the conversation had ended abruptly. She held the phone in her hand and looked at it in disgust, "He hung up," she said before turning her attention to her next assignment, "Good afternoon. How can I help you?" Her smile was fixed but genuine.

"My name is DCI Rosalind Ying and this is DI John Arbogast," she said showing her official ID, "We are here to see a Mister Onur Kocack. I believe he works here?"

"As you might have just heard we are very busy just now. Mr Kocack is out on the moor. We're trying to prepare a site for excavation although the weather is causing us problems. I can page him if you would like to wait although I'm not sure he'll be checking his messages."

"I think it would be better if we went and saw him directly," Arbogast said, "Can you tell us where he is?" The answer was not straight forward but eventually the receptionist, whose name was Gill, arranged for a four-by-four to pick them up and take them out. They had to wear hard hats and high-visibility jackets and both felt foolish as they headed out onto the blasted heath. Arbogast could feel a sharp pain in his ears as the winter winds whistled through him.

"I didn't expect it to be so bloody cold," he said to Rosalind, trying to make his voice heard above the Range Rover's snarling engine.

Onur Kocack wasn't having the best of days. He had made his way to the office expecting progress but nothing seemed to be going to plan. They had to clear the areas around the base of the planned turbines and then dig down. The frozen earth wasn't making for easy going and they had bedrock to blast through, which hadn't shown up in the original survey. Onur shook his head at the thought of the inefficiency of this company but he knew that it wasn't operating on the scale he was used to. And now he had been phoned to say there were two policemen on the way. When they arrived he was surprised that the senior officer was in fact a woman. They tried to ask him questions but the wind was too strong for conversation so they retreated to meet in a small works portacabin.

The cabin had little in it, save for a gas fire powered from a canister, a foldaway table, and six battered plastic chairs. There was a kettle on the table and all the paraphernalia needed for a tea run. The gentle hum of an electric generator could be heard outside competing with the constant groaning of the wind.

"You're a hard man to track down Mr Kocack," Arbogast said, he was surprised at the way the man looked. He had met his wife twice and she had seemed very liberal. Granted both times had been in a lap dancing club but still. The man he was faced with was pushing 40, had a substantial beer belly. He had a calm, strong face with ears that seemed to be pinched in the middle and seemed slightly U-shaped as a result. He had short shaved hair and dark brown eyes. These were now staring intently at both Arbogast and Ying, their focus shifting constantly as he sized up the situation.

"We're here about your wife and daughter Mister Kocack."

"My wife is in Turkey, has something happened?" Onur seemed genuinely perplexed by the question but perhaps this was just a bluff. Arbogast handed Onur the picture Hanom had sent them through the police mobile phone. It was not of a very high quality and had obviously been taken in a dark room. Her face was partially masked by the flash but it had been the best she could do under the circumstances.

"It looks like my wife although it is not a great likeness. What is this about?"

Arbogast explained about his missing daughter and all that had happened in the last few days, "I'm surprised you haven't seen this in the news Mr Kocack. We've been trying to reach you for some time." Arbogast explained the case and Onur Kocack listened.

"I work a lot Detective Arbogast and I cannot find the enthusiasm for local stories. If you say this has happened then I will take you at your word. I find it hard to believe that my wife would allow herself to work in such a place and you say my daughter is missing but you do not know where?"

"That's right, that's right," Arbogast said. He changed tack, "Who owns this company?"

Onur frowned, "What has this to do with my family?"

"Who owns this company Mr Kocack? It may have everything to do with it."

"Moorland Wind is a company in its own right. I have invested much of my own money in this venture but I believe it to be a sound investment. So do my colleagues."

"I believe the Madoch Group has a substantial investment in this venture," Arbogast said, "61 per cent is a controlling stake you might say?"

Onur nodded, "Yes this is true – but there is nothing wrong in that as far as I know."

"Of course not, this is a free country and you can spend your money any way you want to. But the Madoch Group also owns Devil May Care, which as you might recall is where we came across your wife – coincidence?"

The realisation of what the detective was saying was now starting to dawn on Onur, "Look Detective Arbogast I came to this country to make a better life for myself. I do not know what other business the Madoch Group is involved in and I do not care. Mister Madoch sponsored me to come to the UK, and here I am, a partner in my own business. My wife was to visit me soon but I have not heard from her in several weeks. If I can help you in any way I will but please don't accuse me of some crime against my wife. She is the love of my life."

"Do you know a mister Eric Sanderson?" Rosalind said.

"I work with him here," Onur said, prodding his desk, "He is not here today but he has been very kind to me."

"We believe it was his daughter that was travelling with Kovan, your daughter – you do remember her don't you?" Onur looked puzzled, "You haven't once asked about your daughter Mr Kocack – why is that? What's the connection we're missing here?"

This time Onur was more vocal, "Now listen to me Detective I am worried with the news that you have brought me but I care for both my wife and daughter. What you say is a lot to take in. Five minutes ago I believed my family to be safe at home but now you say they have gone missing in this country. What am I to make of this? This might be normal behaviour for you but for me it is like a bolt from the blue. As for Eric Sanderson I have no fight with him. We were looking at pictures of my family just last week and he said that he would love to visit my home in Turkey. One day I hope he still can."

"You understand how serious all this is Mister Kocack. We will need to speak to you again so please don't leave the country. I will assign a police patrol car to your address and I will also need to take phone details to be able to contact you at anytime. We have much to do before we will find your family and we may well need your help. Do you understand?" Onur nodded and they made to leave, leaving Onur to watch them from the office door. Arbogast phoned Onur's mobile from the car just to check the number was correct. When he watched Onur take the phone for his belt holder he wound down the windows and waved an apology, "Just checking – we'll be in touch."

As they edged along the carriageway Rosalind was the first to break the silence.

"What did you make of that?' He's involved somehow isn't he?"

Arbogast agreed that he must be, "But I can't figure out how. There are far too many coincidences in this case for my liking and I don't believe in coincidences. He did seem surprised and he'd have to be a bloody good liar to completely bluff the two of us. I'm not sure he knew the details, that his family were here but he hardly flinched when we filled him in. And you were right about the daughter – he just didn't ask – why not?" As they picked through the arguments on the way home the weather forecaster on the radio said that the thaw was expected at the start of next week.

Mary Clark was scared. The police had come back and said they knew about John, about his role in picking up Kovan. *'But how could they know. How could they?'* Mary still felt weak from her ordeal but her strength was returning fast. Thinking back to the coach she knew that the switch over was supposed to have been straight forward, but something had happened. As she sat in her hospital bed she wished that she could speak to her husband John but they said he had disappeared which was not like him. Mary had been allowed out of bed and she had tried walking but it had been slow painful work. The doctors kept telling her that she needed to build her strength up and eat something, but she had no real appetite. Mary knew she would have to force herself to eat if she was to recover. In the meantime she was a prisoner. The officer outside said that she would be arrested if she tried to leave. *'What do they know? Who else could have known about the arrangement that wasn't already accounted for? Perhaps someone from the ferry?'* What Mary did know was that she was going to have to get out of this hospital and soon.

The investigation seemed to be going round in circles. He had watched as the two detectives arrived at the wind farm but what could they say that could hurt him? He knew they were coming but he did not know the details of what they might ask or what might happen. There had been a lot of talk of family reunions but the plans had changed. The girl was his now to do with what he pleased. She even seemed quite calm. They had drawn together today. She drew a rickety wooden house she said was home. 'When will we go back there?' she had asked. Soon, my darling, he had told her, soon it will all be over. And then there was the mother. He had become angry when he found her with a phone. How was that possible? No matter she will have to be moved soon – perhaps into a new line of work – something more interactive? How delicious.

Istanbul, Turkey, June 25th 2003

Nevizade Sokak was a busy alley full of bars and tavernas. Although tourists did venture there it was predominantly a place where locals gathered to enjoy good food, fine wine, and great company. It was almost always busy which made it the ideal place for Hanom to meet with Onur. He had called at the house every day for the past week. Her father had said he looked sheepish but that he could also see the sincerity in his eyes. She had spent the week thinking of little else. With no school and no studies to occupy her mind she had been thinking only of her adventures, but she wondered if there might be something here for her too. The more she thought of the idea the more appealing Onur became. She did not love Onur, it was true, and it would take time to get used to the idea that she wanted him as more than a friend. Hanom felt guilty about the way she had treated him at her party. She had been angry of course that he had taken attention away from her celebration but she should not have sent him away like that – like a fool. And today as she made her way to Galatasaray Square having crossed the Bosporus at the Galata Bridge she stopped to watch as the ferries and cruisers sailed past but for once it was not their destination that interested her but of those making the journey. She picked out the couples and wondered what twists of fate had conspired to bring them together. By the time she had reached the Boncuk restaurant she had to shoulder her way through crowds of people. Her nerves were getting the better of her now; her stomach was tense with nerves. *'Maybe I should go home, this is ridiculous.'* But she carried on. No-one had ever approached her like that before, had been so heartfelt, and although she thought Onur a fool for having made such an idiot of himself she admired his spirit. He had reserved a table for them and even before she sat down she had already made up her mind to stay.

Glasgow, Scotland, February 21st 2010

Kovan Kocack wasn't sure when she was going to see mummy, her anne (ahn-neh) again. He said it would not be long but it seemed to be so very long. He had been nice to her and brought her lots of toys but there was no-one to play with and she was bored. He said she should call him daddy.

Kovan had been left in a flat in one of Glasgow's high rise blocks. She was unaware of the huge search going on around the country with thousands of man hours being spent to try and find her.

It was a large apartment and had recently been partially redecorated. His organisation owned many flats around the city and they proved useful from time to time, especially in cases like these. There were four bedrooms and only two were occupied. One was his and the other was for Kovan. He noticed the girl was growing tired of his games. He had tried to calm her, to befriend her but she had resisted. He knew that she had been through a lot and understood he would need to be patient before she would trust him, open up to him. He watched as she sat by the window. They were high in the sky he had told her and she was like a princess in an ivory tower. Looking out, though, it was hardly the land of fairy tales. This was a bleak part of Glasgow. The flats looked like they had been forced up from under the ground. Once considered the epitome of 1960s planning, the plans had quickly gone wrong. These towering artefacts of forgotten modernity were now themselves obsolete and would in time be torn down for the next big idea. People were leaving the flats in search of new communities and few remained. This had been useful when the company was looking to buy up multiple properties for next to nothing, allowing a network of safe houses to be established. The neighbours were mostly old people who never asked any questions and refugees who had to wait, sometimes for years, before they were told if they were good enough to remain in their squalid new homes. But the police had been making faster progress than they would have liked. As he looked down on the barren ground he could see young people loitering, kicking cans and searching for violence, anything to pass the time. If they knew what was going on far above their heads then maybe they would act differently. As the self appointed guardian watched the frosty landscape disappear for another day he sat with the girl, watching the city light up. It was another day for people to keep wondering what had happened to the little girl on the bus. It was time to make the call.

14

The last two years had been a wonderful blur. Onur proposed at the same restaurant that they had sealed their bond. They had been given a standing ovation from the other diners in a gesture which still made Hanom smile. Six months later they were married and the happy couple set themselves up in the old family home. That is to say that Onur moved in with her father's blessing, her mother having passed away not long after they had wed.

No-one had been surprised when Hanom had announced she was pregnant and soon there were four souls bound in the rickety walls of the shambling wooden home which had weathered well through the years. It had all happened so quickly and it still surprised Hanom that she had gone along with it. All her dreams had been put on hold with her desire to travel only stretching to their honeymoon. The pair had travelled to the United Kingdom, hardly the tropical paradise of which Hanom had dreamt, but it had been during their month away that Kovan had been conceived. Hanom had never considered having children so young and it had taken some time to get used to the idea that her life would soon no longer be her own. She had heard that people underwent a profound change when they entered parenthood. This had certainly been true for Hanom who no longer felt she was giving up her independence but was opening up a whole new life that had her child at the centre. As the years went by Kovan grew into an inquisitive girl, always questioning what she saw. Hanom's father said she reminded him of her as a child. He laughed when he remembered her mother always scolding her for her far-fetched fantasises. I will not do that, she would say, my child will be encouraged to reach out and take what she wants. Onur was still busy with the city's Metro system. He had done well and was now a senior engineer on the project which was slowly transforming the way people travelled. He explained to her that he was tasked with managing the tunnel system. Hanom thought this a dangerous task and preferred not to know when they were going through the blast cycles. She was proud of him and they lived a good life. He had been pestering her to move from Canturkaran to a new modern home but she felt that she could not leave her father behind when he seemed so happy. They had quarrelled about this but she had won in the end, and they stayed – for better or worse.

Motherwell, Scotland, February 21st 2010

The results of the autopsy came two days after Stevie Davidson's body was discovered, which was longer than normal but his body had been frozen solid and extra time had to be allowed to allow him to defrost – he had become known as 'The Thing' in the morgue. Neither Arbogast or Ying felt the need to be at the autopsy. Arbogast had sat through his fair share. As an investigator you learned a lot about your job listening to the coroner. Now if he was at a crime scene he could spot telltale signs, like the angle a gunshot wound have made, or the height of an attacker who had stabbed his victim – a sight all too familiar in Glasgow with its love affair with the blade. Autopsies were one of those things that people would always ask you 'What's it like?' Arbogast always thought this was a bit like asking a solider if he had killed anyone and just as unpleasant. Arbogast remembered his first time. He had watched as the coroner made a V neck incision into the victim's chest. True to his unwritten rule of attending all major events in his life with a hangover he had had particular problems when the scalpel had started to slice away at the skin, like peeling away wrapping tape on a parcel. He had held it together at first but when the circular saw cracked open the skull he had lost the contents of his stomach which had created a Jackson Pollock tribute on the mortuary floor. He remembered the looks from his senior officer and the others there that day. But with those halcyon days behind him he felt that he had done his time and had happily delegated Stevie Davidson duty to young Frank Simmons, whose eyes had lit up at the prospect. When PC Simmons did report back it was with information they hadn't been expecting.

"We were right about the broken neck but that wasn't the cause of death," Frank said, wincing at the memory. "When you saw his body there were no obvious signs that anything else had happened other than the snap, which was obvious given the way he was found. My god his neck looked strange, almost twisted round 180 degrees." The waiting detectives knew to be patient while PC Frank Simmons collected his thoughts but they could sense they were in for a surprise. "The thing is, though, he had been badly beaten. The bruising had died away but when they peeled back his skin from his torso you could see the marks. He had been beaten viciously with a blunt object although it hadn't broken the skin. The coroner said it looked like he'd been beaten with a club of some sort – one of the marks was in the sign of a cross, as if two people had been beating him or as if he'd been attacked from different angles."

Arbogast had been sitting at his desk taking it all in. He squeezed his upper lip with his thumb and fourth finger, deep in thought. "And we think the beating was the cause of death and that he didn't fall?"

Simmons explained that there were no other problems with Stevie Davidson. There were no abnormalities thrown up other than the break of his neck which had been inflicted post mortem. "The coroner said he'd died of internal haemorrhaging brought on by a sustained and brutal attack."

"Poor bastard," Rosalind said.

"I'm beginning to think our Stevie was just unlucky," Arbogast said, "We know that he does tie into the family but this has all the hallmarks of some kind of gangland execution. It's not been a straight hit and they've gone to a lot of trouble to make it look accidental. The way I see this now is like this: Stevie's driving the bus, wrong place at the wrong time. Mary Clark gets on board with Kovan in Glasgow. The bus isn't going its normal route but the destination's the same, it will just take longer to get there. We think she has arranged to meet her husband, John, somewhere en route. Let's assume it would be the end of the line as that's nearest to her home, so they meet in Shotts."

"But the bus stopped two miles away – stuck in the snow," Rosalind said, "There would be no way to know that was going to happen. When we found her she had no phone on her so presuming the handset was taken she'd have had no way of making a call."

"Unless the child had the phone?" Frank said. Arbogast and Ying had almost forgotten he was there.

"Of course, Kovan," Arbogast said, nodding, "Yes let's suppose Mary gave her the handset to make her feel more secure, maybe she thought she'd be able to speak to her mum – but what about the bus? If John Clark was waiting in Shotts he wouldn't be able to follow in his car – they only have a Fiat 500 – very urban but hardly one for getting through a blizzard."

Rosalind was unconvinced, "Let's suppose there was someone else – possibly John – possibly a third party. Someone was following the bus and when it stopped that's when this happened. The pickup wasn't supposed to happen there, but it did – events forced them to change the plan. They don't need the driver so they take Stevie Davidson up to the church; they improvise and leave him there. Kovan is only 5 and I don't even know if she can speak English. One thing is sure though – she would not have survived the night on her own. Someone knew where to find her and they have her now. I think she's still alive."

Frank interrupted, "Where does Mary Clark fit into this? I sat with her those first few hours in the hospital. She could have died. I don't think her husband would have stripped her and left her to her fate like that and why would she let him if she was involved anyway? It seems reasonable to me that someone is in on this, probably someone we've already spoken to. You might remember Sir, that Mary wouldn't say how she got hold of Kovan. Is it possible she's been played by the traffickers?"

It was a scenario Arbogast had been struggling with for some time "Yeah, it's an angle I just don't get at all. I agree – I think Mary had a plan. I think what she has told us is true, but there's something she's hiding and I don't know what it is. I think Mister Kocack knows more than he's saying too, but what, I just can't say. He's working for a company with serious ties to a firm bankrolled by organised crime, masquerading as a legitimate concern. Maybe we should introduce Onur Kocack to his benefactor?"

"John Madoch?" Rosalind said, "I met him a few months ago and he's quite the celebrity these days. Civic dinners and the big charity man, he's been careful to change his profile. I doubt he'd be so stupid as to be involved here – not directly anyway."

Arbogast considered the ceiling for inspiration, "Madoch may not be directly involved but I can't help but feel someone who works for him is. Mary Clark doesn't have the connections to organise something like this. She's a charity worker with no form and no cash. That her husband is missing is more of a concern than anything else right now as I'd place him in the same league. They're both citizens, not criminals. I'm going to have a chat with my old pals at the SCDEA again and see if they can shed any more light on this. I don't think Hanom will come in until we find her daughter. We should be getting a fix for a location on her mobile soon so hopefully that will help with the search. Frank let me know how it pans out. Rosalind I think it's time I paid a visit to Madoch Group HQ."

He had made the call and the old man was on his way. Hanom didn't know it but she was only a few floors away from her daughter. She had been housed in the same high rise as Kovan but they would both have to be moved. The police had identified her at the club – that much he was certain of, but he wasn't sure how. At the flat they had a strict policy of having no doors locked in the house until lights out. That way he could keep an eye on the girls. Hanom couldn't be trusted to dance anymore and it might be time to keep her sedated, make her really work for her money. When he arrived on the 7th floor she had been in the shower. He waited but she did not appear so he had tried the door which had been locked. He had shouted at her to come out but he could hear she wasn't in the shower even though the water was on. He kicked open the door to find her wrapped in a towel, trying to conceal a phone behind her back. 'What are you doing – where did you get that' He lost control and slapped her with the back of his hand. She fell to the floor with the phone spinning across the exposed wooden floorboards of the bathroom, a forgotten puce relic of the 1970s which hadn't been touched since the day it was installed. The phone had only one number on it. She had sent a picture of herself and seemed to have called the number three or four times, the last time had been seconds ago. Now he understood. He got the house guard to phone the number from a call box. The man who answered simply said 'Yes' but he knew that it was the policeman. He assumed the worst – the phone calls must have been made over a period of time but they could point the way to their current location. That meant they would be able to trace them, and so his hand had been forced. There had been much talk of the safe place – time to find out if it is.

Onur Kocack had appeared quite shaken after speaking to the two detectives. *'What could Onur have to do with this?'* Eric watched as Onur sat fretful at his desk. He was pretending to read the site maps but he could tell that he wasn't concentrating on them.

"Are you OK Onur?"

"Yes my friend but I have just had some disturbing news from the police. They say my family is in Scotland, but that they are not safe. I think they assume I am involved in some way."

"But you aren't of course," Eric said, "the very idea is ridiculous."

Onur was silent for what seemed an age before he looked Eric directly in the eye, "I am afraid that I might be involved. I have a most dreadful secret. One that I thought I might have kept."

Istanbul, Turkey, July 24th 2009

Onur had been working hard. Kovan was 5 years old now. Time had passed quickly and she would soon be enrolling at school. He thought of her often, his darling. Hanom always said that she was her father's daughter. She adored him and would sit for hours while Onur would read to her and teach her. 'A good father is worth a thousand teachers,' she would say and maybe she was right. Kovan seemed a model pupil. She had said her own name

112

after just eight months and could already spell out the alphabet. Onur had high hopes for Kovan. He was earning good money now and had become well known in Istanbul through his engineering feats. The first phase of the Metro had been completed but the expansion continued and it looked likely there would be work left for years to come. His brother had also done well. Karim now called himself a senior director with his 'corporation'. Everyone knew there was more to the business than met the eye but it was never mentioned. He saw his brother less and less these days but they still shared a close bond, which could not be changed. And so it had been good news when Karim had phoned to say he had returned from one of his foreign trips and that he would be visiting that evening.

Hanom had been pleased to hear the news and it would be good to be reunited once more. How many months had it been since they had last eaten together – three, maybe four? He could not remember. All those years ago when Onur had announced he had started a relationship with Hanom he had expected Karim to be angry. The pair had always flirted in the past and everyone had been surprised that the 'dull brother' had won her heart. Yet Karim had only smiled and wished him well, 'Not my type brother,' he had said, 'I prefer more fleeting relationships,' and winked at him, 'Perhaps one day you can return the favour.' There was something sinister in his manner that night which Onur couldn't quite place but no more had been said on the matter.

The brothers met that night in a small tavern, not far from the Kocack family home at a spot which overlooked the Golden Horn. Quiet at the best of times they had agreed this would be a good place to catch up. The bar itself was nothing much to look at. A small door on the street opened up onto a long narrow formica covered bar, which ran some 20 feet before giving way to a larger room at the back. There was enough room for about six tables, each with four chairs. The bar had an exit at the back which led onto a narrow alley, which rarely saw passing trade from tourists. Onur bought two Efes pilsner's and brought them over to Karim who was sat with his back outstretched on the undersized wooden chair.

"Ah brother what times we have known. Look at us now. You the successful engineer, the toast of the city and me, well I have my own wealth now and know no trouble." Onur nodded he could sense Karim was building towards something, "And in all these years I have asked for nothing. Not one thing. When you took the girl I loved from me I said nothing."

"What girl?"

"Oh brother, don't play dumb – your wife. I would have had her for myself but you played a clever game there. I could see that she had changed. My adventures no longer seemed to interest her – perhaps she was not what she thought she was after all. And now all these years later you are the happy family man."

Onur did not understand what Karim was trying to say, "You always said you didn't mind. That you were happy for me."

"Yes that's true," Karim said, "but it was a sacrifice nonetheless. I surrendered what could have been mine for your happiness, as all good brothers should. I feel, though, that you owe me."

"Owe you what? You know I would help you in any way I can."

"It's good that you feel this way as I have a favour to ask."

"Name it."

"You will be aware that my boss is not altogether, well how should I put this, he's not universally respected. He has some unorthodox measures which not everyone approves of."

"He's a gangster if that's what you mean – there's no need to be so cryptic. We all know the 'business' you do," Onur said, sneering rather more than he had meant to. Karim grabbed his brother by the wrist and pulled him close over the table. The cigarette he had been smoking was in the same hand and the smoke was swirling up and into Onur's eyes, causing them to water.

"Listen to me. I have something to ask of you that cannot be refused. My life depends on it. As you know I've been away on business – this time it was New York. I have not spoken of my work but I deal in certain commodities which enjoy high prices in the States. But I have had a problem with one of my people. They have been greedy and my client is unhappy, which is a situation I must resolve. This problem goes high up and involves people that might surprise you – yet despite their status they are not above repercussions. The problem must disappear if you get my meaning. And this is where you come in. All I ask is that you give me access

114

to the new tunnel you are building under the Sea of Marmera. I am not a psychic but I think there might be an accident there soon. You will play no part of course but the site is well guarded and I need help to make this happen. I have never asked you for anything but you owe me your life."

Onur couldn't quite believe what he was hearing, "Brother you must think me a fool if you think I'd agree to this. You want be to be party to someone's death," he said whispering through clenched teeth, "that I cannot do."

"You will agree," Karim said, pressing hard down on Onur's wrist, "There is an occasion planned next week, where there will be a terrible accident. It will be investigated but they won't know who to look for and no-one will be found. Although I ask you this please understand that you have no choice – I have been asked to arrange this. I repeat that you have no choice."

"I have every choice, this is ridiculous." Onur stood up and walked out, not looking back. He was shaking with rage. But Karim was not finished and he caught up with Onur in the alley, grabbing him by the right shoulder, spinning him round. He held him by the throat against the wall. Onur could only look around him trying to work out how this could be happening.

"You think this is a game Onur, something I ask lightly? If you do not do this you might end up having an accident yourself. Look at you the big man – you are nothing – a fat man, living a life of ease. Well you have made a mistake today, a mistake for both of us. Do you think Eser invested in the Metro simply for prestige? This is a project that could last for another 20 years. Plenty of people have died in 'accidents'– you know that only too well but until now maybe you have not questioned why things happened as they did. But this time I cannot arrange it myself – it would be noticed but you could have helped. I promised that you would. I had faith in you brother but I am betrayed." Without warning Karim head-butted Onur and then was gone. Onur sat in shock in the alley, blood dripping down his head and down into the gutter.

Glasgow, Scotland, February 21st 2010

Arbogast thought he'd do Sandy a favour and let him know about the autopsy results before they went out on general release. The press had been quiet these last couple of days and with no new leads to follow the trail had gone dead. There was also an air of public regret now that the feeding frenzy over the 'paedophile' had proven to be less than genuine and 100 per cent off the mark. After a few rings Sandy picked up the call.

"Zander, it's JJ here – you busy?" It always relaxed Arbogast to talk with his old friend. It seemed there were so few people he could be himself with these days without putting on an element of pretence. Sandy was a true pal, perhaps his only friend and that was something which still mattered to him, "It's more business than pleasure but I thought I'd give you a heads-up on the abduction case."

"Long time no-hear John. I thought you were avoiding me."

"I was."

"Letting me back on the case now are you? I thought Stevie Davidson was looking like an accident – and the girl must be dead surely? We've been running a book in the newsroom on how long it'll take for her body to turn up."

"Never let it be said that journalists aren't salt of the earth.

Gentlemen – every last one of you. We've had the autopsy results back in for Stevie Davidson and we're treating his death as suspicious. The release will be going out in about an hour so you should be able to get in first with it if that helps. Off the record, the boy was beaten to death but whoever did it has tried to cover it up."

"Jesus John that's a nightmare – you think the girl's still out there?"

"I do, but I can't say where just now. We've got some good leads but I need this to get some public profile again and if you can help me with this I'll help you out when it's all done and dusted. Another lead, and the one thing no-one has picked up on, is the woman's father."

"The mother or the woman on the bus?"

116

"Mary Clark, the woman from the bus. I think there's a connection with her father. You might remember there was a big scandal about him in the 80s. His daughter accused him of raping a boy who went missing on his estate – guess who?"

"Not Stevie Davidson?"

"Correct, although nothing was ever proved and the case was dropped. Nevertheless his daughter always spoke of a 'secret place' where it all happened. Said she'd been abused too but there was never any evidence. I think there might be something to that case, though, which ties in here. Eric Sanderson works with the missing girl's dad. It's all a bit too cosy. I can't say any more just now and this information most definitely did not come from me, but if you check your archive this should all be in there somewhere. It could do with some digging."

"I'm surprised we haven't come across this already. It should have shown up in the search but of course our new system doesn't read anything past three years ago. We have everything on tape in the archive but we now work off of a server, which only goes back so far. If we want archive we have to digitise the old tapes, which in effect means our archive isn't worth shit. I'll get down to the basement and see if it's still there. I appreciate this John."

"No worries – just do some digging. As long as the focus is on the more tenuous links we may give ourselves more time to wheedle out what's actually happening. My suspicions suggest a link to organised crime."

As he hung up Arbogast wondered if he had done the right thing but of course that was a question he should have asked before.

117

15

Istanbul, Turkey, July 24th 2009

The look Hanom gave him when he walked through the door told Onur all he needed to know about the state of his face.

"Dear god, what's happened to you? Were you mugged or attacked in the street?"

Onur pushed past his wife trying to wave her away. He needed to see for himself – then he needed to think. His brother's rage had been brief but well placed. Judging by the swelling the nose was broken. It had bled a lot at first but now it just felt numb. He could almost see his face throbbing with pain. The bridge of his nose was cut and it looked like someone had sliced at his face with a razor. 'Other than that,' he smiled, 'everything's fine'. Except that it wasn't. His brother was obviously in some kind of trouble. He had never before even mentioned what he did for a living let alone begged for help. That his boss, Mister Ozan, was bad news was well known to the family but they had never voiced their disapproval. Karim had kept out of trouble and they had always hoped he was part of what was ostensibly called the 'legitimate' side of the business. Onur had been shocked when his brother said that there may have been more sinister reasons behind the accidents which had happened at his work. It was true that things had gone wrong from time to time. Three people had died in the last four years but all of those deaths had been accounted for and explained. In building the new Metro system they had to rip up large sections of town and drill and tunnel under others, but for the most part things had gone to plan. As if sensing he was troubled Hanom tried to comfort him. She ran her hand through the hair on the back of his head.

"What's wrong? I haven't seen you like this before. What happened?"

Onur was reluctant to give her too many details. He couldn't, not until he had more information. "It's nothing Hanom – a stranger, looking for money. I was walking down one of the back alleys after stopping for a drink on the way home. I was waiting for Karim but he didn't show. He phoned to say he couldn't make it. A problem at work I think. I'm feeling sorry for myself but the wounds aren't as bad as they look. I'll be OK."

Hanom looked concerned but as she continued to fuss he grew more irritable.

"Please Hanom I must be alone for a while. Please don't worry. I'll be OK," he said, bending over to kiss her softly on her forehead. This seemed to reassure her and he made his way to the top floor where they shared their bedroom. Outside the quiet chatter of passersby drifted through the summer haze. As he sat Onur wondered if it really would be OK.

Glasgow, Scotland, February 22nd 2010

"We've traced the mobile phone." Rosalind said, obviously excited they might finally have a link to Hanom. They had decided to play it safe and had agreed they would not contact her directly. There was a feeling in the team that if they could find out where exactly she was they might be able to figure out what, if anything, John Madoch had to do with the trafficking side of the investigation.

"Good job DCI Ying," Norrie Smith said. He had been reviewing the case and was convinced Madoch was behind the whole sorry mess. "What we need now is solid proof. We've been working on supposition and hearsay for the duration of this case and that won't do – we need to make progress. What have the telecoms people said about where the mobile phone might have been used?"

Rosalind felt she was under intense scrutiny. Everyone knew Norrie was the top man now, and while she knew there was good reason for the change, she still felt as though she had a point to prove.

"From the three calls Hanom has made from the handset we've managed to get a fix on a signal – it seems to be centred on a high rise block in Springburn in the north of the city."

This elicited as groan from the assembled crowd. Everyone knew she meant the Red Road flats. Back in the 1960s the city fathers had planned to leave behind the misery of slum living in notorious estates such as the Gorbals behind and give people better lives in these 'cities in the sky'. But less than ten years later, and with no shops and no hope, the estates slipped into decline and it would now only be a matter of time before they were ripped down. In the meantime they had become host to thousands of refugees and asylum seekers who had been decanted to Glasgow to live alongside the remaining mainly elderly residents who had come to love the flats and call them home. Many of the houses were now uninhabited. There were eight blocks ranging between 25 and 32 floors and everyone knew that if they did not have an exact fix they would have to go round each and every one on foot.

"Yes guys I'm afraid it is Red Road so best get your hiking boots on." Norrie Smith was quick to assemble a team of forty uniformed police to conduct the search. The eyes of the force were on him now and he did not intend to fail. One way or another, this case was getting solved.

Arbogast's second dealings with the SCDEA weren't entirely fruitless. His former colleague Richard Evans told him that the team had been dealing with a possible terror case in Fife and that Madoch had completely fallen off the radar.

"To be honest John we're not really pushing that case just now. We need more gen. He's been very careful so far and as I told you before the girls won't talk. We need to find out where they're coming from, how he gets them in and out of the country before we can nail him. He's not doing anything illegal at the club and his girls all check out, even though we know they shouldn't. If you want to try and find out if anything new is happening I could suggest you try using a CHIS."

"Sure. Who is it that we're talking about here. Anyone I'd know?"

A CHIS, or Covert Human Intelligence Source, was what used to be called a grass. Forces across the country had scores of them on the books. For a small payment scraps of information found their way to an investigation, often making a difference when it was most needed. Arbogast hadn't considered a CHIS as an option in this case but if Rich thought it could help why not sound him out.

"Well he's a different breed this one and to class him as a CHIS is perhaps doing him a disservice given his background."

"I'm interested now," Arbogast said. It was rare that these guys weren't toothless junkies looking for a bit of extra cash to pay for a hit. There were exceptions of course and some information came from gangs keen to roll over a rival. This, however, sounded different.

"The guy's name is Anah Uday. He worked with the British Army in Iraq based out of Um Qasr in the mid-noughties. He was passionate about reform and was in deep with our boys over there. He worked with the SAS in search-and-destroy missions in the north alongside the Americans. His help and contacts were invaluable until his luck ran out. He spoke to one person out of a thousand who he should never had trusted and got a dagger in his eye for his troubles. Not long after that there was an attack on his family in Basra. Twelve were killed including his wife and child. So he turned to his employers for help and they offered him a place to stay and a new life in the UK. I'm sure when he left Iraq though he didn't think he'd be trading places for a squalid life in Glasgow."

"Squalid?"

"Anah Uday was put with the rest of the people seeking asylum in Scotland in the high flats, to the north of Glasgow. He's OK though. He got a flat and can work but he's still living in a shit hole. We found out about him after his story appeared in The Times. Something along the lines of, 'He helped us liberate his country and this is how we thank him.' It caused a hell of a fuss at the time but his misfortune has been useful for us. There are a lot of people milling about up there that aren't allowed to work. For some of them we don't really know their backgrounds as their papers are often lost. Anah helps keep an eye on things; he's involved with a lot of the community groups up there and is well

121

known in refugee and asylum circles. It's possible that he might be able to help you – maybe he's heard something about new people coming in."

"Maybe Rich, but what are the chances? Thanks though." Arbogast didn't hold out much hope of making a breakthrough but he took the number anyway. You never knew.

He was surprised when there was a knock on the door. 'Rata-tat-tat' over and over again. 'There shouldn't be anyone here at this time, at anytime.' He took the gun out from inside his jeans and made his way to the front door. He crept along the side of the hall where the floorboards were the strongest and where he was out of the line of fire, should it come to that. In the spot where the peep hole used to be he had installed a camera which transmitted a picture onto a small screen inside the door. That way he could be sure never to be disturbed unawares. That was the theory. When he got close enough he could see that it was the husband, John Clark. The sight of him there, fidgeting and nervous outside the door made him instantly angry. He unlocked the door and reached out, grabbing John by the jacket lapels and dragging him inside. He pushed him down onto the floor and took aim.

"You realise of course that you should not be here...friend."

"Look, there's trouble. I didn't know where to go."

"You bring trouble to my door when you should have stayed away. You realise the bed you are making for yourself?"

John could see that he wasn't going to get the support he was looking for. He started thinking about a way of improving his fortunes.

"No use looking around now...friend. What is your problem? Maybe I can help put an end to it?"

"The mother has talked – they know about me now although I thought she wouldn't name me."

"Yes I know of this. She speaks to her police friend but no longer. This has been taken care of."

122

"You don't get it though do you?" John had found some of his courage again and had risen to his feet. He tried to calm his captor with his hands, but his host had never been a fan of mime. He grabbed John again, this time by the throat and pushed the gun against his head.

"No it is you who don't understand. You worry for the woman but she will not talk. I will show you." He dragged John along the corridor and kicked open a brown panel door that looked like it had seen its fair share of angry outbursts over the years. Inside the room sat Hanom. She was grey and listless and wore only a dirty white t-shirt. She was sitting with her legs drawn up to her chest and was staring blankly into space. There were red marks on her arms.

"Our guest has taken to some rather unfortunate habits as you can see. Her life will be consumed with things other than the police now. Have no fear. You on the other hand are becoming a problem. You were told not to contact me. I told you this on the night of the blizzard. Yet here you are. I'm afraid you have made a mistake in seeking me out. But listen to me shouting you must be cold, please come in and sit down. I think I have just the thing to make everything much better."

Istanbul, Turkey, August 4th 2009

Onur was on site at the Metro where his team were facing one of the biggest problems of the project so far. They had reached the halfway mark on the new Marmaray tunnel which linked the eastern side of the city to the west. It was important there were no slip ups, as the budgets were already hard pressed. Construction had begun on the metro in '92 and 20 years later there was still a way to go. Today the Mayor of Istanbul, Altan Tirpas, would be paying them a visit to mark the progress and hopefully generate some positive press to deflect attention away from the economic downturn. It had been two weeks since he had last seen Karim and so far nothing more had come of his warning. Although Onur was concerned his brother was still OK he was fairly confident the threats which had been levelled at him had been made in the heat of the moment. As he surveyed the work he had been in charge of he could not help but be proud of his achievements. The tunnel was nearly 30 feet wide and made for an impressive sight. Every day Onur would chart how much farther they had tunnelled, although at times the work was slow going. On a good day they'd make forty metres but they had hit rock and at the moment the colossal TBM's (tunnel boring machines) were only progressing by half a metre a day. All the same it was quite an honour to be visited by the Mayor and his entourage and he would smile when he had to smile before returning to work.

The press arrived on time although the Mayor did not and the tour started about 30 minutes later than planned. He talked to the Mayor about the ways in which they worked and how soon they hoped to complete the tunnel. As he pointed and shuffled his way down the shaft he felt he had finally reached a point in his life where he could say he was content. Photographers recorded their every step and TV cameras would later be unable to shed light on exactly what happened next. As they approached what was considered a safe distance from the TBM, Onur's assistant handed out ear protection mufflers. For this was the showcase – the real wow factor. As the assembled group of about seven dignitaries and twelve members of the press stood and waited as the colossal machine slowly ground into action. The circular cutting head ground down into the rock and processed the waste behind. While it ran, like an enormous crawling mole the machine created the tunnel sides as it went, pouring concrete and sealing the deal. And so it was that the tunnel appeared, little by little, day-by-day and that was the process that everyone was here to see, the monster machine, live in action.

No-one noticed while the roar grew louder that one of the photographers had dropped back to check his equipment. He had stopped pointing his camera at the machine as this was not his intended subject. His employer had given him a very special mission. The photographer had been given the equipment earlier that morning. His Pentax K5 appeared industry standard but with a .22 magnum pen gun installed inside it was guaranteed to be the deadliest shot taken that day. The first person to notice there was anything wrong was the Mayor's PA. Altan Tirpas had raised his hand to reach the back of his neck but by then it was too late. The bullet had severed his spinal cord and he was dead before he hit the ground. About twenty seconds passed before anyone realised what had happened and the silent screaming started. By the time the machines had ground to a halt the press had already been shepherded away. Initially the cause was thought to have been a stray piece of masonry. It wasn't until the next day that the coroner confirmed the mayor had been shot. And by that time Onur had already left Istanbul for good.

***

When Arbogast arrived at the high flats on Coll Road he had already been round the houses. When Rich had told him the CHIS lived in Red Road he had been slightly off the mark. Anah Uday lived in a single block about a mile from Red Road. It sat alone among an avenue of post war council housing and was somewhat out of place. At 26 floors it was 24 floors bigger than anything else anywhere near it. Arbogast knew he was on the right trail as he had been told to look for the burnt out flat in the middle of the block, which was none too promising in itself. These flats had all been re-rendered over the last few years and looked much better than he remembered. But two weeks after the Coll Road flats had been finished there had been an accident. Frank Fields had been enjoying his usual half and a half at his local pub. The landlord was always happy to see Frank as he spent most of his pension there and Frank was glad to see the landlord as he had nowhere else to go. That plus the heating was free and he couldn't afford to warm his own place as the electric fire ate up too much money too quickly. Every night was pretty much the same for Frank. Three rounds of drinks, darts, watch the ten o'clock news then home for 11:00. On his last visit, though, he had rather overdone it. A modest win on the national lottery meant that he had been quite drunk by the time he had got home. Failing in his fight to fend off an alcoholic hunger brought on by five too many pints he had fired up the chip pan before promptly firing up his own home. They found Frank's body next to the cooker. They had picked out bits of tea towel from his face. His case file read that he had slipped and fallen while trying to douse the flames. As Arbogast looked up at the blackened plaster around his 7th floor flat he couldn't help wonder if there was a worse way to go. *'Stupid old bugger.'* And that was when he met Anah Uday, who was waiting for him in the hall outside the office of the concierge.

"Come in here please. It's OK, I have an arrangement."

In the past the high rise blocks all had a concierge on call 24 hours a day. They had lived in the blocks and if something went wrong it was reported and fixed. Now there was one man for eight blocks and nothing got done in a hurry. It became obvious to Arbogast that the office was no longer used, or hardly at any rate. He dusted down a green swivel chair and looked his host over for the first time. Anah Uday was about five feet six inches tall. The story of his eye may have had some truth in it. The eye wasn't covered up but an injury had left a white globe in its wake which gave his host a rather crazed look. His skin was scarred above his injured right eye but other than that it seemed he had at one time been a good looking man, and he retained a sense of dignity that Arbogast warmed to. This was a man who did not mess about.

"You want to know about the refugees yes?" Anah Uday said.

"Not exactly, my colleagues are looking for a Turkish woman who has been taken captive. She's been working out of sex clubs as a dancer but we think she's being held by people – possibly connected to John Madoch. Do you know of him?"

Anah Uday considered this for a while before answering, "I know of this Madoch although I have never met him. His company owns lots of flats in the Red Road," he said, pointing north. Arbogast followed his hand with his eyes then felt like a fool when he ended up staring at a blank wall.

"People come and go at the flats – criminals, associates and yes as you say sometimes prostitutes. Usually no-one asks questions. These are not people that need to be caught. They are small fry," he said, mouthing the last two words slowly, relishing the sound.

"I can't tell you too much Anah but there's a woman we must find. I don't need to speak to her now but I do need to know where she is. She may be the key to an investigation I'm involved with. You would be well paid if we find her."

Anah nodded his understanding, "You have perhaps a picture for me to make finding this woman easier?" Arbogast handed off the garish snapshot he had. The only picture they had of the woman, "You wait here and I will return in one hour."

Rosalind Ying wished the mobile had been traced to anywhere but 'here'. Here was floor 21 of 10 Petershill Court. The DCI cursed the broken lifts and wondered why there was no-one on site to fix the damn things. Fifty per cent of the houses were empty, some with their doors lying open. Some had been used as drug dens while other flats were occupied by refugees who spoke little English. And then there were the little old ladies who just wanted someone to talk to. She had been pacing the floors for two and a half hours now and hadn't even finished block one. The pretence was a neighbourhood watch campaign. To see who opened up and who didn't. When no one answered she stood and listened but so far there had been nothing that was not just run of the mill. *'Run of the mill,'* she thought, *'more like four hours on a treadmill.'* Her calves were aching from the steps and the shuffling along corridors from flat to flat while she shifted her weight from one leg to another whenever she found someone in. Now she stood on the landing of the 21st floor, looking out onto Glasgow from North to South. She had to admit you got a fantastic view from the stairwell. In the distance she could see another block; it looked like there had been a fire in one of the floors.

He had seen them coming, the police officers, going door-to-door, on his floor. He had panicked at first but then he realised he had no need to. He kept very still as the woman knocked on the door. He watched her facial expressions on the camera. He saw the initial determination followed by the waiting, and then she stood and listened with her ear against the door. But there was no movement here and no sound. John Clark was rigid and Hanom was out cold. All he needed to do was wait and then they would be gone. And then she went to the next door, unaware of how close she had come.

Kovan Kocack had been alone for a long time. He had gone and left her. He said he wouldn't be long but he hadn't come back, that she shouldn't move and shouldn't say a word. He said if Kovan said something, anything – when he wasn't here – especially if he wasn't here – then he'd still know. He said that if I was a bad girl then mummy wouldn't come. Not ever again and she wanted to see her mummy. This place was cold. The windows were frozen on the inside leaving ice maidens to glisten in the sun. Every time she touched the glass the cold hurt her. *'Please come back soon,'* she thought as she pulled the rough blanket around her, *'please come back soon.'*

16

Istanbul, Turkey, August 4th 2009

News of the Mayor's death spread quickly and by the time Onur arrived home the enormity of what had happened was only just starting to sink in. The authorities had not yet released full details but Onur was certain his brother's hand had played a part. He knew the Mayor had been shot as soon as he saw the mark at the back of neck. Despite this the event was still being reported as an accident, rather than an assassination. Karim's threats had been real and it seemed that his help had not been needed after all. Onur's mind was racing as he tried to figure out what to do. Karim had suggested he would become a target if he refused to help but the attack had taken place anyway. Someone on the inside had been involved and Onur had come to the conclusion that it had to have been someone he knew. What was worse was that he had been warned but had done nothing. As a thousand possibilities raced through his head a familiar voice sounded behind him.

"I told you this would happen, brother, you really should have listened." It was Karim, dressed in jeans and a t-shirt, a million miles away from the usual designer suits. "You look surprised to see me but not as surprised as you should be. I told you I needed your help but you didn't listen. A terrible shame about the Mayor don't you think? The worst thing is that he wasn't even the target – it was you," Karim stopped as Onur struggled to take the information in, "The less you know about the assassination the better but we only had one shot and it missed the target. You should know that they'll come for you if you stay here."

Onur looked horrified, "What on earth are you talking about? Why would anyone want me dead?"

"Well technically it's not you that's the problem, it's me. My trip to New York did not go to plan. Some money disappeared. I made a mistake and now people are angry, which is natural enough under the circumstances."

"I'm sorry to hear that your stupidity has finally got the better of you but I still don't see what any of this has got to do with me. I work hard and I know nothing of your business. You bring this destruction on my family then turn up with threats." Hanom walked in and stood between them. Karim looked at Hanom then Onur.

"In my line of work brother it pays for employers to have insurance. In my case, the firm knew about my family. It has hung over me from the start. I knew that if I made a mistake I would pay and so would my family and unfortunately that means you. Today's 'mix up' will create a lot of problems. The news is already all over the internet but you can bet the hardest questions will be asked right here in Istanbul. I will try and put this right but you need to disappear, get out of the country."

Hanom was angry now, "Leave? Leave to where – what would you have us do? Onur don't listen to this man – he's a beast – a wicked beast. Why should we listen to you?" she was shouting now and it wasn't until Kovan appeared in the doorway that she held herself in check, "Kovan my darling. You must be wondering what all the noise is about but don't worry everything's OK. Your uncle has had some bad news that's all. Let's go upstairs and see what we can find for you to do."

The two men watched the girl, who was eyeing them uncertainly, sucking on her thumb for comfort. She knew something wasn't right but didn't know what it was, so she started to cry.

"We must leave now brother," Karim said. He had raised his arm towards him and Onur thought at first that he meant to shake hands, until he realised he was now squarely in the sights of a gun.

"What have you got me into?"

"You will be able to return here someday, but you must leave now if you want to live. I warned you this was coming and

130

although you obviously disregarded what I said I've been making plans on your behalf. I have associates in Britain who are willing to give you work. Good work actually in the renewable energy sector. You might even end up quite liking Scotland."

"Scotland?"

"I'm afraid so Onur – that's where you're going and we can even make it look official. I have the right papers. I will arrange for Hanom and Kovan to join you in good time but they will need to be smuggled into the country. We cannot leave a trail. I feel responsible for this brother – please let me try and fix it."

Onur stared at Karim, unable to speak.

"Let me put it another way Onur, if you don't go with me you will all be dead by the end of the week, perhaps sooner. I have a car downstairs that will take you to the airport. It has all been arranged. I will contact you in a few weeks to let you know when the others will follow but you must trust me, this will go smoothly."

"This is ridiculous why should we leave for your mistake? I will go to the police and tell them – this is your problem you must have known this might happen?"

"Ah yes the police, but what would you say to them? That you were given your job after Mr Eser put in a good word for you as a favour to me? That a number of people have died under your watch? That my company is the largest private investor in the Metro? That I am now a wanted man by Interpol? The strands all tie together and I'm afraid they're all hooked on you. You'll be taken care of in the UK. I'll cover your tracks here, it'll look as if you've disappeared."

He stopped talking and fired his pistol, the shot ringing past Onur's head, causing him to grasp his ear in pain. "You will leave now Onur or I will have to take matters into my own hands. This plan cannot be allowed to unravel. You must trust me. You must."

Onur was led down and out of the rickety wooden house without so much as a parting word to his family. His ear was bleeding from the blast of the shot and as he looked up he could see his wife and daughter watching from the window. There was another man with them.

"It's all for your security Onur. We are blood and you should know that I will not betray you. I will guarantee you will all be reunited and soon. Come now."

As the yellow Honda pulled away Onur could not help but feel a growing sense of dread at what exactly his brother had in store for him.

***

Arbogast had been sitting in the little room at the bottom of the high rise flat for more than an hour. He had spent the time checking his emails on his mobile phone. There was no word of progress from the search in Red Road, a work detail he was thankful to have been spared. He could see the buildings where the search was taking place from where he sat. He was glad he would not be going door-to-door in there, which reminded him as he felt a slightly bulging gut that he really ought to try and get running again. He looked up the force Facebook page on his mobile phone, which had been set up specifically for this investigation. They had decided to try to use modern technology to 'connect with people' as Norrie Smith had described it. As his thumb glided over the screen of his handset the blue banded web page appeared. There was video footage of Mary and Kovan at the bus stop which sat alongside video interviews with Rosalind and Norrie. The idea was the same as always, to get people to come forward but the page was still unusual enough to have created its own headlines and it had received heavy traffic. They had had a big response in terms of volume but gained little in terms of quality, meaning there were plenty of people coming forward to confirm what they already knew. Still it kept up their public profile and that was half the battle. What they really needed was a break and he could feel they were close. Arbogast was beginning to think he had wasted his time with the CHIS and that he would be sat here a long time for no good reason. He sighed knowing that it had been a long shot that this guy would have heard anything, and even if the call had come from one of the tower blocks what were the chances the woman was still there? Then his phone rang.

"Detective Arbogast it is Anah Uday here. I may have something for you." The reception was poor and the phone cut out momentarily, "my contact chchchchchch,"

"Hello?" Arbogast said, shouting.

"chchchoch at Red Road, number 10 chchchoch people are leaving."

"Fuck." By the time Arbogast had finished swearing the only thing left in the room to evidence that he had been there at all was a spinning chair and dust mites glinting in the sharp winter light.

Rosalind Ying had had about enough of the search by the time they were three doors in. She knew that if they didn't manage to turn something up the investigation would take two steps back, but she still had a feeling that they were getting close to something. She had been paired with PC James Kerr who she had known from a previous job. On floor 22 no-one had been in. As they made her way to the stairwell leading to 23 Rosalind made up her mind to stay positive. *'Plenty more people to get round.'* She pushed hard against the heavyweight fire doors which creaked under the pressure. She opened the door for James Kerr who climbed the stairs two at a time. DCI Ying made to follow but stopped midway. She had heard a noise behind her. Rosalind looked to her feet scanning the floor, half expecting to see a rat scurry past, but as she looked back down the corridor she realised she was being watched. A man stood arms crossed, midway out of one of the doors she had just tried. When she caught his glance he disappeared back into the house.

"Excuse me...excuse me sir can I have a word please?" She looked back but her partner had gone. She knew she shouldn't proceed alone but curiosity drove her on. 22F, 22E, 22D rolled past until she came face-to-face with a door which was slightly ajar. Rosalind scanned the hall in both directions before deciding to knock.

"Is there anyone there? This is DCI Ying from Strathclyde Police." Rosalind slowly opened the door with her index finger. She was not armed but did have a baton. Passing through the door and over the threshold Rosalind could see there was no one there. The door opened onto a hallway with four doors leading off it, three of which were closed. The walls were papered with a faded red floral print which looked like it had been there for a very long time. There were rectangular patches of brighter colour where framed pictures had once hung and a green and brown shag pile carpet which was matted and worn. There was no sign of life so Rosalind extended her baton and crept down the corridor where a door stood open. As she got nearer she could see a man was waiting by the window. He turned as she got to the door and smiled broadly at her. He seemed to be carrying a phone.

"Come in, I've been expecting you," he said as he raised and pointed the phone. It was only much later that Rosalind realised her mistake. The convulsions which racked her body came from a Taser gun and not a mobile phone. The last thing she remembered before passing out was a delighted smile peering down from above and strong hands covering her face.

PC James Kerr waited at the top of the landing, *'No sign of the boss – she must be on the bloody mobile again.'* After five minutes passed and when she hadn't made an appearance he thought he had better check. Returning to the floor below, he scanned down the corridor. There was no sign of life.

Although Arbogast was only a few hundred feet from the Red Road flats the traffic system was laid out in a way which meant it took him 15 minutes to get there. A combination of traffic lights, wrong turns, and a bad sense of direction meant he went round in circles for some time. When, eventually, he spotted Anah Uday by the side of the road it came as something of a relief. He slowed down the car but Anah walked off into the foyer of one of the blocks, he obviously did not want to be seen. Arbogast parked and followed suit. The set up in this block was similar to the one he had just left but this time the concierge was both available and on site. He nodded to Arbogast as Anah Uday led him into a small room at the back of the office which was dominated by a large pine desk with chairs on either side. There was a perspex screen down the middle of the room and another set of chairs on the other side of the barrier which cut the room in two. The sign on the door signalled this was a 'community help zone' although the advisors obviously did not want to get too close to the locals.

"I think I might have something for your information," Anah Uday said, in his broken English

"The concierge?"

"You need not concern yourself with him, he is of no matter. It is what I can help you with that will be of interest. My friend says there have been many unknown faces here in the last few days. Most of the new arrivals are seeking asylum. Few people choose to live in this area now and as you can see it is slowly becoming a ghetto, well out of the sight of the 'good people of Glasgow'. But there have been many new white faces seen here in the blocks opposite. My friend tells me most are Eastern European. We had many Poles here some years ago but not so much now. My friend says they all women. There is one woman he says is different from the rest. She has darker skin and darker hair, the rest are blonde."

"Would he be able to recognise her?"

"This he will not do but I have shown him the picture and he says he is sure it is the same woman – if not her then very similar."

Arbogast's heart was racing. He turned away from Anah Uday and tried to think.

"And your friend...where does he say this woman is?" Arbogast said, his body still facing the wall but he turned his head round for effect.

"She was in this Tower three nights ago, in Tower 11 the next day and in Tower 12 last night. She seems to move each day. This is why my friend has noticed. It seems odd, yes?"

"Yes it does. I think you've earned your money today. Does your friend have a description of the man who has been with her?"

"He said it was difficult to tell as they always wear baseball caps to mask their faces. He said he was pretty sure that last night it was an older man from the way he walked; he was not like the others. If Mr Madoch's flats are being used he has property on the

14th, 18th, 22nd and top floors of the building," Anah Uday passed a slip of paper with a series of floors and flat numbers, "and this is all I can tell you."

Arbogast tried to raise Ying but her phone was ringing out so he phoned HQ and spoke to Norrie Smith.

"I have an update for you sir. I think I might have found the mother, Hanom. I understand the mobile phone was tracked to the Red Road flats but she might be in Tower 12. I think I should go and have a look." There was a silence at the other end that Arbogast put down to indecision. He knew they needed to act now.

"DCI Ying has been going door-to-door in Tower 12." the Chief said, "I think you better get over there. Be warned though the lifts are out of order."

Arbogast ran out of the building and raced to Tower 12. He should have remembered the weather. The paths had been cleared of snow but the pavement remained treacherous. As Arbogast sped along he did not notice the black ice underfoot until it was too late. His feet gave way beneath him and his whole body collapsed, his head smashing off the side of a rough cast wall. As he lay flat on his back he looked up at the towering blocks in front of him when he realised that there was something wrong. There was smoke coming from one of the flats. As he counted the floors to the fire he already knew the unlucky number was going to be 22. As he picked himself up and carried on he hoped his fears would count for little.

***

Onur Kocack had accepted the invitation from Eric Sanderson gladly. This business with the police had unnerved him. Everything was supposed to be dealt with at this end and he had not expected to hear from his wife for some time. Although the initial plan was to have the family back together very quickly there had been problems and he had been forced to wait it out. He had been checking the web pages of the Turkish press and nothing much more seemed to have come from the assassination, with the investigation having so far turned up nothing of note. There was nothing about him at all save from a piece saying he had been unable to return to work through stress. *'Are they looking for me –*

why did I agree to come here?' Eric had driven him to his home after they had levelled one site for Turbine 102. Sanderson had apologised too many times for the state of his mobile home but Onur said it did not matter to him and that it was good to get out of his own house. When they arrived it was already dark and he had been surprised, despite the warnings, that Eric was living in such a dilapidated old caravan. Onur knew that he made good money and that he must be able to afford something better. As the two men settled into the evening Eric spent the night plying Onur with what he claimed was the best whisky Scotland had to offer. The Laphroig had been hard to take at first but as the night went on he relaxed more and they had enjoyed a night of good food and tall tales. It was well into the evening when Onur realised he had said more than he had meant to, more than he had mentioned to anyone else. He told Eric about his plight and his family who he missed. He told Eric that he had been horrified to learn they were here somewhere in Scotland but that no-one had come forward to let him know. Eric had listened as he had poured over the media coverage and cried when he had recounted what they were saying about his wife and daughter. Onur explained that the police seemed to think he was involved but even he didn't understand what role he had played in the whole sorry saga. The police had asked about John Madoch but what would he know?

Eric had listened and stayed quiet because Eric knew more than he was letting on. He knew that Madoch had dealings on the continent, knew that he was unscrupulous with money, and knew that he owed him more than he could ever pay back. Eric knew, and it was at that moment that he made the decision to do something about it. Onur would be the first to learn his secret but it was a secret that would not pay to be kept for too long. As the night went on and the whisky went down decisions were made.

He left John Clark in the living room on top of an old foam sofa, material which was not made to resist the naked flame. He knew that he would need to act fast as the area was already swarming with police. He consoled himself with the fact that they did not really know what they were looking for and they would never think to connect a travelling family to their investigation. He had offered to let the policewoman 'Ying' leave if she could but she seemed a little under the weather, no doubt she had taken something that did not agree with her. The two of them would look, at first, like two junkies who had gone wrong, which would give him enough time to cover his tracks. He had crossed over to the flat where he was keeping Hanom, who was to share another fate entirely. She would pass quite nicely for an old lady in a wheelchair that had been left behind by the previous owner. He used plastic cable tags to secure her hands and feet to the metal frame and then covered these with a long skirt and gloves. He masked her with a headscarf, while he made sure her face was looking down. For extra docility he had used a dose of rohipnol he kept for special occasions, perhaps he'd use it twice today. 'Let's see how this goes first before getting too carried away.' Before he left he gathered what passed for furniture in the flat and piled it together in the living room. It was old – old and dried out – which would be ideal for his purposes. He emptied a can of lighter fluid and lit it. He sat and watched for a few seconds as the flames took hold. This was the best part of a fire, when the bright orange flames raged powerful and pure, working their way up into an unstoppable inferno. The flat would soon be consumed by smoke and it would be a while before anyone was any the wiser about what had actually happened. As he left, pushing his quarry in front of him, he smiled at how well it had all been going but knew he still had a lot to do. For security he had threatened that fat slob of a concierge with a nice new smile if he didn't play along. He knew he was connected and had passed on his key for the lift which had been 'out of service' now for several days. And now as he reactivated his own private express he dropped down to the 18th floor and collected the girl from her latest bolt hole. She had been excited and asked again if it was time to see mummy. 'Yes,' he had replied 'and much sooner than you think.' As they sailed down the floors the police were still going up by foot. No-one noticed as a man in a baseball cap with his daughter bundled up with hat and scarf for winter pushed an old woman out to the waiting taxi. They would see it later on when looking back at the CCTV footage, but by then it would be too late, far too late.

Arbogast felt light headed and he struggled to reach Tower 12. He thought he had only grazed his head but slowly he had felt the hot blood seep from the wound and drip down into his eyes. His head stung but he forced himself on. He stopped for a second when the window exploded above, with flames and thick black smoke billowing out of the flat and trying to make their way up. At the same time a black Range Rover passed him which he tried to flag down for help but it carried on driving, "Bastards". When he got into the lobby he was surprised to see that the lift was working and that the doors were still open despite what the Chief had told him. Arbogast stood inside and pressed 22 but nothing happened. He noticed the doors had been jammed open and so pulled them together and pressed the button. On 22 he could see the smoke was already starting to fill the corridor and was seeping under a door about halfway down the corridor. As he kicked in the door the rush of air into the room caused a surge of flame which nearly knocked him over. He forced the first door open and saw a figure slumped on the bed. It was Rosalind but she was not moving.

"I'm too late." Arbogast dragged his colleague out from the flat and into the hall before returning to the apartment to see if there was anyone else there. He looked in the other rooms but couldn't see anyone. In the bathroom the shower curtain had been pulled right round and there was no sign of life. The air was thin now and he was struggling to breathe in the heat. Creeping along the floor he heard another crash as more windows gave way in the front of the flat. Arbogast wondered if the building had gas and knew he had to leave. In the corridor he made to smash the fire alarm but it had been vandalised and was out of order. Exhausted he collapsed on the floor with Rosalind's head on his lap. In the distance he could hear the faint sirens of what he hoped would be the Fire and Rescue teams.

It was visiting hour at the Royal Infirmary but as usual no-one had come to see Mary. It seemed she had no-one and was allowed no visitors anyway. *'No matter, I'll be leaving soon and then we'll see who the victim in this really is.'* Mary's mind had turned to her past and the secret place which had ruined her life. *'This time though, it'll be different. This time I'll be the one in charge.'* Mary waited until she knew the shifts were due to change then prepared for what she knew she had to do. There could be no turning back.

17

Istanbul, Turkey, October 7th 2009

Hanom was awake but she kept her eyes closed. Her first instinct was to listen. *'What was it that woke me?'* As a rule Hanom slept with the curtains open so that she was woken naturally by sunlight each day – it had become a habit after Kovan was born. Hanom got up and crept over to the bedroom door. She had felt uneasy since Karim had shattered their family lives. He said he would be back and perhaps this was the time. All she wanted was a quiet life but it seemed she had little say in the matter. Listening intently she could tell there was no movement in the hall and that Kovan was still fast asleep in her room. Her father slept on the ground floor. But there it was again, a slight sound, a quiet rumbling as if someone was moving around below her. The stairs in the house ran up the left hand side of the building with connecting doors on each floor making their way off the painted limestone interior walls. Looking down she could see there was smoke coming from the second floor, and she had to cover her mouth to stop herself from choking. She knew she shouldn't open the door, that the air would make things worse so she ran back up stairs. Kovan was still asleep and was lying on her front with both her hands stretched out in front of her with her hands buried between a wall of pillows as if she was flying. Hanom shook her daughter violently.

"We must get up now darling, but don't worry everything will be fine."

Kovan was not naturally good tempered first thing and did not look pleased to be woken. Hanom grabbed the pile of yesterday's clothes from the floor and lifted her daughter, covering her in the sheets she slept in. When Kovan saw the smoke in the hall she stiffened.

"What's happening mummy, has there been an accident, is our house OK?"

"We must leave because of a little fire but don't worry we'll phone for help once we're safe." Hanom stroked the side of Kovan's cheek to reassure her. This was something that usually calmed her daughter but Hanom could see that the fear was starting to build. Crossing over the threshold and out into the cool night air Hanom allowed for a sigh of relief. She needed to go back for her father. Breathing heavily to try and calm herself down the Kocack women would have seemed calm to a passerby. The fire itself could not yet be seen from the street.

"It will spread soon." The voice startled Hanom and she jumped at the sound, clutching Kovan through fright.

"It's too tight mummy, you're hurting me," but Hanom wasn't listening.

"Karim, tell me this wasn't you. Tell me that you wouldn't stoop so low?"

The question hung between them like a corpse on the gallows. Karim looked as if he was about to explain, to put her mind at rest, and for a second he looked like the Karim of old. But the dark cloud returned and he took a step back gesturing for them to follow.

"You must come now. If you want to be reunited with your husband and if you don't want to die, you must come."

Kovan was weeping into her mother's shoulder. She had never seen adults behave like this before and it scared her. Hanom looked up at the second floor, the flames just visible now under the window. She knew she had to leave, that what lay ahead was uncertain, but at that moment she was sure of one thing: that any love she may ever have held for her brother in law was now lost. If he perished in this fire he had brought on their lives she would be glad of it. She stepped forward and could see there was a waiting car to the side of the house. Another man was in the driving seat. He nodded to her in acknowledgement. Hanom turned and stood face-to-face with Karim before spitting hard. He stood, unmoved, as the saliva ran down his face watching Hanom and Kovan then he smiled.

"Your carriage awaits my princess," he said grabbing her arm, "and before you ask the answer is yes." Karim looked up at the house then down on Hanom and Kovan who were now sat in the back of the car, "Yes your father is dead."

By the time the alarm was raised it was already too late as the rickety old wooden house in Istanbul quickly burned away. The dry, brittle wood cladding sparked like kindling and the house burned like a searchlight in the night. The blaze meant that the rest of the street was evacuated due to the danger of the fire spreading through that close knit community. The fire was not brought under control until late that afternoon and by the time the forensics team arrived there was little left to investigate. The structure had collapsed in on itself and down into the basement. It was another 13 hours before the body was found, and another four days before the blaze was explained as having been the result of an electrical fire.

Glasgow, Scotland, February 22nd 2010

The paramedic found Arbogast collapsed in the hallway of the 22nd floor of Tower 12 with Rosalind Ying unconscious with her head in his lap. At first he thought they might be dead but the Detective's sudden burst of fury suggested otherwise.

"Don't waste time on me take a look at her," Arbogast said. Underneath the soot Rosalind had turned an unnatural shade of blue. The paramedic rolled up her sleeve and nodded.

"What is it?" Arbogast said, concerned and frustrated he could not do more to help.

"Does this woman have a history of drug misuse sir?" Arbogast stared at her blankly before replying as calmly as he could.

"She is a Detective Chief Inspector with Strathclyde Police – she does not use drugs."

"Then I'm afraid that someone has introduced her to the habit. She appears to be overdosing."

The stretcher arrived and Rosalind Ying was thrown onto it unceremoniously before the paramedics disappeared back down into the stairwell. Arbogast followed in convoy. They left in separate ambulances.

"She's in good hands now and the hospital is less than five minutes away. I'd say she has more than a fighting chance of pulling through and she's lucky to be alive."

Arbogast thought that was a phrase he seemed to be hearing more and more these days.

It was 4:30pm at Glasgow Royal Infirmary, which meant visiting time for those lucky enough to have someone that cared. Mary Clark had other plans anyway. Mary had been moved into a private room off the Cardiology wards due to the risk of complications brought on by hypothermia. Although she still felt weak Mary had made a better recovery than she had let on and she was now aiming for an unscheduled visit of her own. Mary knew the first task would be the hardest and that she would need to deal with the policeman before being able to do anything else. Mary had been told the officers had been stationed there to 'keep an eye on her' but she knew only too well that she was under practical house arrest and was being segregated from the rest of the patients, which had given her time to think. Mary had asked about her husband John who should have been back in touch by now, but they said he had gone missing which wasn't a good sign. Looking around the room Mary realised that she had one or two pressing problems. Firstly she had no clothes other than the gown she had been given by the hospital. Her clothes were most likely classified as evidence now. She had searched through all the cupboards and drawers in the room but, unsurprisingly, they had all been empty. Turning her attention to her 24 hour guard Mary was running short of inspiration. Early on it had been that young guy Frank. He had been sweet, trying to talk to her and telling her everything would be OK. That was when they thought she was the victim. Frank had not been as nice to her after the investigation had switched its focus to her. Mary sized up her chances. Frank was a big man and he would be difficult to get past but she didn't feel that she had any

144

choice. The chair was just outside the room and the only time her guard would leave was when there was a nurse in the room. She was always under their watchful eyes. Mary's luck changed for the better about an hour ago. Frank had been replaced by the family liaison officer, DS Mhairi Reid, who was altogether a more appealing prospect. She had come up with an idea, which she was just about to put into action. Mary opened the door slightly and cleared her throat.

"Mrs Clark you know you are not allowed to leave the room unaccompanied."

"I'm not aiming to leave but it's just that I've got," Mary lowered her voice, "well let's just say you might be able to help me with a delicate matter," she smiled in a way she hoped would inspire empathy. DS Reid recoiled slightly at the notion but Mary could see she was weighing up the situation. She rose from the chair before bending in to Mary.

"I'll just get a nurse for you."

Mary didn't waste any time. There was no-one in the hallway and she knew she had to act quickly. She punched DS Reid sharply in the throat, winding her and causing her to bend over. While she was doubled up Mary grabbed her hair and pulled her into the room. She was prepared for this and had shredded a pillow case and now deftly wrapped it around the officer's mouth using it as a makeshift gag. DS Reid was disorientated and didn't have time to realise what was happening to her. She looked from left to right as her brain tried to make sense of the situation. Her natural reaction was to raise her hand, to try to say 'No' but as she rasped and spat onto the cotton sheet she was now bound to her fate. Mary grabbed her by the hair again and smashed her head down onto the floor, once, twice...four times – then quiet. Mary could see there was blood but she knew that could not be helped. The blinds to the room were drawn so she would not be seen if she worked fast. Mary dragged the leaden weight of Mhairi's body into the en suite bathroom. It had been built to be disabled friendly so there was plenty of room to work. The two women were not exactly physically matched but Mary knew the clothes would need to do. DS Reid was about four inches taller but maybe not as wide as Mary. Stripping her of her uniform, Mary shed her gown and got into character. "I'm sorry," she said, bending over to kiss her former captor as if saying goodnight to a lover, "But it had to be this way."

Mary slipped out of the room and was almost caught by a passing Doctor. She quickly sat on the sentry chair before she was seen and nodded to the man as he passed. If he had looked at her more closely he might have seen the beads of sweat which had formed on her brow. Once he left Mary slipped away unnoticed. As she walked from the hospital up and out of the concrete walkway she noticed an ambulance arriving with sirens blazing, unaware that her self-appointed nemesis was about to take her place on the casualty list.

Eric Sanderson had visited Tower 12 earlier the same day. He had been feeding Onur whisky all night while he guzzled on cold tea. He knew that something was going on behind the scenes but had not realised that it might present him with an opportunity. People always asked why he lived the way he did, why if he had made so much money selling land, didn't he sit back and enjoy life. He always said the same thing: that he invested his money into the company and that he was waiting for the long term kick back, his retirement fund. And this was true to a point but his benefactor knew him too well.

John Madoch first approached him a long time ago, around the time when all the fuss had kicked off with the boy and his daughter in the 80s. Madoch had held a knife to his crotch and asked a single question, 'Where is it?' 'It' was what Sanderson considered his life's greatest achievement but also his darkest secret. The 'secret place' had been for his Mary, although he never let her know where it was. It was always a car ride away at night – a long, circular journey which led to the inevitable confrontation. He had made her feel that it was quite normal and in time she had learned to accept it. All until she was old enough to know differently and then she began to challenge and defy him but had never mentioned the big secret. His wife had died of cancer having never cottoned on to what was happening. Eric always imagined she must have known but she had never said anything. He often wondered if she had worried herself to death, always fretting about the little things but never dealing with the big problems of which he surely would have been top of the list. That had been a long time ago but with Madoch the past was never let alone. His 'investment' was more of a security than anything else. His secret was kept and he did alright out of it. Sometimes the 'secret place' would be used by people who needed to stay out of sight for a day or two, but now through a curious turn of events he had a different use in mind. Eric imagined he might even be able to have some fun along the way.

He had squared the meeting with the boss first and so when he arrived at Tower 12 everyone knew what to expect. He had been there and it had been strange to see him after all this time in the flesh. Eric could see that he despised him but that didn't matter – he would do as he was told. The arrangements had been made. Eric told the girl her father was waiting but she didn't seem to be convinced. 'Where is my mother?' she kept asking in Turkish, 'Will I see her soon?' Sanderson had smiled, not understanding what she said in her foreign tongue, and ruffled her hair in what he hoped was a reassuring manner. 'I'll return later, be sure to be ready.' The girl sat playing on the dirty green carpet, and Sanderson thought that she might find herself quite at home, given time.

As he breathed in his lungs were filled with cool, clean, life giving oxygen. Arbogast could almost taste the next 40 years. His face was covered in soot, the dirty black particles having stung his eyes and blocked his nose. When he ran his hands through his hair a thick, filthy grease smeared his hand. In the ambulance they had made him take oxygen although he had protested that he was sure he didn't need it. When he got it though he knew he was wrong.

This was his life for the five minute trip to hospital with the wailing siren marking out the vehicle as one worthy of free passage through the clogged arteries of the city's east end. When he arrived his first thoughts were for Rosalind. He shrugged off the attempts of the paramedics who tried to corral him into the emergency admissions ward for a medical examination, as he could feel he was going to be OK. It turned out that Rosalind had been injected with what they thought might be Diamorphine – or in other words Heroin. Arbogast could feel the investigation slipping away from him. He didn't think there would be too many people out there brave enough to take on the police like this, and fewer still with the nerve to try and burn one alive. Arbogast was sure of one thing though – Madoch was definitely involved. It was his property, two people involved in the case worked together at one of his firms. *'One was Kovan's father for Christ's sake.'* Answering his phone Norrie Smith updated Arbogast on the search.

"They've found another body at the flat. We're fortunate to have caught the fire when we did. It's burned out the front of the building but the back rooms are all intact."

"It's John Clark isn't it?"

"We think so John," Arbogast couldn't remember the boss having used his first name before. "John Clark's wallet is in the building, it was found on the corpse but I can't identify the body yet, the face has been badly mutilated."

"But you think it's him?"

"Well he's the same build and height and the wallet is a fair clue even if we can't be a hundred per cent about it. We'll need to look at dental records as he was badly burnt, but it's a matter of time. Whoever is responsible for this seems to be tying up all the loose ends. And if that wasn't bad enough Onur Kocack has now disappeared."

"What do you mean?" Arbogast couldn't believe what he was hearing, "I thought we had a car on him at all times?"

"Well yes we do. We had a patrol out at the wind farm but his car's still there and there's been a light on through the night at the office. It was only after one of the constables thought to look in that they realised there was no-one there."

"This couldn't get much worse really could it, did you check in with Eric Sanderson?"

"He said Onur was working late and that he hasn't heard from him. The patrol car noted that he left at the usual time, about 5:30. They would have seen if two people were in the car."

"Maybe, look thanks for keeping me in the loop. I'm going to make sure DCI Ying is OK and then I think I'll have a chat with Mary Clark since I'm here anyway. DS Reid can sit in with me."

"Good idea DI Arbogast," he said, hesitating for a second before adding, "and take it easy John. Are you sure you're fit to carry on?"

"Yes sir – we're close now I'm sure we are. Thank you." When Arbogast hung up he opened the door to the emergency room where Rosalind was being treated. He could taste blood in his mouth when he saw that she was breathing through a valve mask, and watched to check the breaths were constant. He didn't see the doctor approach him with an outstretched arm; he was too busy watching as some kind of drug was prepared.

"Is she going to be OK?" he said to no-one in particular. As he was pushed from the room the masked doctor nodded.

"She's in the best possible hands but you cannot be here."

And then Arbogast found himself forced back out into the corridor, faced with a cold grey door and a million questions.

The daily news meeting had been much livelier than normal. Sandy Stirrit knew that he had a good lead on the abduction case. He had explained that the woman found on the bus was the same little girl who had accused her father of raping her in a secluded dungeon in the 1980s. Those old enough had mulled over the juicier titbits of that case while younger reporters watched, asking questions as they tried to remain part of the conversation, hoping to lend some latter day insight. Sandy knew that Arbogast would not have thrown him this scrap if there wasn't something in it but the editor wouldn't touch it.

"Look Sandy, if this ever gets solved, which let's face it doesn't look too likely, then this kind of thing is great. If we're the only ones who have it then it's perfect for a background report but you know the score just now, we can't afford to be upsetting people with age old gossip. We've had our knuckles wrapped a few times recently when we've been accused of taking part in trial by media and we can't afford another scandal. We have had the Scottish Government on already trying to punt a line about secure border controls and sensationalist reporting. The police are already getting pressure to get this case solved and I can't see the

149

justification of going after this guy. Check it out by all means but I'm not putting it on at this stage."

Sandy hadn't been happy at being fobbed off. He was supposed to be the senior reporter but there were few risks being taken these days. He sensed there might have been political pressure judging by the comments about the Government. The Scottish Parliament was still a young institution trying to make its mark and the communications guys were never far away when the reports were 'off message'. The thing that annoyed him was how readily his masters snapped to attention. The fourth estate seemed to be losing its bite. Cuts and rationalisations had left them with an inferior product that less people wanted to watch. It was the same all over but the more it was cut, the worse it got. Sandy wasn't going to let this go. He decided that if he wasn't going to be allowed to actively report on the lead then he was still going to have a bloody good look at it.

Sandy's first stop was to the archive section to root out any coverage they had on tape. He had his answer about four hours later. The case had made the news three nights in a row in 1985 before it died away, the daughter's claim of incest having been dismissed. The reports themselves offered little in the way of insight but he was intrigued by another tape marked 'SANDERSON ARCHIVE'. Taking his time Sandy spooled through and could see Mary as a young girl. She was dressed in a pair of blue denim dungarees and a white baggy t-shirt, topped with the most ridiculous crimped fringe. The grainy film caught the times. It had been a glorious summer's day when the boy had gone missing. This was the next day 'My father did this,' she said directly to the camera 'and he'll do it again, he'll rape another boy and maybe another girl,' then from the background a younger Eric Sanderson appeared and touched the back of her shoulder where she seemed to flinch. Sandy rewound the tape. *'Ever so slightly yes,'* he was sure she had moved. Eric explained that she was upset by the attention and that his daughter had never wanted to allow others onto the land and that the camp had annoyed her. The footage hadn't run of course as it was libellous, although that hadn't stopped the papers, if the old timer's stories were anything to go by. He watched more of the raw footage and was intrigued by the house. It seemed to be circled in birch trees; they didn't look too old, maybe ten years or so. The house sat proudly on the hill, brightly painted in white with black around the exterior windows and round the door. It was a fairly unremarkable old farmhouse. In the background he could see what looked like a well, which sat next to an outhouse, possibly a shower block. There was something about the picture which didn't seem right. He looked and looked but for the life of him he couldn't work out what it was.

Back at Glasgow Royal Infirmary Doctor Ellen Fitzpatrick was doing her rounds. She kept the 'prisoner' for last. She scolded her juniors for calling her that but it was true wasn't it, she was a prisoner more than a patient. Mary Clark seemed to be making a good recovery and she would soon be out of her hair. As long as this whole sorry saga continued her life would be turned upside down. Constant media calls about the state of her health and the round the clock police presence was putting staff and patients alike on edge. Before she even entered the room she knew something wasn't right – there was no policeman at the door and Doctor Fitzpatrick assumed the detectives must have come back to speak to her – maybe they had taken her away. The doctor made a mental note to bring the matter up with her junior staff. This was something that she should have been told about. But when she opened the door there was no-one inside. She became worried when she saw there was blood on the floor. She bent over and touched it, and realised that this was something that had only just happened. As she bent over she could see a shape inside the bathroom through the door which was ajar. Peering into the gloom she gasped when she saw DS Reid lying on the floor. Quickly checking for a pulse the second thing Doctor Fitzpatrick did was to pull the alarm chord.

Mary Clark was loose.

Part 3

18

Glasgow, February 23rd 2010

Every fresh blow shook the plaster from the ceiling. The noise had been constant for 45 minutes and his patience was starting to wear thin. Graeme Short had lived downstairs from John Arbogast for just under six months, and was starting to really 'get to know' his neighbour. Graeme looked up wondering if the ceiling was going to give way and moved to the side of the room 'just in case.' Sometimes dust sieved down through an expanding crack. *'Right that's it, I'm going to go up, whether he's a cop or not.'* Graeme had just put his shoes on when the noise stopped. *'Next time, next time I'm actually going up there and give him a piece of my mind.'*

Sweat dripped from Arbogast's head as he crouched on all fours on the bedroom floor. He had tried to run for an hour on the treadmill but hadn't quite lasted the pace. *'You're still out of shape,'* he thought, gasping for breath. Arbogast had transformed what was ostensibly the guest bedroom into a makeshift gym. The corner nearest the front window was filled by an unmade single bed, which he had taken from his mother's house when he had sold it on. Opposite stood the treadmill which was rarely used, while in the middle of the room sat a bench press and dumbbells. This had all been bought in good faith but the flaw in the plan was that Arbogast lacked the basic motivation to train. Fast food grabbed on the hop and too much socialising in his spare time meant that there were occasions he could barely recognise his own face in the mirror – today it looked fat and fleshy. It was generally true, though, that one good run would pave the way for a three month health kick which got him back to square one and his preferred weight of thirteen stone. Although he had noticed that it had been getting harder to do. Today he would have preferred to have sprinted along the banks of the River Clyde with the bracing gusts of freezing air more refreshing than any session in the gym. But the hard packed ice was making getting about on foot a tricky business, as he had already found out at the Red Road flats. The weather was due to change and the forecasters said that a thaw should come in the next few days. Outside the trees were frosted and beautiful in sharp winter skies. Gone now were the inches of snow which had clung for so long to their bows. It wouldn't be too long before life returned to normal.

45 minutes earlier

Arbogast was running hard. Running to escape the deadlock and running to free his mind. While he ran he reviewed the case. It had been a week since Mary Clark had disappeared. Despite the fact that more than forty officers were deployed in and around the area for the tower block search their key witness had managed to slip through the net, unnoticed in her stolen uniform. Forensics had confirmed the body in the flat was John Clark. He had been drugged, beaten, burned and left for dead in a filthy bath tub. They still hadn't been able to speak to Madoch who had been out of the country but Arbogast planned on paying him a visit later as he had some pressing questions that he needed answered. Sanderson had checked out. He had complained about being contacted by the press about the 1980s allegations. He said he hoped the police hadn't been leaking details. He would have to wait and see how that panned out. Onur Kocack too had gone to ground with all three of the family now missing. Arbogast pushed the machine up into a sprint mode and ran fast for five minutes. He knew there were too many apparently random ties in this case for them to be entirely coincidental yet Madoch seemed to be sitting at the centre. But would he risk his growing empire for the sake of a child. Finally as he gasped for air and inspiration his legs gave way and he stopped, panting and breathless on the treadmill, before collapsing on all fours on the floor.

Walking back into the living room, wiping the sweat from his brow with a filthy green towel, he sat down with his back sticking to the leather, and tried to picture where the investigation was heading. There had been pandemonium at the station after it had leaked out that Mary Clark had assaulted DS Reid and run off. They hadn't gone public at first but one of the nurses had spread the word and before long it was out in the public domain. There had been calls for resignations and the case was made for police incompetency. The politicians had waded into the row, wanting to be seen to be doing something to help. Arbogast hated the process. Politicians would change things for the sake of change, with old discarded methods dredged back up and reused when they should never have been changed in the first place. There had been calls for Scotland's five police forces to be merged into one but with one chief constable to oversee the whole country there were questions about increased political interference. All he wanted to do was find the child.

***

When the door opened the dim light from above flooded in, temporarily blinding them, as their eyes readjusted. The room was no more than 12 feet by 20. There was one damp and pungent mattress and an assortment of cushions, discarded from long dead settees. A slop bucket sat in the middle of the room. Hanom had woken up groggy. At first she thought she might have flu but gradually her memory returned. Hanom felt sick and deathly cold. Her guard returned every few hours, although how long it was really, was impossible to tell. He wore a hooded top which covered his face so it was difficult to make him out. When he came he said nothing, merely pointed, leaving food and sometimes replacing the bucket. She felt that the confined room should be warm but there was a constant flow of cool air so she knew there must be ventilation from somewhere. It was then the screaming started.

***

Arbogast couldn't help but be impressed. Madoch House was the first in a planned street of new office blocks on Clyde Place. In

157

Glasgow's hey day as a bustling Victorian Port the area had been a warren of warehouses and quaysides. Cotton and tobacco harvested by American slave labour had flooded in on freight ships carrying illegally high loads. Later world beating engineering would become the city's main cash cow with shipping becoming a global export. The decline had been slow but inevitable, with skilled labour giving way to mass unemployment. Today the 21st century economy revolved around service sector call centres. The warehouses had given way to 'urban space' and long derelict hangers were demolished, leaving the future in the hands of the speculators. The city had recently built a new footbridge to span the Clyde and it was from here that Arbogast examined Madoch House. The bridge support looked like two arrows poised to fire but Arbogast was heading over not up. Standing at seven storeys tall Madoch House opened last year to much public applause. Arbogast liked it. The architects had tried to be sympathetic to the city's overriding style and had built in a red fingered sandstone facade. It looked new but timeless. At the moment the only tenant was Madoch himself. His office complex occupied the top floor. As Arbogast entered through the large revolving door, he could see that no expense had been spared on the interior. The ground floor was largely open plan with a single central reception desk currently home to a rather bored looking receptionist. Pulling himself to his full height Arbogast approached over the marble tiling.

The receptionist caught him off guard, "DI Arbogast?"

"Yes," he replied, failing to mask his confusion.

"Mister Madoch has been expecting you. If you would like to take the lift to Floor 7, I will tell him you're here."

Arbogast was dismissed and the telephone was raised, "Sending up DI Arbogast for you now sir."

Arbogast watched her on the phone as he made his way round to the lifts. The ground floor had been split by a white marble partition. From outside it had looked like the desk was at the back but on the wall behind reception stood three elevators all of which lay open. Arbogast had the feeling he was being watched. He tried to find signs of hidden cameras as the elevator made its swift ascent but there was nothing obvious. The lift had doors on either side and Arbogast was again wrong footed when the exit revealed itself behind him.

"DI Arbogast?"

When he turned round he was faced by the man himself.

"John Madoch. I suspect you may know why I am here?"

"Yes of course but let's sit down before we delve too deep into the rogue elements."

Arbogast thought rogue elements an interesting choice of words.

"You like my new home detective? I thought if I'm spending all this money I might as well take advantage of the view."

The penthouse was largely open plan and took up roughly quarter of the space of the floor below. The front of the apartment was broken up by white concrete pillars with a glass wall running the length and sides of the building. It was furnished in an expensive corporate style which used art deco as the inspiration and the 70s for structure. White leather loungers mixed with steel framed glass tables and dark wood fittings. At the back there were four enclosed rooms, presumably bedrooms while the exterior was surrounded by decking and an expansive balcony. Madoch led the way, leaving the flat to go outside. Arbogast followed as the manicured interior gave way to a panoramic view of the River Clyde. Madoch still had his back to him when he started speaking.

"Do you like it? The Lord Provost was here when we opened. The council were very thankful that someone finally built something here and others will follow you know. I've invested a lot of time and money here and good things will happen."

"It's the things that have already happened that I'm interested in," Arbogast said, as Madoch finally turned to speak to him face-to-face.

"And what things would they be? Some people would like to consign me to the past. The call me a gangster behind my back, a hooligan, but that's not me. Could a thug have achieved all this? I don't think so."

"And yet your name just keeps popping up Mister Madoch – why would that be?"

"I can't answer that but you should know better than to listen to gossip."

Arbogast changed tack, keen to try and win back the initiative, "Been away have you?"

159

"Yes. My business takes me across the world these days."

"Did you go anywhere special, Turkey perhaps?"

Madoch smiled, "Where's all this leading? I think you should get to the point."

"Let's just say you're in the shit, right up to your neck. An employee of yours, Onur Kocack, has disappeared despite being under police supervision. His daughter has been smuggled into the country and apparently abducted. Meanwhile her mother appears to have been forced to work in one of your lap dancing bars. She's gone too. All this and the daughter of another of your employees was with the girl when she vanished and now she's skipped out of hospital and gone to ground – so many ties that bind you."

"So many loose ends you mean. It seems to be that everyone you need to speak to has disappeared. It's hardly textbook police work."

"Listen Madoch – this case is being watched around the world just now. Two people are already dead for reasons unknown and I don't want to have to deal with any more bodies – this has to stop now – do you understand? I know you're involved and I don't care if the Lord Provost is your fucking rent boy." The two men were close now. Arbogast could smell the stale coffee from Madoch's breath although the man himself was giving nothing away, "Be under no illusions that I will tie you to this and I will find the girl and her family. I can see you've had a good run Madoch but it'll be ending soon make no mistake." Arbogast backed off and threw his arms open, "So don't get too used to this view, it won't be Madoch House for long." He turned and made to leave, his adrenalin pumping, when Madoch shouted back at him.

"I've lost out of this too you know. Kocack's a good man, well connected. I've had property destroyed and questions were asked after John Clark's body was found. I can't afford any more bad publicity. Be assured, though, that you do not want to dig too deep Inspector, you never know what you might uncover."

Arbogast kept walking.

The melting ice was leaving a trail of destruction in its wake. Scotland was not a country that planned for an extended deep freeze. Ice had made its way through cracks and joins in roads and

160

pavements, seeping way down and under the tarmac and forcing it into shapes it wasn't designed to cope with, exerting pressure and destroying the grand design. Then as temperatures rose and the ice melted the roads were left to sink and disintegrate, leaving a sea of potholes and broken roadways. Arbogast cursed the system as he ran into a deep hole which sent a violent judder through the car. He turned down the radio to listen for damage, fearful the jolt had burst a tyre, but after a few seconds he was satisfied there was nothing wrong. As he drove through the streets of Glasgow he knew that they would need to stay close to Madoch. The investigation was still in full swing but the absence of Rosalind had slowed things down, sapped the morale of the team. They still couldn't understand exactly why she had been attacked. Perversely it had also strengthened their resolve to catch whoever was responsible, but with so little progress being made it was starting to become difficult to see when the case was going to break. The loss of Rosalind had been hard to take. She had been dazed and confused and hadn't been making much sense since the incident at Tower 12. The doctors said that she had suffered some kind of breakdown and she had not spoken to anyone yet, she hadn't seemed able. It was to her bedside that Arbogast was heading.

Generally speaking Rosalind Ying was not looking her best. Arbogast had been shocked to see how pale and sickly she seemed, lying in her bed staring into space. The Doctor said there was nothing wrong with her but that she had yet to communicate what had happened at Red Road. Arbogast stood silently inside the door. He had bought flowers from the hospital shop but saw that several people had already had the same idea. Her bedside was covered with cards and messages from concerned friends and family. He thought again of his mother and her situation, *'What if it had been me?'* That was the first thing he had thought of, *'Selfish John, selfish,'* yet the question remained.

"Is that you John?"

Arbogast looked up and saw Rosalind was looking at him, "Hi Rosalind. I thought I'd—'

"I was hoping you'd come."

"—What happened? Look I know it's been hard but I need to know, this case is slipping away."

"It was him John, the man in the flat. It was him."

"John Madoch?"

"No John, it was Onur Kocack. I'm sure of it. I didn't see him for long but I'm sure it was him."

"Onur Kocack? You do know he's gone missing."

"Oh John I feel I've failed everyone. It all happened so quickly," Rosalind said. She couldn't face him anymore and was on the verge of tears. "The door was open and then there was this face – his face – and then he just lunged at me, I thought it was the end of me."

"You'll be OK Rose." He had never called her that before and wondered if he might have overstepped the boundaries of their friendship but she made no comment so he decided to try it again.

"Rose, I need to know if you are a hundred per cent certain it was Onur. Forensics has found multiple traces of DNA but nothing that connects with anyone we have on record."

"I'm sure it was him. The only thing that was different was the rage. He seemed so passive when we spoke to him. This time though..."

"I'm going to go after him Rose. I think I might have a chance but I'll need to go my own way. I tried this by the book once and it didn't bring me anything but a headache. I'm not going to make the same mistake again."

"Be careful John, these guys aren't shy. Don't leave yourself wide open or they'll nail you. They've shown they aren't frightened. I don't want a bedfellow John."

"Really? Well maybe you don't know what you're missing." He winked at Rosalind, who blinked back slowly. They both had their own thoughts on what might just have happened but that would need to wait.

Onur sat in darkness, considering where it had all gone wrong. His relocation was supposed to have been temporary but as time went by he could sense things would not be changing for the better anytime soon. Eric Sanderson had been sympathetic to his plight but Onur had drunk too much, glad nonetheless to have finally confided in someone. Onur felt that none of this was his doing, that he had simply been drawn into some kind of conspiracy; a pawn in someone else's game. Eric said he could help and that it would all be OK after the Tower but so far nothing had changed. Hours had turned to days and Onur was aware that he couldn't leave now, he couldn't even go outside. Eric Sanderson had said the Police were looking for him, that they'd been here asking for him. Of course he had said nothing, how could he. As Onur sat waiting he suspected that Eric was a far more accomplished actor than he appeared. And so the waiting game began for Onur. He waited for news, waited for food. He waited and kept waiting.

Bishopton, February 23rd 2010

The signs of decay were obvious and Eric Sanderson knew that it would only be a matter of time before his world crumbled around him. He had ventured inside the house for the first time in several months the day after the crack had widened. The temperature felt warmer and for the first time in weeks he could feel his face when he worked outside. Eric had noticed a change in his old home when the snow first came. The house itself had sunk slightly, only by an inch or so, but it was undoubtedly starting to shift again. The surveyors had identified an old mine shaft beneath the house but he never thought the void would claim the home which had always seemed invulnerable. But as he made his way through the ground floor Eric Sanderson could see the extent of the damage. The house was not carpeted but had rugs throughout, to mask the ancient floorboards. What had once passed for the living room was now dominated by a huge crack which had splintered the floorboards wide apart, big enough that you could put your fist through the hole. Eric knew that he shouldn't be here, that it was dangerous, but he sensed his misfortune might still present an opportunity, if he played his cards wisely. From the basement Eric could see the damage went deeper than he feared. The floor, which had been cut into a limestone base, was cracked wide open too. He dropped a nail down to see if he could gauge the depth of the hole. The

163

distant clatter indicated it was worse than he thought. What he needed were the right tools.

Sandy Stirrit had driven out to try and talk with Eric Sanderson but there was no-one home. He had been struck by the farmhouse which, having looked so well cared for in his archive footage, now seemed on the verge of collapse. He took the opportunity to have a look round. The shower block remained although it had seen better days. The caravan sat alongside it. *'Maybe he used the water supply from there?'* Something was missing though. It was a few minutes before Sandy realised that the well had been removed. Looking around it seemed obvious to Sandy that someone had been here recently. The snow had turned to slush and there were newly made tyre tracks which looked like they had been made by a 4x4. Sandy knew he was wasting his time. *'Maybe the editor was right?'* He stopped on his way out and thought for a moment, while the engine hummed against the cold, steam rising from the bonnet. Sandy took out his camera and spun it in the direction of the house. While he was here he might as well take some footage. If anything came of this it would be good to have some wintry GV's. But Sandy wasn't alone. From the top floor window of the condemned house he was being watched.

He thought the only way it could have gone any better would have been if the policewoman had died, but you couldn't have everything. He now had them all in place and it had been much easier than he could ever have imagined. He had used the intricate system of dungeons which he had inherited to keep them within feet of each other, yet completely blind to the reality of the situation they were facing. He drugged the woman at night while the daughter was left to wonder. The old man seemed to like her but those games couldn't be allowed to continue. He would end this tonight. They had waited long enough. He would make it easy on them, give them a choice. Tonight had been a long time coming. Treachery and assassination had failed to win the day and so it had come to this. They had agreed of course. He could not have

164

acted without their support and their connections had been invaluable. Of course they had pinned the whole thing on the wrong man. It hadn't been hard to copy his writing and his personal details had been easy to get hold of. Just a simple trip into the bank – a transaction to move funds, sanctioned by him of course and there you had it – embezzlement. The type of deal Mr Eser didn't take kindly to. And so the wheels had been put in motion. The hounds were out to find my brother and I am leading the pack. Thinking back to the Tower he wondered if the police had seen him, would they be able to identify who he was? He doubted it was likely. If anyone, they would link this to his brother. Karim knew that he had played this perfectly.

19

Glasgow, February 22nd 2010

'What was she looking at? Maybe she knows? Keep walking, keep walking,' Mary Clark powered forward on pure adrenalin. For a moment she thought she'd been caught, but when she was spotted by the doctor she had managed to bluff her way through. Leaving Glasgow Royal Infirmary Mary was amazed she hadn't been recognised. She looked down to examine her borrowed trousers and laughed. To mask the length she had rolled up the legs and then tightened the belt. None of the clothes really fitted but it seemed that people avoided looking directly at you when you were wearing a uniform. Mary had been cooped up in the hospital for more than a week and had enjoyed a constant heat of about 25c so the first gusts of freezing air which met her on the esplanade came as a shock to her system. 'Where now?' was the question of the moment. Mary's first problem was that she didn't really know where she was, although she knew that she wasn't far from the city centre. Outside the hospital piles of ice lay by the roadside, blackened by pollution from the city's traffic. The dreary mounds would lie for weeks after the thaw, a fleeting reminder of the big freeze. Mary became aware of heavy traffic. It took a few seconds before she realised it came from the M8 which lay parallel to the road outside the hospital with only the pavement and crash barrier to separate the two carriageways. Mary opted to follow the traffic and headed west. She started on foot downhill, along the perimeter of the hospital, passing by the multi-storey car park and the Victorian sections of the hospital, past the Cathedral. In the background Mary could see the Necropolis so she knew to turn right along Cathedral Street which would take her back into town.

It wouldn't be long before she was back in civilisation. Mary caught a glimpse of herself on the black glass window of one of the buildings at Strathclyde University. She looked awful, pale and drawn and much thinner. She also realised that she looked 'wrong' in the clothes she was wearing. Checking through the pockets of the black jacket she found a purse and a mobile phone. The purse had less than £10 in it which was disappointing. More intriguing though was the range of credit cards: Visa, MasterCard and a number of store cards. These might be more useful. Her first thought was to look at the mobile phone. *'She might be a cop but I bet she's as lazy as the rest of us.'* Sure enough there were the codes stored on the phone: Visa as 9854 while MasterCard was 7767. *'Bingo'.* She knew she wouldn't have much time to use them but she was confident enough they would not be cancelled within the hour. If she was quick she could restock and then go to ground.

Her first port of call was to the John Lewis department store across from the bus station. Here she got everything she needed: a job lot of jeans; dresses; jumpers; gloves; hats; boots; bags; underwear; and a warm winter jacket, which she knew would be essential. Smiling as she punched in the pin number the checkout girl asked if she would like to take out a store card. Mary laughed and explained she was in enough trouble as it was without taking on more credit. They had both laughed at that. The check out girl said she 'understood' what she meant. Next stop was Jessop's to buy some photography equipment; this she thought would come in handy, while Sainsbury's metro store provided the food she needed to get her through the next few days. She knew the cameras would have picked up her movements. At a cash machine Mary entered the pin again.

WOULD YOU LIKE TO MAKE A WITHDRAWAL?

"Yes please." Mary withdrew the maximum which was a generous £400 and then repeated the action at the machine next to it for the other card, in an action she thought would make her movements harder to trace, telling the woman behind her the machine was broken and the queue dully shifted over behind her.

Mary knew she would have to get out of the clothes. It had been almost an hour since she had left the hospital and so far she had managed to avoid causing a scene. She put £1 into a public toilet and entered. Stripping off the police clothes she kept the baton and handcuffs. The toilet stank of chemicals and the plastic corrugated sides were stained with the black marks of stubbed out cigarettes. These portaloos had a reputation for being popular with risqué lovers at the weekend but Mary fancied few would be as risqué as her. She dressed herself in comfortable clothes and took the camera out and hung it round her neck. The rest she stuffed in one of the cavernous bags she'd been given from the department store and stepped back out into the world. She wandered down Buchanan Street as a tourist, making sure to look up and point her camera every so often and then made her mind up that she needed to get out of sight. Dumping the bag with the clothes and boxes into an industrial bin, left unlocked in an alley, she felt prepared. As she walked among the people of the city: the office workers, the students, the horseback police and the tourists, she knew that none of them would spot her. They would be looking for someone dressed as a policewoman, certainly until they found out about the transactions. Her final act on camera was to buy a one-way ticket to London at the kiosk at Central Station. After that she left the credit cards in a bin inside the station pub, and then boarded the train. It wasn't due to leave for another ten minutes which gave her time to change clothes again. Disembarking she waited on the platform and waved to an imagined someone. *'That should throw them off the trail for a while.'* She now had nearly a thousand pounds in cash and she knew what she had to do.

Eric Sanderson returned to work on Sunday afternoon. The security guard, Charlie, was surprised to see him.

"Alright Eric? I wasn't expecting a visit from you today."

"No rest for the wicked and all that."

"Any sign of Onur yet?"

"Listen Charlie, Onur's been living in a nightmare. He's been lying low these last few days, helping the police with their inquiries about his family. It all looks to have been sorted out but there are a couple of things that still need to be finalised before they go public with the details. You need to keep quiet on this – mum's the word?"

"I've no gripe with Onur but—"

"If I hear you've been talking you will have no job – understand?"

"—Sure...sure. I don't want to make waves."

"I don't mean to get heavy Charlie but it's been hard for him. It'll be fine you'll see. How are things going here? Have we had any joy with pile 104?"

"Well you can see for yourself the weather's improving which should speed things up. One of the boys said given a little bit of luck we might even be able to get the project back on schedule."

"That's excellent news. Catch you later Charlie and just remember – you don't know a thing."

Eric sat at the wheel of his car chewing on his fingers. He was nervous. Eric knew what he was about to do was dangerous, but if it worked he could blame Mary and take the credit for finding the girl. *'Yes, it's worth a try. I just need to wait until the site is cleared.'* Eric was fairly confident that the police had lost interest in him. Detective Arbogast had phoned to say that Mary had gone missing from hospital and that he must tell them if she made contact. They said they would be making another public appeal and that they might want him to help to try and find her through a statement to the press. He had growled something about hell freezing over but said he'd think about it. It seemed to Eric that he no longer figured in the investigation which was an unexpected bonus. *'Mary seems to be their main suspect which suits me fine, it's about time the little bitch got her comeuppance.'*

The stock room was under lock and key and security had an eye on the place 24 hours a day. That was in theory anyway. In reality Charlie the overnight security guard was a 67 year old man who was just there to make up the numbers. The security system was archaic to say the least. Madoch's business empire had started on the road to legitimacy by channelling drug money through 'security' agencies. Staff appeared on the payroll with no real job description. Intimidation and protection had been his line, up to the point where he no longer needed to make his money the hard way, but the security arm lingered on. Here at the wind farm it was felt high tech security wasn't needed so they had brought in some antiquated VHS recording systems to help the flow of money through the company's various arms. Old Charlie just sat and read the paper through the night. He was happy and no-one else really cared. Distracting him had been easy.

"I saw some teenagers on the site from my office Charlie. Could you check it out for me?"

"No problem boss, they'll run when they see the torch," Charlie said, before disappearing into the dark of evening. In the security room Eric pressed stop on both machines and then left. The licensing requirements for storing explosives were strict and they were not permitted to keep them on site for more than 24 hours. But with blasting due to take place tomorrow the latest batch had already arrived. As he pressed the security code into the external pad the door clicked open, causing the internal light to flicker on. There were around forty bags of ammonium nitrate and eighty gallons of fuel oil. This was only of any use in confined spaces. They would drill down into the rock, pack in the ANFO and then set it off with dynamite. There were six boxes of dynamite, one of which he opened, depositing half the contents in his holdall. It would be his job to set the explosive for the blast the next day and when the job failed he would complain about poor quality product. He might even get a reduction on the next order. This was the beauty of the plan, only he and Onur had access to these supplies and even though the order book stated how much was there, there would be no-one to suggest it all hadn't been used. He packed the small brown cylinders into his bag. The sticks measured around 20 cm by 2½ cm across and they all had one magic ingredient: nitro-glycerine.

Mary knew what she was about to do went against everything she stood for, but she had no other choice. She kept a low profile that afternoon, spending three hours in the Odeon watching a terrible fantasy film she had picked for the length alone and used the opportunity to catch up on her sleep, exhausted by her efforts so far. She wouldn't be able to use public transport as she might be seen. Mary needed a car. If she was going to avoid any unwanted questions she was going to have to steal one. Mary knew just the place to go. In the cinema toilets she changed clothes once more, this time into a tight red Lycra dress and high heels. She wished she had bought some makeup but reasoned that it probably didn't matter. Making sure her police baton was handy she left for the red light district, a place she had worked for years trying to support the women who were abused. *'Well tonight I'm giving it back,'* she thought as she made to the corner of Anthony Street and Newton Street. She dumped her bags in bushes nearby where she managed to cut her hand on thick gorse. She smeared some of the blood on her lips to give her some colour and stood by the corner. After about 15 minutes Mary was approached by another woman who seemed angry.

"Think you're taking my spot tonight? I don't think so. You'd better move or there will be trouble believe you me. I'm not in the mood for arguing so take a walk. ARE YOU STILL THERE BITCH?"

Mary froze, she knew this woman. It was Maggie Deans. Maggie – who had once come to her after being stabbed by a punter who didn't want to pay. Nothing happened of course, that was the tragedy of it. Mary turned to face Maggie head on. She said nothing at first, allowing Maggie the time to figure out what was going on.

"Mary is that you? Mary Clark? But why would...are you not?" The question was left hanging.

"Yes it's me Maggie, they're looking for me. I was attacked and left for dead. You know what that's like. The thing is I know who did it and I think I can do something about it. The police want to blame me but I know the truth. We've been friends for a long time. Maybe you think I'm just one of those do-gooders out to ease their own conscience and maybe I am, but tonight it's me asking you for help. I need a car."

Maggie Deans nodded. She didn't really understand what was going on but she could see from Mary's face that she was deadly serious. That was a face she knew only too well.

"I'm not going to ask what's going on – I have a feeling I don't want to know – but I will do this one thing for you. Stand back and be ready."

Maggie took Mary's place on the kerb and about 40 minutes later the transport arrived. As the car crawled along the kerb, the window descended allowing the victim's face to leer out. Mary had been expecting someone older, someone fatter and more repulsive but this was a young man, quite good looking, who came to a halt not six feet from her. Maggie leaned over to make her deal from the pavement. Mary was fast and brutal. She pulled Maggie aside and pulled open the door on the driver's side. He'd been smoking a cigarette, trying to look cool and it dropped out and rolled down below the car as he was propelled from the haven of his driver's seat.

"Not wearing your seat belt – naughty boy," Mary said. As his head passed her body she swung low with the baton, the skull cracking under the pressure. His prostrate body lay on the ground.

"He's still moving, I think he'll be OK," Mary said, with a wink to Maggie and then she took her place in the driver's seat. The engine was still running and moments later she was on the motorway and heading south. As Maggie watched her leave she picked up the half rolled cigarette from the ground. It had been a joint.

"Every cloud has a silver lining," she said, inhaling deeply, "Are you alright down there son? I think you've been car-jacked." Whatever it was he said he didn't sound too happy.

As Eric drove off with his illicit cargo, he made a mental note to berate Charlie for his lax security the next time he got a chance. By the time he arrived back at the farm it was late on Sunday night. Karim was pleased with the haul and was even happier with the latest news.

"They think Onur is responsible for the Tower – they've issued a picture."

Eric nodded. He had also mistaken Karim for Onur the first time they had met. He had been called into Mister Madoch's office for a meeting on 'operational matters' which meant that there was a delicate matter which needed his special attention. The two men had a long standing agreement. He hid people and no-one asked any questions. That time had been different though. He had greeted who he thought was Onur, 'What a surprise to see you here,' but the surprise was his when he was told this was the brother, Karim. Mr Madoch had told him his services were needed but that this time there would be four people staying with him, one of whom might be staying a bit longer than the others. Mister Madoch did not appreciate his 'weakness' but he fed it all the same. Many times he had turned the other cheek, each time building a stronger case against the hopeless human being that was Eric Sanderson.

Earlier this week Eric had been told he was to pick his passengers up at Tower 12. Meanwhile he was to convince Onur 'one way or the other' to seek refuge with him. Karim had sat and said nothing and Eric sensed he would have to be careful. Eric thought about the subsidence at his home and he knew that his capital was literally sinking; that once his secret place was exposed he was in danger of becoming surplus to requirements. For the time being Eric agreed to the plan but he knew that he would need to make a change and soon.

Back at the caravan Karim and the girl slept in the spare rooms while Eric lay awake, wondering how to take the initiative. It seemed odd that he was getting a minder this time. He suspected Karim might be here to finish off a few jobs and that he might be top of the list. He tried to put the matter out of his mind and reached for a bottle of vodka from his bedside table. Watching the clear liquid fill his glass Eric knew that he had taken to drinking more than was wise under the circumstances. Leaving the glass he took a deep swig from the bottle and almost retched as he swallowed finger after finger of the cheap sharp liquid. The vodka spilled from his mouth when he pushed the bottle away, thin rivulets of alcohol dribbling down the side of his face. Eric knew what he had to do. Whatever happened he was sure it would be on his own terms and that Madoch could go to hell.

Bishopton, February 22nd 2010

It took Mary less than half an hour to get to Bishopton. Soon she would be back at the farm, back with dad, the very thought made her feel nauseous. She thought back to the day she first met Hanom, the day that fate handed her a gift. Hanom had said her employer planned to bring her daughter into the country at Hull. Kovan would be smuggled by van but they were using a tried and tested method and there was no doubt she would get through safely. Mary's job was to take over at the ferry. She would meet a man called Oskar at the ferry terminal and he would hand over Kovan. Oskar worked for Hanom's boss. Hanom said she had not met him but that he was working with her family to make sure they were reunited. It might be that she could not leave so they had arranged for Mary's husband, John, to meet them in Lanarkshire. Mary said she had a safe place to take the child. She had mentioned her father, but not his history. But it had all gone wrong. A man had appeared while she was still on the bus, forcing her to strip. He said he meant her no harm but that she couldn't leave. He left the engine running and she had gone along with it. It had been warm at first but when the engine stopped – she shivered at the thought of it. It had gotten so cold and the next thing she remembered she was in hospital which was when the questions had started. It had all seemed so straight forward. She had meant to put the past to rest but now there was no sign of John and she seemed to be the suspect for a crime she had not committed, not in the way they thought.

Mary parked the stolen car inside the ruins of an old farmhouse she had known as a child. It hadn't been lived in for more than 60 years and was now nothing more than a shell. There was only a dirt track leading to it from a side road and it was not a spot people would be likely to come across anytime soon. Mary put the car into first gear and tried to steer it over land that was still frozen with thick black ice. She struggled to steer the car as it slid, the wheels spinning through lack of purchase. Frustrated at her slow progress she stopped and took stock. She took the floor mats out of the car and placed them in front of the wheels, ramming them as far under the tyres as she could. Then she climbed back in the car, took a deep breath and turned on the ignition. She smiled when the car roared back into life. Mary had left the door open so that she could look back and see the wheels in motion. She put the car in first gear and then leaning out of the car she gunned the motor and pressed the accelerator. The car lurched forward and spun into the ruined building, causing loose masonry to fall on the roof and bonnet. She screamed but then stopped when she realised that she had escaped uninjured. The car spluttered and juddered before coming to a halt. The job had been done. The car was partially obscured by the ruin and wouldn't be easily seen from the road. Mary changed back into her winter clothes and began the final mile of her journey.

As she walked along the deserted back road her mind wandered back to her childhood. The area brought back painful memories and that was one of the reasons she never came back. That, and him. The man who had lied and postured for so long no-one could think him capable of doing anything untoward. He: beloved father, a man of the people. If only they knew what he was really like. She winced when she thought of the secret place, of the lengths he went to try and hide its true location, but she knew it was on the farm, somewhere. And now after years of waiting she had come so close to uncovering him, of allowing his mask to slip. But the bus had changed things. She knew she had to avenge his victims. She had found it hard to believe that the driver was Stevie Davidson. In truth she hadn't recognised him but the irony was that he had now become her victim. She had tried to use him once before and had been called a liar.

'Now he's dead and I should feel something for him but I just can't. If I allowed that to colour my thinking I wouldn't be able to do this and if I never do anything in my miserable life – this will be it. I hope you are feeling perky, daddy dearest, as tonight we're going to change the rules.'

Mary stopped at the bottom of the lane she knew so well. In the distance she could make out the ramshackle frame of her old family home, silhouetted in the night sky. But it was the other place she was interested in and as she made her way up towards the caravan she could see the master was still at home. Mary prepared herself to settle down for the long haul.

20

Glasgow, Police HQ, February 22nd 2010

It took the team three hours to put a trace on DS Reid's credit cards. After five hours a full description of Mary Clark had been broadcast around the UK. The first question that had been asked was 'where is she going to go?' When they realised Mhairi's purse had been stolen they drew their own assumptions.

"If we can trace the cards we'll have a good idea of what she's up to," Arbogast said. Their HR records showed that Mhairi banked with HSBC. They pulled in the paperwork and got a copy of her statements from the bank without too much resistance. From there they could see that she had standing orders with both Visa and MasterCard. A few hours later they sat looking at the latest credit card transactions.

"She's a fast worker I'll give her that," Arbogast said, as they pieced together her movements. "She left the hospital and made her way to town, stopping off at the first major store she came to and went on a spending spree. I'm going to need someone to go to the department store to take statements. I think we can safely assume she's no longer in police uniform." Grim looks were exchanged around the room. They all knew Mhairi Reid was in a bad way. The doctors said she had a brain haemorrhage and so far hadn't been able to speak. If the case hadn't been personal before it certainly was now. Arbogast found the last few entries on the card statements the most perplexing.

"Mary has withdrawn £800 using both cards, which amounts to the daily limit so we know she has cash – and then we have the train ticket."

VIRGIN rail Glasgow – London 8765 £113.70

"Let's assume she wants us to believe she's on the Virgin train bound for England, probably London. Did she actually get on?"

Norrie Smith had arrived, "I'll get some bodies down to the station to check the CCTV. The transport police should be able to help. Do we know if she has family and friends in London? Maybe she's trying to leave the country?"

Arbogast considered this as he leaned back in his chair, trying to picture what might have happened.

"I don't think she has sir. Most people would have panicked given the situation but she's kept a cool head. I agree with you on the CCTV – we need to check it out. I'll get onto our colleagues in London to see what station the train would go to."

"It's London Euston sir." PC Frank Simmons had been battering away on Google and was staring at a long list of departure times, "The nearest two trains leaving for London from the time this ticket was bought both terminate at Euston."

"Right well we've got plenty to work with. What I want is a picture of Mary in the shop and hopefully from the station. We need to go public with this as soon as possible. I have an idea to put a cat among the pigeons too, but I'll need to check some things out first."

The Chief Constable was nodding in agreement, "Right team let's get on with it. I don't need to tell you we've had two officers assaulted in the last 24 hours in connection with this case so let's assume we're already ruffling their feathers. We can't afford to make mistakes now. I need you all to do good police work." There was a chorus of approval around the room as the team got back on the case. Arbogast had already left the room.

Central Station was an enormous glass cavern situated right in the heart of Glasgow. It was one of the busiest stations in Britain with around 27.5 million bodies passing through it each year. Arbogast stood on the concourse by Platform 1. He knew that tens of thousands of people would have been through here today. It was late now – nearly 11:00pm. The last trains of the day would be leaving within the next hour. Of the many shops only Burger King remained open. A travelling man stood teetering by his suitcase trying to co-ordinate a burger from hand to mouth. He hadn't noticed the salad cream dripping down his suit jacket. 'That will be one for tomorrow, let's hope he has a spare.' The person Arbogast was here to see was he ticket inspector. Craig Johnson had been on shift since 2:00 that afternoon.

"I'm on till midnight then I'm away."

"Can you remember seeing anything odd earlier in the day?"

"We get all walks of life through here Inspector," Craig Johnson said, nodding towards the travelling man who had now dropped his burger on the ground, and was making moves to retrieve it.

"Yes I can see that but did you notice anything odd, someone acting strangely? We're looking for this woman."

Arbogast showed Craig a picture of Mary. Craig moved his flat station cap back and scratched his balding head.

"Now you're asking. Look I couldn't tell you if I've seen her or not. Maybe she did come through but unless she was breathing fire I doubt I'd have noticed. You remember the drunks, the troublemakers but it's been quiet today. Sundays are like that."

He stopped to think for a while. "There was one thing I suppose," Arbogast tried not to look too animated, "But I'm sure there's a reason for it. There was one woman who got off the train and came back through before it left. She didn't get back on. That must have been about 6:00. I remember because I'd just come back from a break."

Arbogast was disappointed. "It can't be unusual for someone to wave a loved one off on the train now can it?"

"It isn't, but they have to do it from this side of the platform." he pointed to the security gates in front of him, gates which blocked access to the platform, "But since we beefed up security you can only get on and off the platform if you have a ticket. If someone had asked to get through I would have remembered. This woman must have had a ticket but she didn't travel."

Arbogast raised himself onto the tips of his toes, "Mister Johnson, you are a star." Arbogast made straight for Network Rail, who ran the station and had an office above the ticket booths. He had four officers checking CCTV with pictures of Mary Clark to try and make a positive identification.

"Change of plan lads, let's check footage between 5:30 and 6:30pm. We're looking for a woman leaving the train, someone that doesn't get back on." At first they couldn't spot her. It wasn't until the saw a woman wearing a large winter sports jacket and hat waving to the carriage and then making her way down through the gates an under the camera that they got their match, "Gotcha," Arbogast smiled, "you're still here."

After searching through other footage they established Mary had left the station by the North West exit at around 6:15. They had rushed out an enhanced picture of her to all news outlets late that night. Arbogast knew this would be big news tomorrow. It had made the websites within an hour. *The newsrooms will start filling up in around two hours. It's going to be busy but the Chief will have to deal with that part of things. I'm sure he won't mind the profile.'* Calling back to the office Arbogast found the address for Mary's workplace. The Phoenix Centre was only a five minute walk from the station. Arbogast didn't think Mary would be bold or stupid enough to go there and he knew they had already phoned. He decided to check again just to put his mind at ease.

The Phoenix Centre was open through the night. It had to be. The city's statistics for violent abuse against prostitutes were not great. There had been ten women murdered in the last nine years. Some had been raped and beaten; others abducted and left in isolated rural areas. One had even been thrown from a moving car on the motorway. Her body had bounced off rush hour traffic and several cars had simply kept on driving. But all the cases had one thing in common and that was that no-one was ever caught. Arbogast knew those incidents were the high profile ones, the cases the tabloids loved, but there was never any mention of the nightly beatings from pimps and punters, of rogue police taking advantage of their protection, or simply of the dangers posed by drugs. Glasgow was no Amsterdam. There were no glass windows, no vivacious mannequins offering sexual adventures. Glasgow was the real deal with women forced into punting their bodies to pay for unsustainable drug habits. Not such a problem at first but over time the ravages of trying to manage the habit took its toll. As Arbogast walked through the red light district he could see that some of them looked half dead. The scrawny, other worldly faces told their own stories – toothless crones touting for business. The thought of a good time was a bitter irony which would end in premature death. But it was unfair to say this was true of everyone. Some were just desperate and it was desperation which Arbogast saw when he entered the drop-in centre.

"Are you police?" one girl said with a sneer. "Fancy some company," said another, giggling. He knew that he would have few friends here. Arbogast was sympathetic to the idea of legalised prostitution. At least with brothels the girls would be safe and he would have fewer murders to solve. He spoke to the woman running the centre, a name he instantly forgot. She told him she had been shocked when Mary's name had appeared in the papers 'such a nice girl' she said but really she had nothing to say. *Just another dead end,'* Arbogast knew the woman was telling the truth, that she hadn't seen Mary. It seemed as if his prey had simply vanished. As he turned to leave he saw one woman staring at him and when she caught his gaze she turned and left too quickly. Arbogast rushed out after her, tripping on a chair leg. He was dazed for a second, lying flat on his back while he was laughed at 'Oops there he goes, while your down there why don't you make yourself useful,' he could still hear the cackles as he made his way back out into the freezing winter's night to find the disappearing woman, but she was gone. There was a fog hanging over the city tonight. The area was poorly lit at the best of times and seemed even less so tonight. In the background he could see the masked orange glow of the street lights trying to find clarity through the gloom.

"Is she in trouble?" said a voice from the fog. Arbogast spun round to find the woman from inside. She looked to be in her thirties or forties but could be 21 for all he knew. She wore a tight green mini-dress and blue stiletto heels. Covered in a warm winter jacket she was smoking a Kensitas Club through dried out lipstick. He thought she looked a little like the actress Sigourney Weaver.

"Is she in trouble?" she repeated.

"Is who in trouble?"

"You know who I mean."

"I'm afraid I don't."

She shifted her weight from right to left, "Mary, wee Mary."

Arbogast nodded "Could be. I'm sorry I don't know your name?"

"That's right you don't." Arbogast thought she was unsure about him but he couldn't help but wonder why she had come forward.

"You can call me Maggie."

Arbogast nodded, "So what do you know Maggie – can you tell me about Mary?"

"I like Mary, she was good to me, took the time to see me through when I thought I might not be able to go on. She saved me in a way." She grunted, "But the details don't matter. What I want to know is – are you trying to help her?"

There was a long silence. Maggie took two long drags from her cigarette, with the ash hanging precariously as the contents sagged in a bid for freedom.

"I won't lie to you Maggie, Mary's in trouble. She's done some stupid things. She sees herself as a victim but maybe she's just caught up in something she can't control. What I do know for sure is that she's another name in a growing line of people who are getting hurt: people that are disappearing and turning up dead. I don't want her to be another figure, another casualty. She's in it up to her neck, but she's messing around with the wrong people."

Maggie nodded; she knew the kind of people he meant. "I'm not telling you anything officially detective...?"

"Arbogast, John Arbogast."

"Well Detective Arbogast she was here earlier, dressed like a tart. I didn't recognise her at first. In fact I almost gave her a good slap but I could see she was scared. Mary said she needed to get away, that people were looking for her. She attacked a punter and took his car. He's OK, a bit beaten up and he'll have a bugger of a headache tomorrow. She drove off in his car, a Ford Mondeo. It was white. A 54 plate."

And then she stopped and Arbogast knew he would be getting nothing more. "Just find her Arbogast," she said and left. Arbogast watched as Maggie made her way off into the gloom, trying her luck and hoping for a quiet night. He wished her well and went home.

The screen flickered to life as the machine rumbled into action. Slowly as the desktop loaded and came to life, icon by icon, Arbogast wondered what to make of his earlier encounter. He logged into his computer and then typed up notes of what Maggie had told him. He emailed the description of the car and sent them through the HOLMES team, to be added into the mix. This could be a major lead. A national search would go out for the vehicle later that day; hopefully it would be easy to track. Anything travelling on the major trunk roads was clocked by the traffic camera network, registration plates were logged and people were easy to track. It would take a couple of hours though which meant he had time to relax. Sleep. He poured himself a large whisky and sat back down at the screen. He clicked on his favourites bar and then was back in his other world.

Hey there, flashed the message on screen. She was framed in a box and sat on a bed, a Chinese girl who looked a bit like Rose.

Hi.

What's your name?

JJ

Hey JJ, You wanna have some fun?

She sat in her underwear moving from left to right showing off the goods.

Let me see you.

Hey bad boy

He watched as she undressed for him. He watched and then slowly lost track of the time.

CTRL Alt Delete

February 23rd 2010

When he woke up he felt as if he had only been asleep for a second, but when he checked his watch he saw that he had been out for four hours.

"Fuck." He had set his alarm but then must have switched the phone off. He had nineteen missed calls, all from the same number. He didn't need to check his messages and phoned in straight away.

"Sorry boss," he explained that he must have dozed off.

"John it's going ballistic in here, where the hell have you been? We have a press conference today and they all want to know where we are with this. I'm going to tell them about the hospital but I'm going to keep the details on the car vague."

Arbogast could see the sense in this, "Yes tell them we are looking for the driver of a white Ford to come forward. We should say it was last seen in the Anderston area of town. Meanwhile we can check the traffic cameras."

"That's already been done John; we haven't all been asleep on the job. The roads were quiet last night. The driving conditions weren't good with the fog. We've spotted two white Fords matching the description. One was on the M74 heading south but it's the other one that caught my attention."

"Tell me it was on the M8?"

"Yes. A car fitting that description was seen heading west on the M8. I think our girl may have been paying a visit to daddy."

"I'll go down now. What time's the press call?"

"Twelve."

"OK I'll phone in before then but expect to see me there."

"Don't take any unnecessary risks. I'll have a patrol car sent down. Happy hunting."

February 22nd 2010

Mary had been careful not to make any noise as she approached the caravan. It had been icy and she had been careful not to give herself away by the crunch of the gravel driveway. Slowly she made her way to the back of the trailer. She crouched under the main window and listened. Mary had expected the quiet hum of the TV but there were raised voices inside, a foreign male voice which she didn't recognise.

"You will do as you are told. This has been planned to the last detail and I expect you to do your part."

Mary heard her father protest but then there was a scuffle and then a crash. She raised herself onto her tip toes to see if she could catch a glimpse of what was going on inside. It was a dangerous move and if they looked out and saw her there was little she could do to hide. She could only make out the top of his head, a dark mane of hair swept back round his ears.

"Now do you understand?" the voice was harsh. "Yes I understand," replied her father. In the background she thought she could hear a child crying. *'I'm going to need to revise my plans. Maybe the other man will leave.'* Mary crept across to the old house and checked the doors which were all locked. Thinking back she turned over a large stone in the driveway and found what she was looking for, the spare key. The rock had been stuck hard into the ground and was difficult to move so she assumed her father had forgotten it was here. As she walked through what had been her home Mary was struck by the silence. She froze when she heard a door open outside and for a second she thought that she had been discovered. From the front of the house she could see a beam of light shining through the windows. She bent down and held her breath. Then the door closed again and the light was gone. Mary made her way to the top floor and opened the door to her childhood bedroom to be faced once more with the memories which refused to die.

February 23rd 2010

Arbogast arrived at the farm at around 8:45am. He had rushed down a mug full of espresso from his DeLonghi Perfecta. It had cost a fortune but he could only function in the morning with strong coffee so the investment paid for itself on a daily basis. He felt wired – it was part coffee, part exhaustion, and part adrenalin. When he arrived at the Sanderson farm he realised it had been nearly two weeks since his last visit, although DS Reid had been down a few times. He thought of her and prayed that she would be OK, not that prayer was a currency he valued, but he still had hope. The landscape had changed. The last time he had been here the countryside had that magical quality that new snowfall brings. But it had started to melt away and the dead grass and blackened trees were beginning to show themselves. The thaw always brought with it the shock of the old. Deep snow hid the world, masked reality and concealed its secrets. The rubbish people dropped into a snowstorm would emerge through the ice, leaving a wasteland, as if an iceberg had slid over the country leaving behind it the detritus of countless careless moments.

The farm stood midway up a hill, poised on a brief plateau. The birch trees that circled the house had been swept back by the wind, like a hand pushing down on long grass on a hot summer day. His own car was an eight year old Nissan which wasn't made for ice. He had to abandon it halfway up the hill. It was probably fairer to say that the car abandoned him. The Nissan had lost all traction and the vehicle had spun nose first round 180 degrees and was facing back down lodged between the raised verges on either side of the drive. Arbogast left 'old faithful' in reverse and walked the rest of the way. There didn't seem to be anyone around although the Range Rover was still there. Arbogast rapped the metal door for longer than was necessary. He waited but no-one came so he tried the door which to his surprise was open. He pulled it towards him and stuck his head through the door. "Hello?" he said, but found no response. He looked behind him, checking there was no one there and then he entered. He knew he shouldn't, he had no right, but then again it had been left open so why not. All the rooms were empty and apparently unused. A bottle of vodka sat by what he assumed was Sanderson's bed but

185

there was no sign of anyone else. Confused he left the caravan and surveyed the area. Behind the caravan was the shower block. Arbogast made his way round and had a look. He assumed this was where the water came from. The block had seen better days. What had once been small white wooden windows where now rotting frames which wouldn't last for much longer. There were two doors at either side, one marked MEN, the other WOMEN. He tried the door on the women's side but it was locked. The rust on the hinges suggested it hadn't been opened for some time. The other side was open. He walked in and was struck but the unmistakable stench of sewage. Arbogast covered his mouth and nose with his jacket sleeve and went into have a closer look. The block itself was nothing special. There were four shower cubicles and a urinal which was separated from the washing area by a flimsy plaster wall, which was crumbling in places. He assumed the tiles had once been white but they were now stained brown, strangers to detergent. The floor was cleaner; someone had been in here recently. Arbogast remembered that Sanderson said he drew his water from here. There was something about the shower block that was gnawing at Arbogast but he couldn't place it. He would store it at the back of his mind and come back to it. Leaving the block he decided to have a closer look at the house but was stopped in his tracks. Standing outside, Eric Sanderson stood wiping his hands on what looked like an oil rag.

"Detective Arbogast, get lost did we?" he said smiling from ear to ear, "I hear that you have managed to misplace my daughter – she's always been trouble you know."

Arbogast didn't like his tone, "I've been looking for you actually Mr Sanderson. I wondered if you might have seen your daughter, but I couldn't find you."

"I was in the old place."

"Really, I thought you said the house was out of bounds?"

"Quite right but I fear that Mother Nature has forced my hand. It's the thaw you see. The house is becoming unstable. As you can see it's dropped an inch or two these last few days and I'm afraid the mine workings below may be ready to claim her."

"Being a bit dramatic aren't we there sir?" There was something different in Eric's manner today. He seemed more confident.

"I've been having a look around the old place, taking what I might need but it's become quite filthy. But let's not stand around outside Detective, come into my office."

He gestured to Arbogast to make his way to the caravan.

As the metal door scraped shut Mary watched from the house as her father took the Detective inside. She smiled and knew that her time had come.

21

Arbogast was staring intently at Eric Sanderson and he knew that his instinct had been right, something had changed. This was not the same reserved man he had encountered just a few days ago. He seemed relaxed, almost as if his troubles had disappeared. Arbogast saw no reason to beat around the bush.

"Has Mary been here Eric?"

"Mary?"

If he knew anything Sanderson did well to cover his surprise.

"I have good reason to believe that she may either be here already, or will turn up soon. Either way she's in trouble."

Eric was examining the cuticles on his right hand, which was loosely clenched, "And what do you suppose I can do about that?"

"You don't seem overly concerned."

"Why should I be? I've told you about what happened in the past – there's no love lost between us."

"Even so she's still your daughter – flesh and blood. I'm sure you were...close...at one point?"

"I don't think I care much for your insinuations Inspector."

"Listen Eric I think you might know more about this than you're letting on but right now you know I can't prove anything."

"How inconvenient for you, detective."

Sanderson was about to say something else when he was cut off.

"But here's the thing – this case has turned into quite a circus. We're holding a press conference in a couple of hours in Glasgow and I think you're going to be our star turn. You see, like it or not, your daughter is missing. I think she's in the immediate area and I think she wants to see you. But we want her to know you want to see her so you'll be asking her to contact us, to give herself up."

"Are we back to this again? Why should I agree?"

"It'll look good for you. I know there are a few press people circling round just now, keen to dig up old stories and paint you up as a dirty old man. Whatever happens next this will help you and it will help us too. This case started off fairly simply. We had a known sex offender on the run with a young girl. But it's all changed and I can't quite pin down a motive. Your daughter doesn't seem to have good reason to be involved in murder and abduction but she's pushed herself out there. She's become involved. Looking at the bigger picture all roads seem to be leading to your boss right now."

"What's John Madoch got to do with anything?"

"That's my business. I want you to come with me and publicly call for Mary to turn herself in. Don't take long to think it over because I'm not really giving you a choice. It's either that or I'll take you in and I'll have forensics down here with a fine tooth comb. Technology has come a long way since 1985 you know."

"I hear what you're saying and but I really don't have a clue where you get your ideas from. I'm an engineer and a busy one at that. I'm at a key stage of the excavations for the wind farm. I have blasting to do today and this press conference of yours – let's just say I don't have the time."

"There'll be time enough for that too, maybe. Get your coat."

As they left the caravan Arbogast noticed that Sanderson hadn't locked up.

"Feeling safe?"

"There's no-one here that will bother me and I really do have nothing worth taking."

"We've all got something, Eric."

As they recovered the car from the ice Arbogast noticed that a patrol car had arrived and was parked at the bottom of the road. He stopped on his way past and got out to speak to the constables.

"Alright there? I need you to keep an eye on this entrance. I appreciate the owner's coming with me but we still expect his daughter to make an appearance. Here's her picture. If you see anything – phone it in. Failing that I'll be back in a couple of hours."

He got the resigned nods he expected from the PCs who were embarking on what would no doubt be a tedious and largely thankless task, but it was this kind of donkey work that split pain-in-the-arse cases like this one wide open.

Mary Clark watched her father leave with the detective and wondered what was going on. There was a patrol car too, which complicated things slightly but she could wait. The old house was creaking and groaning, in a way that was new to her. It seemed to be troubled, waiting for something to happen, to soothe its aches and pains, and it wouldn't have long to wait. As Mary negotiated the stairs down to the ground floor she could see what the noise had been. Her father had been pottering around for close to three hours. She had toyed with the idea of confronting him there and then, but this wasn't the right time. Not yet. As she looked around she could see that he had been busy, with tools scattered everywhere, although she couldn't see what he had been working on. It occurred to Mary that her father might be trying to cover his tracks but she was determined that the trail of tears would end here. *'I know Kovan is here somewhere. Madoch's men told me that they would bring her here. I have never known exactly where it was but now I have the chance to find it.'* As she looked around she was surprised at how little her childhood home had changed. She had managed to escape and find a life of her own but it was as if time had stood still. There was something appropriate about the damage Mother Nature had wreaked on this old pile, as if the bricks and mortar were finally ready to give up her secrets. And then she saw the picture. It was taken outside behind the house. It had been a bright summer's day and it showed her sat in her father's knee on the old wooden garden bench, with her mother leaning in with her head nestled under his chin. *'The happy family. What a joke.'* As she took the picture off the wall her old life came flooding back, the picnics and the Christmas time memories – but they all faded away when she remembered what he had done to her, time and time again. Mary felt anger growing inside her as she welled up at the thought of the secret place, their secret place. A sudden rage overcame her and she threw the picture across the room, recoiling when the glass shattered into a thousand pieces, the frame cracking and breaking. Mary collapsed onto the floor hugging her herself close with her arms clasped around here knees.

She didn't hear it at first but through her tears she became aware of the noise. A dull thud she thought must have been her own heartbeat but when she stopped and listened she realised that there was something or someone else in the house with her. This scared her at first but then if the noise came from a threat she reasoned that she would already know about it. Mary walked through the ground floor but could not identify exactly where the sound was coming from. She tried the door to the basement. It had always been locked when she was a child and she could never remember having actually been in there. Outside the door the noise was louder, a muffled banging noise and then what sounded like a muffled scream.

"Help me," it said, again and again, "Help me – let me out."

She tried the door to the basement and was surprised when it opened. The space was divided into two sections. The first had access to steps which led outside to the garden. The floor was cracked and when she looked up she could see it went right through the building and that she was directly below the living room. The second part of the basement was another enclosed room which took up the west section. Mary could see that the door was locked but it was here that the noise was coming from.

"Hello?"

"Hello – who is that – can you let me out please? I cannot breathe in this coffin. I must find my wife and daughter?"

The voice was foreign although Mary could not place it, although it sounded familiar.

"Wait. I'll help. I'm not with the man who locked you in." Looking around Mary could see there was no key and there were three mortise locks to be opened. "I'll be back." She knew where the keys had been kept before, but returning to the kitchen she found nothing save for rusting cutlery and aged utensils that were long past their prime. Returning to the basement she looked for an axe or saw, anything that could help her cut through. And then she saw the chainsaw.

"Stand back I'm going to cut you out," she said, pulling on the starter cord. Again and again she pulled achieving nothing but fruitless splutters until, suddenly, the saw roared into life and she got to work. It was hard going but 15 minutes later she had managed to cut a hole that was big enough through the wooden door for the prisoner to crawl through. She watched as he made his way to freedom, his lush dark hair and dirty black suit made for quite a contrast. As he raised himself to his full height she screamed.

"It's you, my god what have I done."

It was another full house at the Pitt Street auditorium. They had agreed to keep it short and sweet. Chief Constable, Norrie Smith, was going to give a brief update about yesterday's 'escape' while Eric Sanderson was to be the star of the show. He hadn't been keen and tried to leave when he saw the number of people, cameras, and microphones that were waiting for him. 'I can't do TV, I just can't,' he had argued but they had insisted he would not need to do interviews, and that the press conference itself would provide all the material that would be needed. A number of satellite broadcasters were there too so the whole thing was to be covered live across the UK and abroad. Arbogast was pleasantly surprised to see Rosalind Ying back in the saddle.

"Hey there, are you sure you should be back so soon?" he said, touching her arm. Rosalind still looked like death warmed up but she was obviously determined to make the best of a bad situation.

"What and let you close my case, I don't think so. How's Eric doing?"

"He'll do his bit. This routine will give us a bit of breathing space. I've got a car down at the farm and I'll be driving him back after this. I think I'll have a look around the house."

"With his permission of course," she said, as a broad smile lit up her face.

"Naturally," They watched from the sidelines as the media consumed the Eric and Norrie show.

"He's not too bad," Arbogast said, nudging Rosalind, "you'd almost think he cared." From the corner of his eye Arbogast saw a hand trying to get his attention. It was Sandy Stirrit.

"I'll be back in a minute." Rosalind nodded as Arbogast made his way into the press pack.

"Fancy seeing you here – I thought you were going to go to town on this for me?"

"I tried but they wouldn't bite. Too scared of legal action but this is all good stuff," he said nodding to the press bench. "Do you have anything else for me?"

"Strictly on the QT we're looking into one John Madoch."

"John Madoch – Glasgow's favourite gangster?"

"He's over this like a rash. Hanom Kocack was being forced to work in a lap dancing bar owned by Madoch while the husband, Onur, is working at Moorland Wind out at Eaglesham. Eric Sanderson works with him, and then as you know Sanderson's daughter is also involved. Far too many coincidences to be coincidental don't you think? We're saying nothing publicly at the moment but it would be worth you digging a bit deeper. Madoch's involved but we can't prove it yet. And you being a good fellow of the press I'm sure he wouldn't object to a few friendly questions."

"OK JJ, I'll have a look into it. He's certainly keeping a lower profile these days but he must still be connected. Cheers."

"And when I've cleared this one up we can have a jar or two?"

"Definitely JJ and listen, who's the lady you were pawing a minute ago?"

"I'm sure I don't know who you mean. Are you not meant to be working?" They shared a smile which said it all and then Arbogast was gone.

"That went quite well then Eric," Arbogast said, "Are you happy enough with the way it panned out?'

Eric was sat in the back of the Nissan with Rosalind Ying while Arbogast drove back down the M8.

"Aye well I wouldn't want to do that every day but I did OK. I hate to think how I'll look but if it brings Mary in then I suppose it's been worthwhile."

"That it will be Mr Sanderson – that it will be."

Rosalind was checking for media coverage on her mobile. The footage was already available on the BBC and STV websites while all the major papers had fresh details on the case online.

"Looks like they've gone for it a big way, let's hope it was worth it gentlemen."

No-one spoke for the rest of the journey as the car powered on, heading back to the Sanderson farm.

"It's you, my god what have I done?" Mary said, repeating herself. She knew the face. It was the face from the bus. It was the man that forced her to strip at gunpoint, the man who had strayed from the plan, the man that had nearly been the death of her. He reached forward and grabbed her wrists.

"What is wrong with you woman. Who are you?"

Slowly Mary calmed down. She realised that there was something different, something in his eyes.

"I feel like I've met you before?"

"You have my word that we have never met. Have you seen my wife, my daughter?"

"Kovan?" His eyes lit up at this then his expression darkened.

"Who are you? Why have you let me out?"

Mary explained that she was here for her father, that they had unfinished business and that she could not allow him to inflict any more pain on the people he held close.

"But I still feel as though we've met. You look like the man who left me on the bus. I could have died there. You look so much alike."

Onur thought on this for a few seconds before it dawned on him who the other man must be.

"I think I understand your problem. I also think that it is not safe to remain here."

Mary found his English hard to follow at times but she realised that he meant what he said.

"Is the other man here?"

"He is my brother and I have not seen him for some time, since the day I left Turkey in fact. That he is here is a worry to me. We must leave."

"I can't leave. I'm here for my father and I won't go until I see him. I'm involved in this. I believe your daughter is here, maybe even your wife too. I was approached by Hanom to pick up Kovan and take her to a safe place. That safe place is right here. My father will know where it is but he is not an honourable man. If he has your daughter then I fear for her safety. If we leave you might not see them again. My father is up to something, he's been working upstairs. I think he's planning something so we must act while he's not here."

They left the house by the back door which was invisible from the road. If they slipped around past the shower block they should be able to reach the caravan unseen from the road. Mary's heart was beating fast as she raced for cover.

There had been an accident on the M8 just past the airport, which had held them up for 45 minutes. Moving at a slow crawl they left the carriageway to take a back road to the farm. Sanderson insisted it would be quicker and they bowed to his local knowledge. Travelling through the isolated single track roads Arbogast was struck by how bleak the landscape looked. Dead reeds and long grass were matted together with small islands of ice clinging on as the snow slowly melted away. Cattle roamed freely – once more able to graze in open pasture, free from the constraints of recent weeks. Life was returning to normal. They passed old farmhouses with modern bungalows built beside them; ostentatious gate mounting's more reminiscent of Dallas, Texas than the nearby village of Houston, Renfrewshire. An old ruined farmhouse flashed by and before he realised why Arbogast had slammed on the brakes, the back tyres skidding on the ground frost.

"What the hell are you doing?" Rosalind said. Eric caught his breath as the seatbelt dug hard into his chest with the force of the emergency stop.

"I thought I saw something," he said, reversing the car slowly back up the road.

Getting out, Arbogast stood in the middle of the road and stared at the building. 'What was it that caught my eye?' It looked like just another abandoned building. All that remained were the two gable ends and the front wall which was obscured by thick trees which had sprung up around the entrance and windows. The walls were black with age and thick with moss and then he saw it. There was a crack in the front gable end. It was new damage; he could see newly ground sandstone and the clean side of a recently displaced stone. A dirt track led round the back and Arbogast followed this round to get a better look. There stood the white Ford Mondeo. It had been rammed into the building and the front end was covered in rubble. Branches had been placed over the car and that was why he hadn't seen it straight away from the road. He called in the forensics team.

"It probably won't tell us anything we don't already know but at least we will be able to confirm that Mary's been here." The two detectives twisted round in their seats, "It's not too late to change your story Eric," Arbogast said, "If you know where she is now's the time to come clean." Eric sat back in his seat and answered the question with a blank stare.

Mary ushered Onur into the shower block when she was sure they hadn't been seen.

"I can remember when they built this place in the 1970s. We had a lot of people camping on the farm and we decided to put it up — my father said we could charge more that way and it seemed to make the place more appealing. For years I knew my dad had a hiding place, somewhere he knew he wouldn't be disturbed. I was always blindfolded when he took me there — he did things to me." Her face clouded at the thought of what had happened, "But I could never work out where it was. And then not long ago it suddenly struck me that it might be here. The outhouse isn't connected to a sewer so we've always had to use a septic tank, which we emptied regularly. Thinking about it, the tank was emptied far more regularly than it should have been, given that it was only really used at certain times of the year. And in here somewhere," she said wiping away the dirt from the floor, "is the panel to get down to the tank, which might just be bigger than everyone thinks."

Mary scanned the floor. She had never seen the entrance herself but knew it must be here somewhere. There was one tile with a metal edge instead of grout. She pushed this down and the tile sprang up. Beneath it was a horseshoe shaped handle which, when pulled up, revealed the way down to the tank.

"Voila, the trapdoor," but whatever it was Mary expected to find she was disappointed. Below her was a deep tank which reeked of chemicals and human waste. Her nostrils filled with the stale stench of decomposing excrement but there was no sign of human life. Her disappointment was short lived.

"Did you travel all this way just to revel in shit?" Mary thought it was Onur speaking but it wasn't. Behind them Karim had appeared with a Glock for company.

"Move and I promise you I will shoot."

Arbogast, Ying, and Sanderson waited on the forensics team at the ruin before continuing to the farmhouse. Arbogast slowed when he reached the patrol car and Rosalind wound down the electric windows.

"Anything to report?"

The PC in the driving seat was the first to reply, "It's been very quiet ma'am." She could tell the officer was trying to impress her but 'very quiet' rarely did it.

"Eh, good work. For now you're needed elsewhere. We found a car about a mile or so back and we need to close the road. Think you can manage that? We'll be here for a while. I'll be in touch when we need you back – should be about an hour." As they the two nodding dogs retreated up the country road, Arbogast parked at the bottom of the dirt track to avoid trying to navigate the ice rink ahead.

Karim Kocack had taken his captives back to the caravan where he was confident he could not be seen from the road. He stood keeping a watchful eye over his prey in the lounge area, while his gun kept the peace.

"You had the right idea Mary, but you really should have stayed in hospital or done the decent thing and died on the bus, which was my intention after all."

Mary had that feeling again. The one she had as a child. The one that meant it didn't matter what she wanted as what was about to happen would happen regardless. She had gone from hunter to hunted in the blink of an eye and she knew that her efforts had been a complete waste of time.

"Push the table on its side." Karim said, pointing the gun at Onur, "I'm sorry it has to be this way brother. I'm sure you had hoped for better, but if it's any consolation you will soon be with your family."

The table top was mounted on two steel poles. After struggling at first Onur managed to flick over the table towards the back wall, revealing the outline of another trap door, which had been obscured by the dark rubber tiling and the table itself.

"Now lift up the hatch please." Onur hesitated for a second.

"Why is this happening Karim, why does it need to be this way?"

Karim flashed forward and dealt a glancing blow with the gun butt to Onur's head, causing him to crash to the floor.

"Do as you are told brother, the time for talking is over."

Onur pulled up the trapdoor which revealed a narrow wooden ladder with rounded edges.

"Down," Karim said, "You first." he pointed the gun at Onur who disappeared down the ladder and was followed by Mary. As Mary climbed down Karim pushed down on her head with the sole of his shoe. She cried out and fell. Karim was down the steps quickly; he had practiced this many times and was ready. He flicked on the light switch, which illuminated a narrow corridor which had two metal doors at the end. Karim pushed them forward and then threw Onur the key and told him to open the door.

"Please don't kill us," Mary said, sobbing, "I'm only here for my father." But her cries went unheeded and the metal hinges creaked as the door opened. Out of desperation Onur lunged at his brother but had been off balance from the start. Karim kicked hard and caught Onur on the legs forcing him face down. He then grabbed him by the shirt and pulling him along, threw him head first into the blackness. He pointed the gun at Mary, "Now you – unless you would prefer to do things the hard way?"

Five minutes later Karim was sitting upstairs in the lounge. He placed a book in front of him and an empty cup for effect. He could see the shapes of three people approaching the caravan, all of them unaware of the welcome they were about to receive.

22

Secrets of 1985

It was quiet now and the silence carried its own warning. It was impossible to say how long it had been – alone in the darkness she had lost track of the time. She knew what she was expected to do and was always keen to please, given the alternative. There was no-one to miss her at home, where she was mostly ignored, and when her father came there was little to do but obey. It hurt if she resisted and so she had learned to accept it and now did what she was told. All that she had for comfort was a bed of cushions from a discarded couch and an old, sodden mattress which carried the now familiar smell of decay and parental dereliction. After several hours the hatch opened and he appeared like a fallen angel, with the stars sparkling behind him. She could feel his breath as the cold night air breezed through the room, expelling old air and bringing an end to her long wait. Mary could see his smile and soon she knew that she would taste his fury.

Bishopton, February 23rd 2010

Mary woke up from her nightmare and realised that despite the memories this wasn't the way it had happened before. She knew this was the same place. This was the first time that she knew exactly where she was – that she now knew how close to home the abuse had been – close enough to the house that someone should have heard her scream. This time, though, she had company. When she had felt the weight of the boot on her head she had slipped on the ladder, landing roughly on her left arm. She lay there at first, too scared to cry out, the memories of her childhood flooding back. The pain too seemed familiar, but she had been too weak to resist then. Mary fought back tears and tried to focus. In the darkness she could hear a rustling but she couldn't locate the source. The blackness was all consuming, the sense of seclusion absolute. She could see nothing. After what seemed like an age something reached out and touched her leg. She cried out then quickly clasped her hand over her mouth, surprised she would have been so quick to give herself away.

"Is that you?" she said to the darkness.

"I think I am OK," Onur said, "I thought Eric was my friend. How can he know my brother?" The voice trailed off leaving Mary fearful of what was happening. The shuffling noise again caused her to shift her position; to try to look for the wall she knew wasn't too far away. Perhaps if she could find some sense of proportion this wouldn't seem such a hopeless nightmare.

"He's my father," Mary said, whispering, "and he's a bad man."

As she sat in the dark Mary couldn't quite believe how quickly her plans had unravelled. All she wanted to do was to find this place, make sure her father was with the child – then phone the police. Let him rot in his own hell, the same one that she had been forced to live in since the age of 5, one that nobody had ever believed.

"He is my father and this is his secret place."

"This..." Onur's words hung in the air like a knife poised for attacked, "...is his secret place – the safe place?"

Onur had agreed with Sanderson that his family would be safe in the secret place but this was not quite what he had imagined.

"My family is supposed to be here with me. Sanderson said we would be reunited but why is Karim here? I fear for our safety. My brother has brought me nothing but bad luck these last few months. He said he would save me but it seems he has other plans. You say you know this place – is there a way out – can we escape?"

"No I don't think so. I have never seen past that door and I have been brought here many, many times. My father is a sick bastard – a child molester and rapist. He might seem like a good person but let me assure you he is a devious little cunt and not to be trusted."

The words startled Onur as he began to realise the full extent of his situation. "My daughter is here already. I know this from what you have said." Onur started to weep, "Oh god what have I allowed my family to become involved with. Kovan is only 5, she's a child."

Mary understood what he was going through, what they were all going through. She fumbled through the pitch blackness with her arms outstretched. Zombie like, she found Onur and took him in her arms. Together, for a while, they found solace.

A short time later they became aware that they were not alone. Their embrace was broken by a rattling sound, like metal on wood.

"Is there somebody else down here?" Mary said, trying to locate the source of the sound which had cut through the silence. Mary was startled when a light appeared by her side.

"Don't worry it is only my phone," Onur said.

Mary laughed, "Who are you going to phone – you'll get no reception down here."

"Yes but the light might help us."

Onur must have landed on his phone and the screen to his blackberry was cracked and inky beneath the glass but the soft glow still managed to cast some light on the situation.

"It's not very bright."

"It's better than nothing."

He held up the handset to meet Mary, lighting up one side of her face like something out of a cheap horror movie.

"We can only see about a foot ahead but maybe it will help. I cannot say how long the battery will last so we need to make the most of the time we have."

Moving together they crawled towards the source of the noise. They stumbled when they reached the mattress, the smell both familiar and repellent. Mary thought it strange that a simple smell could bring back so completely a time, place, and experience. Mary was becoming scared, very scared. The source of the rattling had been another door at the back of the room. Mary struggled to remember it. She was sure this had only been a single large room before but she could see that a partition had been built and they sat now in front of a door.

"It's metal."

Onur passed the phone to Mary as he tried the handle with both hands. It was a sliding door that had been built to slide inside the partition. Onur stroked the surface trying to get an idea of what he was dealing with.

"There are no hinges," he said, knocking on the surface to gauge its thickness.

"Can we open it?"

They both jumped back, startled, when the door rattled again.

"Beni saliver, beni saliver," The voice came from the other side of the partition.

"Beni saliver," Onur said, whispering the words, "It's Turkish. It means let me out – my god."

Onur stood up as far as he could and tried the door again, this time with real effort.

"Hanom, Hanom is that you?"

"Beni saliver." she said, again and again and again.

"HANOM," Mary could see that Onur had lost control. In desperation he thrashed against the door, which was steadfast and unlikely to give way. Mary looked behind her, watching for signs of light from behind, but there was none. She grabbed Onur and forced his mouth closed with her hand.

"Shut up. You must be quiet or we'll be in trouble. If they hear us what do you think they'll do?"

Onur was struggling and Mary had difficulty restraining him, but as the logic of what she said slowly sunk in he seemed to realise she was right and stopped.

"My wife is behind the screen Mary. If we have no hope of leaving here I at least want to see my family again, do you understand?" He said the last words as he turned his back to her. Onur was convinced he could find a way through. He turned his attention to the wall, tapping gently. The wall had been set in some kind of rough cast material but the surface itself did not feel solid. "It's a hollow wall made to look stronger than it is."

Onur suddenly disappeared back into the gloom. "Where are you going?" Mary said, scrabbling to pick up the phone, which was lying on the floor shining upwards, before the timing mechanism kicked in and they were plunged back into darkness. Onur was on the mattress. He felt around and it wasn't long before he found what he was looking for. The material was ancient and damp and not difficult to tear.

"We can use this to get through." Onur tore away the padding and ripped out one of the rusting springs. He cursed as the jagged end ripped through his index finger, the warm blood mingling with the metal. Returning to his task another spring was released and handed to Mary.

"Use this to scrape away the plaster, use the hook end and maybe we can get through."

Mary nodded and they got to work.

"Well thanks for the lift," Eric said, turning to the two detectives and smiling, "I'll need to be getting to work, busy day and all that."

Arbogast just stared at him, "While we are here maybe we could have a look around?"

Eric looked at Arbogast then Ying, his eyes flickering between the two of them looking for a sign, something to tell him everything was still OK. "Really Detective I'm a busy man, some other time maybe." He turned away and stood with one leg on the first of the three small wooden steps which led into the caravan. His hand pushed down on the metal handle and the door quivered open, held in place by the nervous hand of its owner.

"Well we're here now Mr Sanderson," Rosalind said, "so if it's all the same we'll just have a nosey, no harm done." Rosalind gave Sanderson one of her most genuine smiles before starting to make her way towards the shower block behind the caravan.

Casting a look around Sanderson could see that Karim was in the caravan, staring straight at him, gun in hand. He nodded at him through the window and Sanderson knew what to do.

"OK, have it your way. Let's have a look." He let go of the door handle and it clicked back into place, "I'll come with you."

The three of them made their way to the shower block when Arbogast broke off and doubled back. "I'll just have a look around the house."

"It's not safe, you can see it's moved these last weeks. It's the thaw."

"I'm a big boy Mr Sanderson so don't you worry, I'll be fine. If you would be so kind as to assist my colleague I'd be forever in your debt." Sanderson could only watch as he ambled over to the old house.

Rosalind stopped at the doorway and looked into the shower block where she could see the outline of the hatch from the dirt which had been disturbed.

"It's been a while since this place saw any detergent." she said, looking round to see a rather anxious looking host.

"You know we don't use it anymore."

"We?"

"The family, me I suppose I meant."

"Yes you don't see much of your daughter these days do you Mr Sanderson. Not too close anymore are you. I'm sure you must miss her."

"Not really. We don't get on."

"I seem to remember a lot of fuss here at the farm a while back. A lot of talk about abduction and sexual abuse, none of it proved of course but shit sticks doesn't it?" Rosalind turned and smiled at Eric Sanderson, watching to see what his reaction would be. Perhaps he would look away, tell her something with his eyes. But if there were clues to be had from body language then no-one had told Eric Sanderson who was looking right past her, staring at the hatch.

"Your daughter talked of a 'secret place' where it all happened. It doesn't seem those tales she told ever left her and look at the mess she's in now. She's mixed up in a lot of trouble. She assaulted a colleague of mine. DS Reid is in a bad way – you met her of course – nice girl. Looks like it could be touch and go with her. It would be very bad news if she didn't pull through wouldn't it?" The question came as Rosalind crouched down looking for a way to open the hatch. "And then there's the past. It's never far away you know. Just open up one door and bang – there it is. Back in the 80s Eric, when all those policemen were here the

205

last time – they didn't find anything, did they? No secret hideaway. But then we're a stupid lot really aren't we." Scraping and pulling Rosalind found what she was looking for. Pushing down the tile popped up to reveal the steel handle below. She lifted up the horseshoe shaped ring, "Well well, look what I've found."

By the time she looked up again Sanderson was already on her.

Karim watched from the safe haven of the caravan as the detective circled the house looking for a way in. He knew there was only one easy option so when he vanished from sight Karim came out of hiding and followed. *'I hope you like surprises Inspector.'*

It was slow work and hard going but Mary and Onur were making good progress. Between them they had uncovered an area of around four square feet. Their hands had been ripped apart by the rough wall so they had tied strips of the sodden mattress around their knuckles, which acted as makeshift gloves. Behind the first layer there was more plasterboard. Onur was trying to punch his way through and his skin started to tear from his knuckles.

"I can feel it give way."

Onur was sweating through a lack of fresh air, and was dirty from the dust which had engulfed their space. Finally his hand broke through, grasping at thin air before coming to rest on another wall at the other side. Slowly but surely the wall gave way. Onur stopped scraping; his hands cut to ribbons. They had uncovered a large section.

"It'll be enough to get through," Mary said.

Nodding Onur started to kick at the other side, "Prop me up."

Mary pushed hard on Onur's back and he kicked with all his strength, his thick steel toe capped work boots pounding away at the plaster, which crumbled under the force.

Hanom had woken under a cloud. She felt sick. She had vomited and was shivering, unable to think. *'Where am I?'* Every time he came she passed out. She ached all over, and could no longer see out of one eye. She touched the orb but it felt soft and mushy to her probing fingers. Slowly, she pushed herself back against the wall and raised herself into the sitting position. "Where am I?" This time she said it out loud and then she heard the voices. She held her breath and listened. She struggled to make out the words but there was someone there. This had never happened before, always the light came and then the blackouts. The door shook and she gasped, *'Not again, not again, not again,'* she chanted, hugging herself and waiting for the inevitable. *'Why won't it open?'* Hanom tried to focus on the door and then she saw the light, a green glow underneath it and then voices, scared voices. Crawling to the door she hoped for the impossible, for relief, "Beni saliver," she cried. It had sounded like her husband but it couldn't be – it must be her mind playing tricks on her. She knew the bastard Karim was her captor but if it was him surely he would just use the key. After a time the crashing began, not from the door but the wall. There was nothing at first but slowly the noise became louder. Then her small room filled with dust and debris as the wall crumbled away. She buried her face in what remained of her clothes, trying to breathe. She was terrified of what might happen – of what new terror might await her.

"Got it, we're through."

Onur crawled through the hole but could see nothing in the darkness, "Pass me the phone." Mary slid the handset over to him. Onur sat up and pressed the keys, bringing light to the new room.

"Hanom – Hanom it's me, your husband. It's Onur my darling. Are you here?"

He moved forward with one hand holding the phone, the other trying to feel for a sign of life. Then he found her, shivering, bloody and abused, but alive.

"Hanom," he said, placing his hand on her leg, caressing it.

This couldn't be true thought Hanom. She screamed, her arms and legs thrashing, resisting, "Beni saliver, beni saliver," she cried as Onur forced his arms around her and held her tightly.

"Kovan is here," Hanom said eventually through her tears, "but I have failed her, failed her so badly. I sat here and listened to her screams as that beast attacked her but I could do nothing."

Mary say quietly and watched determined that if she ever got the chance she would tear her father limb from limb. *'All I need is a second, just one second and I'll rid this world of his twisted depravity'.*

Rosalind's head hit the wall and cracked off the tiles. Sanderson had kicked her in the head, with the force of it sending a spear of pain through her body. If the blow had landed on her windpipe she might have died but it had caught her around the jaw. Winded and wounded she lay on the ground, unable to react.

"I've had about enough of you now Detective. I asked you to leave but you had to look."

Rosalind turned her head. The world seemed to have shifted 90 degrees south and she could only watch as the hatch she had discovered only seconds ago was fully opened.

"I'm sorry it has to be like this but I'm afraid you've left me no choice. People just won't let the past be. I know that my habits might not be to everyone's taste but I have never killed anyone. No-one died Detective."

Rosalind was moving now, crawling across the room, but Sanderson grabbed her legs and pulled her into position. She tried to reach out but couldn't seem to control herself. She was thinking, though, coming back to her senses but it was too late. Sanderson spun her round and then pushed her legs over the hatch so that they hung over the edge. She could feel herself being hoisted into a sitting position when he whispered in her ear.

"I really am sorry it has to be like this but I think you've worked your last case."

Rosalind could feel his breath on her neck, shuddered as she heard him breathe in her scent. She was coming round now and sensed she had a chance.

"Goodbye Inspector," he said kissing her softly below the ear, "A final present for your journey." Rosalind's mouth opened in a silent scream as he punched hard on her back. She struggled to turn around but then the foot came, pushing against her back. She fell. Turning in midair Rosalind tried in vain to reach out for something, anything to keep her from falling. But she could not move fast enough and when the bottom arrived unannounced the world went black. The hatch closed. She was alone.

Sanderson stood and looked at the hatch. There was no going back. It wasn't going well but he still had options. Closing the door and wedging it shut he made his way back to the caravan. He needed to speak to Karim. They would need to deal with Arbogast – the meddling bastard had caused enough trouble. Sanderson was glad the DI wasn't armed as that meant Arbogast was already at a disadvantage. Sanderson opened the door, expecting to see his partner but he had gone. Looking over towards the house he thought he saw movement and realised that it might not be so difficult to resolve this situation as he had feared.

Arbogast entered the house through the back door, the only one that was open, the key still in its lock. He trod carefully, cautious of the building's shifting foundations. He checked upstairs first. There were signs the building had been used recently. *'They must be here somewhere.'* Satisfied that there was no-one in the upper floors he found himself at the head of the staircase which led down to the basement. Arbogast had his back to the wall as he made his way down, avoiding any creaks and groans from the warped and decaying structure. The two rooms were empty. One door was torn to shreds and a thick film of fresh sawdust carpeted the stone floor. Arbogast stood and looked around, trying to figure out what had happened when he heard a scraping from upstairs. He had company. Arbogast found a length of wood stacked at the back of the room and tried it for weight. *'Right now would be a good time for backup – why did we send away the guys in the patrol car?'* Making his way back up to the ground floor he peered round the timber frame of the basement door and looked around. He saw nothing but his nose twitched at the scent of cigarette smoke. The basement opened up into the hall. Directly across from the door he could see into what must have been the living room. On a table sat an ashtray holding a smouldering cigarette, the smoke swirling up in the crisp winter air. Holding his makeshift club like a baseball bat Arbogast looked left and right as he made his way across the hall and over to the living room, ready to strike. But again he was disappointed to find the room empty and was surprised when he heard the click behind him.

"It's loaded Detective so don't turn around."

Arbogast didn't move. He recognised the voice. It was familiar – familiar, but different, and in no way friendly.

Sanderson went to his guest's bedroom and found the metal briefcase under his bed. One gun was missing. Checking the remaining Glock was loaded he went back to the lounge and slid back the table. He went through the hatch and down the ladder, knowing this time would be more difficult. When he opened the door to the room his vision was obscured by the small particles of dust from the rubble, which scratched at his throat as he inhaled. His heart beat quickly as the adrenalin took over. He moved forward with gun in hand ready to act, peering into the murky space, trying to find them.

"Where are you? Better come out now."

Sanderson saw the hole in the wall and laughed, "Have you burrowed your way back to happiness Onur? You always did like to tunnel."

Sanderson took out his keys and opened the metal sliding door. This was his proudest achievement, this secret place and he would not give it up. The door opened. There was no light in the room so Sanderson moved to shine his torch when he saw a dim glow in the background. He stopped for a second and could see the outline of three people huddled in the darkness and then a voice rang out that he had not heard in a long while.

"This is for you, daddy dearest."

Sanderson was clearly visible with the bright naked bulb from the hall lighting up his silhouette from behind. Mary hurled the phone at him. Eric noticed the dim green light swinging into vision. The phone struck him on the forehead and he swore as he staggered back two steps but they were on him before he knew what had happened.

23

Eric saw the light flicker, getting closer with every spin. When the crack came he knew that he had played the situation all wrong. The mobile phone struck Sanderson on the forehead, between his eyes, causing him to drop his torch. The metal clattered on the concrete floor and the light went out. His reflex had been to shoot, but in the dark his senses were out of kilter and his aim was wild. The bullet sank into the concrete wall as screams of retribution filled his ears.

Mary knew it was her father, she knew his stench and she knew she would only get one chance. So many times she had been a prisoner here. So many times the hatch had opened and the light had blinded her before the horror began. *'So many times before. But not today, and never again.'*

Mary could see her father quite clearly. There could be no mistaking it was him. He had a torch in one hand while the other was masked from view. In desperation she threw the phone. With all her strength she hurled the handset at him, her mind watching in slow motion as the handset pirouetted through the murky air, sailing towards its target. She snapped to when she saw the torch drop and ran screaming at him. She knew she was not alone and this time was going to be different. This time she was calling the shots. This time it ended.

Arbogast turned around and he found himself looking at a familiar face.

"Onur?"

"Who I am is unimportant. What you need to realise is that your investigation is now officially over."

Arbogast realised he was going to have to work with limited options. He decided to play it safe.

"I only need to find the girl. I can make the rest disappear."

From the back of the house he heard a noise.

"The girl?"

Karim nodded, "And so you see that you have found the girl. Congratulations Inspector but this was never a case that was going to be solved. It can only end one way and that way, I am afraid, will not be good for you."

Arbogast looked around and realised he might not leave this room and that no amount of logic would save him. All Arbogast could see was the gun aimed straight at him, the dark nose of the barrel pointing to the end of the line. When the shot rang out he went into an involuntary spasm, closing his eyes and waiting for the sharp pain he knew was coming. Arbogast stood with clenched fists and white knuckles, his head angled away from the gun as if that futile gesture might have saved him, but nothing happened. The shot had been from outside. When he opened his eyes it was just in time to see the gun nose flare, this time it was closer to home.

***

John Madoch stood looking out over the Clyde. This venture with Sanderson and Karim was starting to become rather messy. He had got involved as a favour to his colleagues in Turkey but it was supposed to have been relatively straight forward. Madoch knew that it was time to get rid of Sanderson, while his benefactor needed to dispose of a renegade operator. Sanderson's daughter popping up by accident had been the icing on the cake. The snow had caused problems and the operation had spiralled slowly out of control ever since the first flake dropped slowly to earth. John Madoch went inside and sat at his desk, running his hand along the 1930s mahogany as if checking for imperfections. He picked up the phone and dialled.

"Is that the newsroom? I'd liked to speak to Sandy Stirrit please. If you could yes, it's rather urgent."

212

***

Sanderson was knocked onto his back and Mary threw herself on top of him. She grasped around in the darkness and found the round end of the heavy metal torch. Lifting it above her head with her thighs gripping her father's sides she pounded his torso and head. Three, four times her anger rained down on her father, years of pent up anger released in one long primal scream. Then a hand grabbed her from behind and pulled her off, threw her back.

"That is enough."

As Mary looked up she saw Onur had the gun. Sanderson was still alive, "That is quite enough." The room was silent, so quiet they could hear each other's breathing and the low groans from Sanderson, who was barely moving. In the background they could hear a voice. Hanom followed the sound into the back room and pressed her ear to the wall.

"It's coming from here, there must be another room."

Rosalind Ying had had better weeks. When she came to, she was face down and choking. She awoke with a start and cleared her throat, retching and spluttering as she clamoured for air. She breathed in deeply. The stench was overwhelming. Crouched forward on all fours Rosalind vomited the contents of her stomach; her hands were inch deep in excrement. *'Where am I?'* Then she remembered the hatch. *'Sanderson.'* She looked up but could see no light. *'I'm in the tank which will be airtight and sealed. I don't have much time.'*

She screamed.

"There it is again," Hanom said, "It sounds like a woman. We have to help her. I think she's in pain."

Mary looked at Onur, "Give me the gun, this is my battle."

She stood up and walked over to Onur with her arm outstretched.

"Please give me the gun."

Onur presented the gun face down on the palm of his hand.

213

"Don't worry," Mary said, "We will find your daughter."

Mary looked at the gun. She had never used one before but she knew how it worked. Her father had already fired it so she knew the safety was off. She straddled her father once more, pinning his arms to the ground with her legs. She placed the gun to the side of his head above his right ear and whispered.

"Who is in the next room?"

Sanderson looked at her with fear in his eyes. His face was caked with blood which was already starting to harden; thick streaks of red matted his white hair.

"I don't know what you mean," the sound audible only to Mary.

She squeezed the trigger slightly, "Who is next door and where is the girl? You have one chance to redeem yourself, dad, take it."

He started to protest, "I don't kn—" but the shot rang out before he had the chance to say anything more, "The next time I won't miss" Mary said. She had fired off what was to be her final warning.

"It's the detective – the woman – she's in the septic tank in the shower block – she's still alive – I only needed her out of the way. The girl's in the house." There were tears in his eyes.

"All your good work, undone – the shame of it all." Mary stood up aimed at his chest and fired.

The fourth shot was muffled and definitely outside. Arbogast lay writhing on the floor, with the pain from his shoulder causing him to spin round as his legs thrashed out.

"Be still." When he looked up he could see the man with Onur's face staring down at him, "I have something to take care of. And this is something we can all do together."

Arbogast didn't see the kick coming and was almost relieved in the split second when the force pushed him back into oblivion.

Karim lifted the Detective's limp arm and dropped it to the floor satisfied he would pose no problems. The shots had come from the caravan. Making his way to the front of the house he stood and watched, looking for movement, for a clue to what was happening. The door to the caravan burst open and he saw his brother run out with gun in hand, followed by two women. They looked to Karim as if they had stepped out of hell, covered in dirt and blood they squinted at the force of the sunshine, unfamiliar after their confinement. He knew this would be the best time to act. Unlocking the front door he drew his gun and ran out to meet them.

Making their way up and out of their dungeon Mary, Onur and Hanom did not know exactly what to expect but they were armed and had purpose. Emerging into the caravan they heard a shot from the house.

"Kovan," Hanom said, "My daughter – he has killed my daughter." Hanom raised her hands to cover her ears, to block out the unfolding drama but it was no use. Mary stood back and raised the gun, pointing at Onur.

"We must think clearly. Who is here and what are we dealing with? I only expected to find my father."

"I know my brother is here. Karim was to be our saviour but now, well now I don't know what he's capable of."

Then, without warning, Onur lunged at Mary knocking her back against the flimsy partition wall, which bobbled under her weight. Onur grabbed at Mary's shirt, taking the gun from her before pulling open the door and running out into the bright sunlight.

"Stop," Mary screamed, but her protests came too late. They had barely made it out of the door when a shot rang out and Onur fell to the ground. His mirror image was charging at them, arm raised and gun aimed right at them. Onur had fallen. Taking the gun she doubled back to the shower block, leaving Hanom to care for her husband. Mary slipped and fell trying to race around the corner. The firing had stopped and she was back in relative safety. She knew she didn't have much time. Scanning the floor she saw the clean marks scraped through the months of filth on the tiled floor and found the handle to the hatch. The door sprang open and Mary looked down, searching for signs of life.

"Hello. Is there anyone there?"

"Don't you fucking dare come down here. I'm a senior police officer and you've made a fucking big mistake."

Mary smiled. "I'm a prisoner too but I need your help officer and you need me to get out of this shit pit. It's Mary. Mary Clark. I think I've killed my father."

***

Sandy Stirrit sat back and wondered what had just happened. John Madoch had phoned him and told him that he had unearthed 'a conspiracy' among certain of his staff and that he would be taking his case to the police. It had been suggested he might want to take a camera crew to the Sanderson farm, where he would be able to document the end of a rather unsavoury episode which he said was threatening to tarnish his good name. He had then hung up. Sandy had been in the game long enough to know that he was being set up for something, but it was something big.

***

The rush of fresh air which came when the hatch opened was the single most terrifying moment of Rosalind Ying's life. The fresh air didn't quite mask her situation but she knew she now had hope. After what seemed like an age the light from above was blocked out and for a second Rosalind thought her reprieve was only temporary. But it had been Mary Clark. She had lifted one of the doors from the toilet cubicles free from its hinges. They were flimsy but long enough to use as a ladder down into the gloom. Rosalind used the bolts at the side of the door for a foothold and after several unsuccessful attempts she emerged like a swamp rat at feeding time. The two women looked at each other.

"You know you'll have to come in after this Mary," Rosalind said, "but what you've done now will be taken note of in court. For now, though, I need your help."

Mary nodded and raised the gun. "Thanks for the pep talk but for now you'll do as I say – let's go."

Mary ushered Rosalind back out of the block and the two made their way outside.

"They were right here," Mary said.

216

"Who were?"

"Onur and Hanom – Onur was shot."

"There," Rosalind said, pointing to the house, "I think I saw movement inside."

Mary shook the gun at Rosalind, "Let's go."

***

Sandy Stirrit told the editor that he needed the satellite truck and that tonight they would have the scoop of the year. He had been vague on the details but had convinced the team there was something in his phone call from Madoch. After a few carefully phrased questions the police had pointed them in the same direction and while it might come to nothing they decided that they could not risk missing out to the competition. Now driving down the M8 Sandy hoped he had made the right call. He would be at the farm in 20 minutes.

***

Karim dragged Onur back into the house with the help of Hanom, who had decided not to argue with the gun. He dumped him beside Arbogast who was still out cold. Onur sat with his back to the wall, his eyes boring into his brother with a growing hatred.

"Just like the old days brother," Karim said.

"What is this all about? I feel this charade has run its course. What is it you want with my family?"

"With your family? Well there's a thing. Do you remember those summer days, years ago when we three were inseparable."

Hanom watched, edging closer to her husband, nervous about what might be about to happen.

"How we laughed and planned the adventures we would have. Hanom here only had eyes for me in those days, but fate had a different plan."

"Get to the point Karim."

"The point is that there's been a grand deception playing out in our lives, a deception which runs to the core of your supposed family – a deception which has brought us here. Hanom, our daughter is in the next room." Hanom's eyes widened, "Bring

217

her to her father." Hanom looked at Onur, who could see that her eyes had welled up. She turned and left.

"You see Onur I never liked that you took my place at Hanom's side. She was my prize, not yours, but when you proposed, well it seemed to change things. And all on the night of her 18th birthday – you'll remember it well. You were a laughing stock."

"You weren't there. What happened was fate."

Karim laughed, "Fate yes, but not the way you think. I came to Hanom that night and on many others too. I am not accustomed to people saying no to me and I made the situation quite clear. The child is mine, Onur. Kovan is my daughter not yours. All these years you have been the family man, admired and respected while people have feared me. Where is the justice you might ask? But the last laugh is mine. This has all been for you, for my revenge and for what will be my family."

Onur was speechless. Hanom and Kovan had appeared at the door. Hanom held Kovan with both arms draped around her chest from behind, holding her close. It was Kovan who spoke first.

"Daddy Karim has been keeping me in a tower. He says I'm his little princess but I did miss you and mummy. Now we can all live together." She looked up at Hanom who was staring at Onur.

Hanom broke the silence, "I could not tell you for shame my love. He came in the night and threatened your life. He said he would say nothing if I agreed. It has been a dreadful secret but it is you that has been Kovan's father, not this...animal," she spat at Karim but he didn't move.

"All this time Karim and you knew. Were you so consumed with hate? Everything that has happened: the assassination in Istanbul, our flight into hiding – all that just to get to me. I don't understand."

"I am connected brother and I can disappear. We all can and you certainly will."

Arbogast had come round now but he lay still with his eyes closed – listening, trying to think of a way out.

"Look around brother and what do you see? Nothing but the seeds of your own work. Do you know the police are looking for you? They think you are me, such is our likeness."

"We are nothing alike."

"I have never thought so, but perhaps I have been wrong. Many people have confused us for each other, even the policewoman. She should have died but the mistake was to my advantage. It all comes back to your notion of fate."

Karim pointed the gun, "Game over."

Sanderson felt like death. He had lain looking up at the ceiling unable to move for some time. His body ached. He had been beaten and shot, fortunate the bullet had passed straight through, missing his heart. Slowly and painfully he turned himself over and made his way back to the surface. Raking through his bedroom chest he found what he needed and made his way back to the family home for what he knew would be the last time.

"Move," Mary said, the gun pointed in the small of Rosalind's back. Rosalind was nervous, unsure of how she was going to get free. She could see they were going to the farmhouse and watched for signs of life inside. The back door was open. She focused on the bronze hexagonal handle, looking for a possible break, but Mary was focused on Rosalind and before they reached the door she swung the gun again and knocked her down. Checking that she was out cold Mary took out her handcuffs and bound the detective before entering the house. Slipping in through the front door Mary stood unheard in the hall and listened. She heard the story from brother to brother and understood what she had become part of. Mary watched as Karim pointed and said "Game over." Standing perfectly still she aimed and fired. The shot left only a small hole in the back of his head but the front was blown away, the contents smeared over the floor, with thin rivulets of blood sprayed onto the Kocack women.

Arbogast knew that if he was going to do anything now was the time – but he was badly concussed and the events of the next few minutes would spin by in a blur. Onur sprang forward and prised the gun from Karim's hand. At the same time the walking corpse of Eric Sanderson crashed through the door brandishing a large hunting knife. Mary turned, surprised as Eric plunged the knife deep into her chest. Mary's eyes bulged in disbelief as father and daughter collapsed to the floor. Onur stood having retrieved his brother's gun. Perhaps he had meant to attack his brother but he was now very dead and getting cold. Outside Arbogast could see the outline of two uniforms coming up the hill. *'Here comes the cavalry – they must have been sent back from the ruin.'* Mary was lying on her side, a thick pool of blood was beginning to form around her and her father now had her gun. It was pointing at Arbogast.

"Time's up officer, for me anyway. Take the family and go."

Onur had been staring hopelessly at the lifeless figure of his brother. He raised the gun to point at Sanderson.

"This was your doing my friend."

"No Onur I was only told to keep you here. The child was a mistake and I can say nothing to make that better. But this is the end of the road for me. My family line ends here." With his free hand he took out a single stick of dynamite. He motioned to the crack in the floor by way of explanation, "There are five more planted in the foundations. I have been in the pocket of Madoch for years. He came to me in the 80s after finding out about my secret, but he was good to me. I hid people here during the dark days and he allowed me to indulge in my...well I make no excuses. The heart wants what the heart wants. I am what I am and I don't expect you to understand."

Arbogast stood up, holding the side where he had been shot, and made his way over to Onur.

"Give me the gun," he said, softly, laying his hand on Onur's wrist, edging towards the warm steel of the chamber.

"It's over. You have your family and he's going with me."

Onur released the gun and Arbogast stood back.

"We're leaving now Eric."

Eric nodded as Hanom took Kovan through the front door, the girl's hand reached out for Onur who followed silently. Arbogast stood and watched Eric Sanderson for a few seconds. He had raised Mary's head onto his lap and sat stroking her hair. She looked happy.

"I've made too many mistakes but this was my worst, allowing that man to corrupt that family. I have no more words."

"You can't leave here, you know that."

Sanderson nodded.

Arbogast turned and left, leaving the Sanderson family alone, for the last time. Sanderson took a cigarette lighter from his pocket and waited.

The timber had stood firm for 160 years. Today the wooden supports creaked and groaned under the increasing pressure of earth and rock from above. Melted ice dripped through fissures and slowly weakened the limestone. The land had started to reclaim the house the previous winter and the great thaw of 2010 meant that the bedrock under the Sanderson Farm could no longer take the strain. Above the chasm and inside the house, Eric Sanderson lit the fuse and shared a final tender moment with his daughter as the flame worked its way down towards its final destination.

Sandy Stirrit's TV crew arrived as Arbogast emerged from the farmhouse. Sandy stopped when the explosion hit. The house quivered briefly before disappearing under its own weight into a cloud of rubble, filling the void below.

"Get the camera on now," he said, but the tripod was already down and the camera had caught every moment. Watching TV that night the pictures caused a sensation. The report also featured aerial shots, taken later in the day, which showed the extent of the blast after the dust had settled. Where the farm had stood was now a one hundred foot crater, the house reduced to nothing – the landscape transformed. Sandy Stirrit told his viewers about sinkholes caused by mine workings. Footage from earlier in the day showed five people being taken to hospital. One was understood to be the missing girl.

As the ambulance pulled away Arbogast allowed himself to fall into a deep sleep. Exhausted he consoled himself with the fact that at the very least he had found the girl this time. He had found the girl but failed to solve the case.

Epilogue

Daily Record, February 24th 2010

EXPLOSION UNCOVERS PAEDO RING

The 5 year old young girl missing from a bus in Lanarkshire two weeks ago has been found along with her mother and father following an explosion at a farmhouse near Bishopton, Renfrewshire. Kovan Kocack, Hanom Kocack (36) and Onur Kocack (43) had been held prisoner in an underground sex lair at a farm, which has been used by an international paedophile ring. Chief Constable at Strathclyde Police, Norrie Smith, said this marked the successful conclusion of the largest manhunt in living memory, "This is the end of a massive search for a missing girl, which has uncovered a circle of sickening human trafficking that sadly is becoming more and more common. I am pleased that we have reunited a family torn apart by a criminal gang. We have had our best people working on this and I would like to thank everyone involved for their tireless dedication."
Following a tip-off from Glasgow businessman, John Madoch, police arrived at the property to find the owner Eric Sanderson (56) had blown up his family home. Our sources suggest he had used dynamite stolen from the industrial site which he worked at as an engineer. Eric Sanderson was inside the building at the time along with

his daughter Mary Clark (34) and an unknown third man, thought to be a Turkish national. Daily Record readers may remember that Sanderson made headlines in 1985 after his daughter Mary accused him of abusing both herself and a young boy. At the time the allegations were ignored but it has since emerged that the driver of the bus Kovan Kocack was taken from had been driven by the known sex offender, Stevie Davidson, who was recently found dead at the Kirk o' Shotts in Lanarkshire. A major investigation has now been launched to locate the rest of the paedophile ring, which has been operating across Scotland for some time.

John Madoch said he had come forward with the information after it was discovered a case of high explosives, meant for levelling foundations at his Moorland Wind development on Eaglesham Moor, had gone missing overnight, "Eric Sanderson had been acting oddly for some time but it wasn't until he started asking questions about his co-workers that I started to become genuinely concerned. My company had brought Onur Kocack over from Istanbul to use his expertise during the construction of the wind farm. He was helping police with investigations into the abduction of his daughter when he went missing too. When the dynamite was reported missing from my site I suspected that Sanderson might be involved. I only wish I'd acted sooner and then maybe this tragedy could have been avoided."

Read more on p 2,3,4,5,6,7,8

Arbogast sighed as he put down the newspaper. *'If only I'd acted sooner.'* He could not believe the nerve of John Madoch, who had come forward and painted himself as the hero of the day. By the time he had left the farmhouse there was already a full blown media circus outside. Sandy was there along with a flotilla of uniforms and armed response teams. By that time of course there was nothing more to be done. The Sandersons and Karim were gone and Arbogast doubted that they would even find a trace of them. The truth of the matter was that the huge sinkhole which now occupied the space where the Sanderson farm had once stood was far too unsafe to merit further investigation. In his working life Arbogast had only seen total destruction like that once before, when he had to investigate a gas explosion in a small town. There had been nothing left. It had been a detached house and the force of the blast had taken away the sides of the two neighbouring houses. The only thing that survived in one piece was a fridge freezer which had been blown up on to the neighbour's roof. Three generations of the same family had been asleep inside. And so it was with the Sanderson farm. The mineshaft discovered below the house had finally given way. The deep frost that had penetrated the limestone beneath had melted away to leave unstable holes in the rocks which could no longer support the weight above. Thousands of tonnes of earth simply shifted from topside to fill the chasm below. The force would have torn the three bodies to shreds. Arbogast sighed again. He was being praised for finding the family, for reuniting the girl with her parents, but he didn't feel like a hero. Five people were dead; three officers including him had been violently assaulted, but they had found the girl and that was what the press and his superiors were focusing on. Maybe he was being too hard on himself but Arbogast felt as if he had failed, as if he had been once step behind all the way and had only got the result through sheer luck. The whole thing was obviously tied into Madoch but it seemed that would be impossible to prove. Arbogast had taken all the accolades for coming forward at a pivotal time but in reality he had changed nothing, other than to shift the blame away from himself. Having considered the case Arbogast felt that maybe Onur had been right, maybe their lives were bound by nothing more than fate and what had happened was meant to have happened just the way it did. Karim had been so confident of taking his brother's place at the head of the family but something had gone wrong. He had gone wrong.

A few days later DI John J Arbogast paid a second visit to Madoch House.

"The hero returns," Madoch said, from behind his desk, "My congratulations on all the good work Inspector. I'm glad to see the family made it through."

"Cut the crap Madoch I'm not here on official business. You know your role in this. What was the brother doing over here?"

Madoch considered the question, slouched back on his tilting leather chair, arms draped over the rests. He had pulled in his chin for effect in a gesture which made him look fat.

"DI Arbogast you know I have a past – but it's just that – a past. I live in the here-and-now and let's say I have created a certain reputation for myself. The business with Sanderson was getting out of hand."

"You knew about him – tell me about it?"

"Before we start," Madoch stood up and moved to Arbogast. He frisked him, "A precaution." Satisfied he didn't have an extended audience Madoch sat back on the edge of his desk, "Eric had certain rather disgusting vices which I turned a blind eye to but his money allowed me to turn myself around. It made us both very rich."

"So where do the Kocack family fit in? Was the girl just another child for him to corrupt with your blessing – don't you think you have a responsibility to the families you turn a blind eye to?"

"I thought this time would be different. Onur had been doing good work for me. He was having trouble at home but he worked hard. I was going to help him get his life back on track. At first he told me he had money problems with what he called 'bad people' in Turkey but it was all for show. His brother was setting him up. He was angry about Hanom but he was reckless. His people wanted to tear up the contract. These things have a habit of working themselves out."

"So you wanted to help Onur, is that it? And by forcing his wife to work as a lap dancer and putting his daughter in the care of a killer and a paedophile you thought you'd be doing him a good turn. Do me a favour!"

"I had nothing to do with the wife, but my girls aren't badly treated. They're well paid. Most go home after a year or so and are none the worse for their little adventure. The one big variable was Mary Clark. She was contacted by Hanom independently. We like to keep our girls safe so we let them out, but we keep an eye on them if you know what I mean. When Mary got involved the whole plan just got a lot simpler. With Sanderson being such a close associate I already knew there was somewhere to hide the girl. Bizarrely Mary wanted to take the girl there too; I think she wanted to set her father up – to expose him for what he was. Karim wanted to go back to Turkey with them. He had already arranged a way out by boat. Either way Sanderson was going to be dealt with. It was all meant to be quite straight forward but it got complicated. He made things more difficult and had quite a temper. What surprised me most though was Onur."

"What about him?"

"He knew about the whole thing. I'm afraid that I was sucked into his plan too. Onur wanted his daughter out of the way. When you spoke to him I'll bet he never spoke of Kovan much did he? He knew what had gone on between his wife and brother and had wanted to deal with his situation for quite some time. He just didn't have the means. When Karim was being pressured in Istanbul it was Onur who came forward and suggested a plan of action."

"All this was down to Onur?"

"It was all just business. I have associates in Turkey who were concerned about reputational matters. Karim was becoming a liability – he was a loose cannon and making waves where he shouldn't. He dealt with the US side of the corporation and they weren't happy. I suppose now everyone's happy, more or less."

"This whole thing was a set up." Arbogast sat down, deflated, "A set up to get rid of Karim – but Onur clouded the whole process. But that means..."

"Don't be too quick to judge, it is after all a rather grey area. Needless to say I have spoken to Onur. He's agreed to take

231

over Sanderson's workload. I am pretty sure the Home Office will grant permanent visas for the family. They've been through a terrible ordeal and to be trafficked like that – it wouldn't be safe to return home would it. They can live out their lives as one big happy family. Now if you wouldn't mind Inspector I am very busy."

***

DI John J Arbogast and DCI Rosalind Ying were both awarded commendations for bravery. They had stood and smiled as the cameras clicked and flashed, said the right things when they were asked to and then later retired to Rab's to mull over the events of the last few weeks.

Sandy Stirrit had taken up Arbogast's offer of some evening hospitality, "Do you think the Kocacks will be OK?"

"Who can say, it certainly looks like Onur's landed on his feet regardless of his motives. I've spoken to Hanom and she seemed quite calm about it. And anyway, we've no evidence to back up Madoch's claims about Onur, so we're stuck with his version of events." Arbogast shook his head. "I just don't know. Here we are, toast of the nation, but what did we do? The girl could still be getting abused. She's in danger."

"But you got the family out John, put your ghosts to rest," Rosalind said. She was sipping at a large glass of Pinot Grigio, looking more relaxed than she had done for weeks. "And for your information something has been done about Onur."

"What?"

"I phoned social services. If Kovan is Karim's child there will be a DNA match. That will make life difficult for Onur and it'll back up your version of events. We may have a case yet. More importantly Kovan could end up living with her mum – in safety."

"I can't say it makes me feel any better."

"You've got to stay positive. It's not all bad – Mhairi Reid's doing OK too. She'll be back with us in a couple of months."

"That is good news," Arbogast said before turning his attention to Sandy, "One thing has me puzzled, though, why do you think Madoch phoned the newsroom?"

"He knew I'd been looking into Sanderson. Maybe he just saw his chance. The strange thing was I had looked at the archive footage and there was something I couldn't work out and I know what it was now – it was the well."

"What well?"

"In the 80s footage there was an old well which had a pointed roof and a wall round it. But it wasn't there. On the old reels the well was where the caravan is now. That must have been where he got down to his dungeon. The source must have run dry. He'd have had much more privacy getting down through his caravan than climbing down through the well entrance. How many people do you think he had down there? It makes me sick to think of it."

"Hey, we're meant to be celebrating and this case is closed," Arbogast said, "The investigation into the paedophile ring has passed over to the SCDEA. Trafficking is their thing so maybe they'll have better luck, maybe Madoch will trip up – let's hope so."

All three thought the same thing but no-one said a word.

"Look guys I've had it, I'm going to call it a night," Rosalind had gathered her coat and was looking to leave, "You two have probably got a lot of catching up to do anyway."

"I'll walk you out Rose, are you alright for a drink Sandy?"

"I'm fine John, take your time."

When they left the pub torrential rain was bouncing off the tarmac and the streets were deserted. Arbogast walked Rosalind to the taxi rank, sheltering under a clear, domed, red rimmed umbrella.

John stopped when he noticed that Rosalind was upset.

"You're crying Rose." The roar of the rain almost drowned out his voice, the torrent sounding like a million marbles being dropped on a tin roof.

"We could have died John, both of us. I've never been in that situation before."

"The kind of situation where you know if you don't act you might never get the chance again?"

Rosalind looked at John but said nothing. The mist of the rain which engulfed them blocked out the rest of the world and in that moment John knew. They shared a kiss.

She pushed him away slightly, but with no real force, "I won't stay with you tonight John. I don't know, it's just too soon – so much has happened. But I want you to know that I want to. I'll come back to you when I can."

"Thanks Rose – I'll be in touch. You can count on that."

The taxi arrived and she broke away and left. John watched the cab until it had turned up into George Square. Without the protection of the umbrella he could feel the rain soaking through his clothes, rivulets of water running down his back but it didn't seem to matter.

***

Arriving at the nursing home Arbogast was surprised to see his mother had another guest, an elderly man in his seventies. He watched from the window.

"Who's that?" he asked the duty nurse.

"That's John," she said, "He comes here every couple of months."

Arbogast sat and watched for a while. The man got up and gave his mother a peck on the cheek and then left. He walked past Arbogast, giving a nod of recognition. *'Polite, but who are you?'* Arbogast considered asking but then decided he couldn't be bothered to hold a conversation. He went and sat by his mother who was back in her usual spot in the middle of a large semi circle of patients. They all looked pretty much the same although some were farther gone than others. One woman looked like she was still quite compos mentis but he supposed she would soon go the same way, otherwise why would she be here? Arbogast sat and watched his mother for what seemed to be an eternity, thinking – remembering what had gone before. She sat staring into space quite unmoved by the chaos which surrounded her, although she seemed more animated than he had seen her for some time. She was moving more, her face twitching. Expressions of surprise and confusion flickered over her face, each one instantly replaced by another.

"You don't know you're born mum." It was a phrase she had said to him so many times in the past. She turned to face him and her eyes lit up.

"I love you Johnny," she said beaming with bright eyes and then looked away.

"What did you say mum, what was that?"

But her mind had retreated into its perpetual confusion. For a moment, though, she'd been back – she'd been something like the woman he remembered. As his thoughts drifted to the farm and through the course of the investigation, Johnny Arbogast held his mother's hand and shed a tear for his own disappearing world.

About the author

Originally from Ayrshire, Campbell Hart has lived in Glasgow on-and-off for the last 20 years. A qualified broadcast journalist he spent ten years working in commercial radio and at BBC Scotland before moving into PR. His debut crime novel 'Wilderness' was inspired by real events and the bitter winter of 2010.

The second book in the Arbogast trilogy 'The Nationalist' is coming soon.

For more details visit: www.campbellhart.co.uk